Don't Take Me Home
Following Wales At Euro 2016

By Jonathon Rogers

ISBN: 1540510387
ISBN-13: 978-1540510389

To Alan, Diane, Janine and Lorna.

Thanks to Jack Williams for his support and help.

CHAPTER 1

I was surrounded by a scene of unbridled joy. Grown men in tears embraced their friends, clasped in bearhugs four or five deep. Others furiously punched the air and bellowed until their throats cracked. A pair of middle-aged women jigged around uncontrollably, whooping with glee. As for myself, I was stood motionless with my hands on my head, incredulous at what I had just witnessed like an innocent bystander at a roadside accident. Little did they know it, but the streets of Zenica were about to play unwitting host to the biggest party in the city's history.

While my disbelief was in stark contrast to everyone else within my vicinity, one thing kept us in common - the red shirt of the Wales football team. A jersey that for so long had been a symbol of ridicule, pain and embarrassment was now being proudly adorned by 725 of us who had trekked across land and sea to the centre of Bosnia and Herzegovina to support our team, our country. It was soaking the tears of many when I was suddenly torpedoed to the ground by a blur of sheer excitement and crunched against the litter-strewn floor between two rows of red plastic seats.

"We've bloody done it! We've bloody done it, Scotty! I've waited 58 years for this!"

"What do you mean, you silly sod? You're only 33!" I laughed. That was Dafydd, or Dav as we both preferred, my best friend since the age of six when we were forced to participate in a primary school nativity play and both realised our dislike towards acting was proportionate to our love of swapping football stickers.

"You know what I mean! This is the best moment of my life!" he screamed firmly down my earhole which had already sustained the figurative bursting of an eardrum once it had been announced that Wales had qualified for their first major international football tournament since 1958 - Euro 2016.

Dav helped me off the ground and I handed him his trademark red, yellow and green bucket hat that had spilled onto the warm concrete that made up our row of one of the stands inside the Bilino Polje Stadium, which was being shaken to its foundations. Never did the architects of this crumbling relic of a ground in the back end of the Balkans ever believe that its capabilities would be tested so fiercely by so few, but Welsh sporting history was unfolding right in front of our eyes, and it was glorious.

It had been a very different scene just 15 seconds earlier. As the final whistle was blown my heart had sunk to the pit of my stomach and I was rueing the one swift pint I had agreed to have with Dav in the White Horse down the road from Westminster Abbey. That well-meaning solitary lager had led to a half-dozen more, and a drunken conversation in between mouthfuls of suspect kebab meat that would lead to an expensive 1,257 trip to a country that I wouldn't have been able to throw a dart at, even if I'd have possessed the accuracy of Phil Taylor.

But unlike most plans made over a few glasses of Carling hurtling towards the wee hours, this one had stood the test of a hangover and by the middle of the next day the savings account had been raided and flights had been booked. The location, the difficulty of getting there and the cost had been inconsequential - this was a chance for Dav and I to witness together our tiny little nation join Europe's top teams and book our place at a major finals.

We'd only needed a draw to make it and having remained unbeaten in all our previous qualifiers, including beating the mighty Belgium on a night I'll never forget - or rather remember - in Cardiff a few months earlier, it looked a certainty. But two second half goals had punctured the hardy souls who, like us, had abandoned reason and logic to take time off work and pilgrimaged to the far corner of the continent - and we looked set to trudge home disappointed like the bad old days.

There was still one more game to go against group whipping boys Andorra, who had managed to lose every one of their eight qualification matches, and even if they had pulled a Neville Southall-sized miracle out of the hat and drawn against our newfound, mighty squad of sudden superstars, then Wales would still be in the draw for the finals. But there lay the problem: this was Wales, a country that when it comes to football had always managed to grasp gallant defeat from the jaws of certain victory.

Our footballing history is littered with hard luck stories, such as the dodgy referee who gave Scotland a penalty when one of their players punched the ball to ensure we missed out on the 1978 World Cup, or Paul Bodin - bless him - entering the nation's lexicon for misfortune when his tame penalty was saved and another chance at World Cup glory was ended in 1993 at Cardiff Arms Park.

I was 20 when I took my place inside the Millennium Stadium 10 years later, already naively planning a summer travelling around Portugal to see us at Euro 2004, and stood alongside Dav, his dad and our other close mates from university, Ieuan and Matt, waiting for it to be confirmed. 90 minutes later, tears streaked through the red dragons painted on our cheeks as a single goal for the visitors meant that my Lonely Planet guide to Iberia would be consigned to a shelf in the Red Cross shop.

Scarred by the past, nothing was being taken for granted and so I longed for our spot in France to be secured as soon as possible. But a 2-0 defeat wasn't going to do that. Angry, gutted but not at all surprised, the referee's whistle had been the signal for me to turn on my heel, make a quick getaway and wallow in pity inside the windowless, flea-ridden single bed hotel room we had opted to share a few days earlier. It had seemed like a five star establishment with a balcony overlooking the aqua blue Adriatic Sea when we had initially arrived, full of hopes and dreams.

However, I had my exit blocked by an unexpected sight - Dav on his phone. Back home this would be nothing out of the ordinary; he would be constantly checking his Facebook account for messages or frantically swiping his chubby fingers through Tinder in a usually fruitless search for a female friend. But this was abroad, and Dav is known for being extremely tight-fisted (or frugal as he describes), thus the unwillingness to spend on his own hotel room or even a bed in the same one as mine, meaning I would endure a night perched precariously on the edge of the mattress cwtched up next to the large, beanbag-like physique of my best friend. His data roaming had been off switched since we arrived at the airport just in case, and the withdrawal symptoms were palpable as he pawed away at his virtually useless device, all but the calculator app he used to work out the cost of his beers during the afternoon's warm-up.

"What are you doing, mate?" I asked concerned.

"Trying to find out what happened in Israel," he replied nonchalantly, scratching his bum chin. For the second time in a matter of seconds confusion reigned supreme - Dav was simply not a follower of world affairs. Back in our school days he'd once answered a question in a geography test with a drawing of the world map and attempted to gain a mark by 'showing his working' as he'd been asked to do in maths.

"What are you talking about?" I responded.

"The Israel-Cyprus game - remember?" he said, and suddenly it all made sense. Israel had needed to win that match to keep pace with Wales and force our Andorra game to be meaningful three days later, but they were certainties to win that one against inferior opposition.

"Bloody signal; I can't get online here - there are too many people," he grumbled. I looked around and many other fans were doing the same - some were even trying to call relatives back home to get an indication of whether we had been given a lifeline. It seemed pointless to me, so forlornly I looked towards the pitch where the subdued Welsh players were shuffling around with their socks already rolled down, congratulating the Bosnian players with muted handshakes.

Suddenly I caught a glimpse of a figure in a black suit and jet black hair running towards us, fists clenched in the air. It was the unmistakable figure of Chris Coleman, the Wales manager and mastermind of our recent success - and his emotions could only mean one thing. News had filtered through that Israel had lost and tonight's game had been irrelevant - Wales had made it to Euro 2016 after all. Cue the unbridled joy.

***

"Are you online yet?"

"No, I'm still waiting for this bloody computer to finish starting up."

"Jesus Christ, man, I told you years ago that you need to move with the times and get rid of that thing. I think they launched Moon expeditions from that back in the 60s."

"Bit harsh. It still works; it just takes a little time, that's all. Besides, not all of us can afford a shiny new iPad every time a new one comes out."

"Whatever, mate, just hurry up and get online."

Dav and I were on the hunt for tickets. Two months had passed since that balmy autumn night in Bosnia which only got better from the moment our dreams had come true. After Coleman and co had finished celebrating possibly the greatest defeat in sporting history, the 725 continued their party in the bars of Zenica as we took advantage of the favourable exchange rate to buy bottle after bottle of what looked like champagne but barely a drop was drunk; instead it was doused over anyone dressed in red, white and green until they were left in a sticky, sweaty mess.

The Bosnian fans, still buoyant after winning the match, had joined in with our revelry but retreated to their respective beds after a few hours of scarf swapping, beer toasting and sharing retro terrace chants. A blood red sun adorned the sky before those of us with a Welsh affiliation would follow suit, having refused to let the night end until it was astronomically impossible.

Even though I awoke to the sight of a naked, drooling Dav sleeping at the foot of my bed, with just his Wales flag draped over him poorly covering his modesty, weary smiles were still etched on faces as we all met again at the airport hours later. Knowing my work output would have been even more minimal than usual due to sleep deprivation, airport hopping and a raging hangover, I had thankfully hastily booked some time off work the following week so I could also take in the Andorra game, which was an occasion it seemed the whole country didn't want to miss.

Pushing offcuts of copper pipes, ball valves and a tickertape parade's worth of receipts onto the floor, I squeezed myself into the passenger seat of Dav's battered Transit van that moonlighted as a vehicle, an office and seemingly a café, due to the crushed polystyrene coffee cups and ketchup-covered napkins scattered across the dashboard. He'd kindly offered to drive us down the well-trodden path that is the M4 to Cardiff for yet another homecoming which followed the usual traditions: me falling asleep as soon as we got off the M25; Dav waking me up with Tom Jones' "Green Green Grass Of Home" crackling out of the startled speakers as we crossed the Severn Bridge; cheering as we hurtled past the sign that said "Welcome to Wales" which prompted the immediate winding down of the windows as we filled our lungs with the fresh air of God's country, ignoring the fact that we were still on a motorway alongside hundreds of vehicles with emissions billowing out of every exhaust pipe.

A decade of life living in London meant that trips back to the motherland had taken on extra poignancy, but this particular voyage would be special. As always, the pair of us met up with our uni chums, Ieuan and Matt - friendships forged once again over football and despite Dav not going to university - at a small, warren-like pub called The Cottage, which was a long goal-kick away from the Millennium Stadium and always rammed with fans for the big games. It was there that the war room-esque strategic planning regarding our quest for tickets was born.

"Right, so it's agreed," I said. "We all create accounts beforehand, log on to the ticket website at five minute intervals in alphabetical order and go for a game each."

"First name or surname order?" said Matt, a Health and Safety Officer for Cardiff Council who could always be trusted to seek out the finer details of any plan, no matter how tenuous or boring it might be.

"Surname - so Hughes, Jones, Thomas and Williams" I replied.

"Thank you, Captain Obvious!" sneered Dav.

"I'm just making sure you understand you're first - after all it's going to take you a week to get that computer of yours up and running."

"You've still got the same one you had in uni, Dav?" Ieuan exclaimed. "Unbelievable. Wasn't that Windows 95 or something? Does it take cassettes or do you load the Internet onto it via a floppy disk?"

"98, actually. And, yeah, it's fine, don't worry. I can't afford a new one now anyway - got a £120 data roaming charge from when I was in Bosnia." Everyone immediately burst into hysterics. "Stop taking the piss -whose round is it?"

"It's yours, Dav," we chimed in unison.

The drinking, banter and jollity continued where we had left off in Bosnia and before you knew it our voices were among a choir of 33,000 others inside the Cardiff City Stadium, belting out the national anthem, shoulder to shoulder, and giving the "Gwlads" plenty of gusto. For once the football hardly mattered; our star men Aaron Ramsey and Gareth Bale would eventually get the goals as Wales won 2-0, but we were all there as a nation to share a moment of history and look forward to what would be a magical summer.

But that all depended on getting our hands on some tickets, and our best laid plans were in ruins. With Dav's computer slower than John Hartson attempting the 110 hurdles, and Ieuan forgetting that he was on holiday in Lanzarote with his girlfriend on the day UEFA released the all-important first batch, I knew that we were up against the entire Welsh nation as well as England fans, after we had been paired with the old enemy whose doorstep I now reluctantly relied on for shelter and money.

It was the game everyone from the principality had wanted, and when both teams were put in the same group, my thoughts immediately turned primal - I simply had to be there just in case we won. I'd have taken losses against our other group opponents, Slovakia and Russia, if it meant that we could just get one over those white-shirted, red rose, dragon-slaying repressors - after all we were going to France to enjoy ourselves and were happy to win that particular battle even if they eventually won the war.

As I waited impatiently to enter the online ticket portal, it looked as though my only company that day, as two nations swarmed across the Channel, would be Gary Lineker on the telly in my front room in Clapham. But that was until a text came through from Matt.

"Dav - have you got a text from Matt? He's made it in!"

"Get in! What can he get?"

"Waiting to find out now."

"Everything going OK, Mr Thomas?" came a familiar voice from behind my seat that made me hastily hang up on Dav, scramble for my mouse and try and open the Powerpoint presentation that hadn't seen any changes all morning. But it was far too late to salvage the situation.

"Yes, fine thanks, Graham," I replied to my boss Graham Mortimer, the chief executive and self-titled Brand Guardian of Underscore Design. Swivelling around to face him, I was greeted by his tall, rotund figure blocking out the majority of the fluorescent lighting that kept me from squinting around my small section of an open plan office, where a number of the usually lifeless workforce had also spun their seats to see what transgression had caught his attention.

"Trying to book tickets to the football are we, Scott?" he said, from which I guessed that my quickly-open-Powerpoint plan I'd conjured up an hour before had failed miserably.

"Err yeah, I was just having a quick look whilst I wait for some artwork from Poundland regarding the Quavers campaign."

"Oh, OK, well seeing as you have a minute then, can we touch base on what you've done so far?" he said, desperately trying to conceal the smirk on his face. I knew exactly what he was doing as I had given him a run through of these same plans during a 'deep dive' days earlier; he was simply trying to stall me and prevent me getting tickets. Knowing I couldn't get away with saying that his company was no nearer to a lucrative deal than they were 48 hours previously - mainly because I was trying to come up with a foolproof plan to circumnavigate UEFA's ticket website - I was forced to talk him through the same plan for 20 agonising minutes.

"Great stuff, keep up the good work," Graham insincerely stated after wasting both of our time and retreated to his office, probably to create the latest industry buzzword. With the coast clear, I returned to the website only to find out that I had been sent to the back of the queue 'due to inactivity.' I was crestfallen.

But when I checked my phone, Matt had come up trumps. 'Got 4 tix for Slovakia game!' said the finest text message to grace my phone since Angharad Morgan had agreed to be my girlfriend back in Year 10 after I'd failed to pluck up the courage to ask her face-to-face. She would dump me three weeks later for Gary Davies in Year 12 - who had become the first lad to pass his driving test and got a car - without even a hint of a cheeky kiss behind the maths block.

But screw you, Angharad, you tease, screw Gary, and screw Graham - I was going to Wales' opening game of the Euros! I busted out a mini fist pump at my desk and decided now was the perfect time for my fourth cuppa of the day, especially as my mug was graced with a photo of Ian Rush celebrating one of his record-holding 28 goals for Wales. It was a mediocre tally for someone of his quality, who had represented for his country for 16 years, but it perfectly reflected how pitiful Welsh footballing achievements had been until now, and I was going to be there as a new era dawned and everything changed forever.

The rest of the working day evaporated in a flash. Had Graham wanted to see the Quavers artwork again the next day, then I might be in trouble - because suddenly, slouching in my chair, sharing the same piece of grey carpet as 20 other beige people all trapped for eight hours day between beige walls was going to be the cash cow that funded my summer in France. I despised my job, but I was resigned to the truth that it was where my future lay. A dream of an exciting career in the vibrant world of graphic design, which had me scrambling for a pen and signing up to three years at Cardiff University, had only yielded a role with Underscore designing newspaper adverts for those companies who couldn't afford to go to one of Soho's top advertising agencies. This had handcuffed me to a third of my life expectancy paying off the loans for tuition fees, Smirnoff Ices and tins of Sainsbury's Basics sausages and beans.

But now I suddenly had the fear of my contract being terminated. And, with the Euros on the horizon, I immediately felt a sense of duty and loyalty to the firm that had given me my break over a decade earlier, and vowed that, after an afternoon of imagining, in slow-motion, Ashley Williams lifting the Henri Delaunay trophy above his head as red and blue confetti fluttered around him, I would be the best graphic designer that Soho, Madison Avenue or anywhere in the world had seen. It would be like when Gary Speed picked up the pieces after the snoozefest that was the John Toshack era; the quality was there, but it just needed to be tapped into and soon the improvement would be for all to see. Well, at least the 20 dullards sat grinding their teeth at their desks anyway.

To help with my new-found drive, I went to the stationary cupboard and pulled out a 2016 desk calendar. Ironically for a graphic design company, it had no theme or pattern to it, just a black and white, bog-standard calendar. But it was perfect for what I had in mind for it, which some newfangled expert probably calls a visualisation technique to create 'blue sky thinking' or some other ridiculous guff that they'll then charge an idiot like Graham thousands for and spend it on fold-up bikes and kale. I opened my desk, navigated around the mint wrappers, unopened letters and empty notepads, and pulled out a red felt-tip pen which had not seen the light of day for a while as after I'd scribbled furiously on a fresh jotter, I drew a big circle around one date in the calendar: Saturday 11th June 2016, the day Wales played their first game at a major international championship since a teenager called Pele scored the only goal to knock us out of the 1958 World Cup. Whatever happened to him?

As was customary, I watched the final few seconds of the day count down on the large black and white clock watching over me at the back of the room before hitting Start and Shut Down on my computer, which had gotten more and more satisfying as the years at Underscore had passed. A minute later I was strolling through Carnaby Street, politely declining the droves of fundraisers eager to sign me up to whatever unwashed charity's t-shirt they had decided to pull on that day. Normally I just stared a hole right through them to try and brush the cheeriness off their faces and make them realise that when they trade in their temp job for the real world, they too will act the same way when asked to graciously part ways with the wages they had just earned yearning for five o'clock to arrive.

Nope, they wouldn't get to me today because nothing would. It didn't matter that a black cab yet again flagrantly ignored the Highway Code when I was about to step onto a zebra crossing, or that some girl with pink hair and bowler hat stopped walking right in front of me to try and create instant fame on Instagram for a pigeon minding its own business. It didn't matter that a German tourist at the ticket barriers refused to believe he had insufficient funds on his Oyster card, or that a Chinese man with a dust mask on coughed in my face on a tube train hotter than an apple pie in a microwave.

I was going to the European Championships to see Wales - and my mood refused to alter.

Even my iPhone could feel the happiness radiating through my body and spookily Frankie Valli's "Can't Take My Eyes Off You," a staple of our late-night crooning after a few shandies on various away trips in far-flung lands, was shuffled into my ears as I exited Clapham South tube station.

For once I didn't notice the crack in the window pane of the front door of my extortionately rented one-bedroom apartment on the high street, or the blaring sirens of the police car and ambulance as they raced past. I closed the door behind me, scooping up the pile of post scattered on the laminated flooring. As I walked into what passed up as my kitchen, I separated the takeaway menus, council magazines and business cards for professional cleaning services from the letters that had actually included some sort of postage.

"Hi, honey, are you home?" I shouted out.

"Alright. I'm in here," came a voice from just around the corner in the living room section of the flat; but I should have realised her presence from the nail polish fumes that instantly attacked my sinuses like someone sticking a hundred needles into my brain. Turning the corner, I was greeted by the sight of my fiancée, Victoria, who was blowing furiously at her feet to get her recently-applied red varnish to dry quicker. Blaring out of the TV was some god-awful reality show about some American housewives pretending to be in shocking situations when they just happened to have four cameras pointing at them at the precise time - you know the kind. She craned her neck around to look at me, and grunted, "Any of that for me?" Sadly she meant the post.

"Yeah, there's a letter for you, and something addressed to both of us," I replied, and chucked them on her lap.

"Oi, don't do that, you might get nail varnish on the sofa, or worse I'll have to do another coat. Have a look what's in the one addressed to both us and read it out to me. I don't want to smudge these nails."

She never was interested in how my day went anyway. I picked up the purple envelope addressed to 'Victoria & Scott' and ripped it open.

"It's a wedding invitation from Sarah and Craig."

"Ooooh exciting. She rang me yesterday when I was in the bath, so I knew it was on its way! I've already been online looking for hats. What does it say inside?"

"To Victoria and Scott. Sarah and Craig would like you to join them as they celebrate their marriage at St John's Church in Great Rissington at 2pm on Saturday 11th...". Suddenly my heart leapt out of my mouth, catching my breath, and my eyes screwed up wishing I'd not seen the end of the sentence. My body went limp for a millisecond. For fuck's sake.

"Keep going," Victoria said.

"At 2pm on Saturday 11th June."

CHAPTER 2

The Victoria who was bent double on a leather sofa, slapping on coats of nail varnish and virtually ignoring my presence, was not the girl I'd fallen head over heels in love with in university, moved to London with to continue our blossoming relationship and eventually allowed me to slip a diamond ring on her finger.

I had first clasped eyes on her during freshers' week just days after I had started at Cardiff Uni. Having grown up in a small Victorian town that lived off past glories called Llandrindod Wells, situated in the bullseye of Wales, surrounded by rolling green hills, I arrived in the nation's capital like a rabbit in the headlights. I had only uprooted 70 miles, but Cardiff was a world away from my sheltered upbringing, where everyone knew their neighbours, their postman and even the brothers that worked in the cobblers.

I was intimidated by the city boys who seemed to be so much more brash, confident, trendy and well-built than me. My halls were packed with them, and even by the end of the first getting-to-know-you party on day one, they had developed a clique where membership merely required a love of protein shakes and hair gel. Having taken one look at my scrawny frame and terrible posture, they cast me adrift almost instantly. I rode their coattails to the student union that first night before they managed to shake me off as soon as we got inside. The union quickly became a second home for me, carpeted by sticky snakebite with the stale aroma of a teenage boy's bedroom.

After wandering around aimlessly for a while, a trip to the toilet followed. As I relieved my body of the horrendous initiation shots that had been forced upon me - not to mention the three litres of Strongbow I'd inflicted upon myself to build some Dutch courage - I could just about make out a slurred conversation in the cubicles next to me over the pumping bassline of So Solid Crew's 21 Seconds.

"Honestly, we're going nowhere under Sparky. Nowhere. We're useless - we drew 0-0 draw against Armenia a few weeks ago. There is more chance of you scoring tonight, mate, than that shower of shite."

"Give it time, butt; Hughesy knows what he's doing. Bellamy is the future; he's been tearing things up for Newcastle recently, and Simon Davies is tasty. Hang on, do you reckon I've actually got a chance?"

"Poor Giggsy. He dribbles, and dribbles, and dribbles, and crosses and what does he look up to see? Nathan Blake up front."

"I was chatting to that fit Catherine girl in the dorm earlier, she looked keen. Does she have a boyfriend?"

"I mean, Nathan Blake. Nathan bloody Blake."

This was the in I needed. After a good shake, I washed my hands and lingered around the basin for these two hiccupping football fanatics to do the same, praying that they didn't turn out to be another couple of meatheads with a David Beckham-inspired mohican, in stripy Topman t-shirts and cargo pants. However, my Blind Date-esque reveal took an eternity and the other loo users splashing around in puddles of piss were giving me funny looks as I attended to my already preened spiky hairstyle, complete with frosted tips.

Eventually the two voices emerged, and their pasty, pimpled skin alluded to hours spent cooped inside deprived of sunlight which could only mean they were fellow Championship Manager addicts. Their eyes were drowning in whatever booze they had been polishing off all evening and they just staggered straight past and burst out of the door as dry ice and laser beams crept into the bathroom momentarily from the dancefloor. I rushed to follow suit, and fortunately when they had taken up a position at the bar they hadn't changed topic.

"It's not as bad as Bobby Gould, butt - I had to put up with him as manager of Cardiff too! Made me want to stop going to Ninian, but I didn't."

"He gave Nathan Blake an international cap. He needs shooting, that Gould."

"Yeah, he was crap, wasn't he?" I hastily chipped in uninvited. "I mean, anyone desperate enough to find a Welsh grandparent for Vinnie Jones to solve our midfield problems has got to have a screw loose."

"You're not wrong there, butt. Who are you again?"

And that is how I came to know Ieuan and Matt. Cardiff lads born and bred, they had been complete strangers until about two hours earlier, when they moved in next door to each other in their halls and shared a pack of Stella. A night of shunning the DJ's attempts to tap into our fledgling repertoire of poor dance moves was instead spent discussing all-things football: Ryan Giggs' rumoured move abroad; if my team, Aston Villa, could hold onto the hot managerial property that was John Gregory; how mental on a scale of one to 10 was Sam Hamann, who owned Ieuan's beloved Cardiff City; and Matt moaning about English fans' bravado after recently beating Germany 5-1 ("I mean, Carsten Jancker is a poor man's Nathan Blake").

This continued for the next few days as we spent very little time diving head-first into our courses but instead battering FIFA 99 in my tiny bedroom, which had consisted of a single bed and a wonky shelf when I moved in. By the time we had been coaxed out of it for another night out a few days later, the only decorating I had attempted had been to pin up posters of Villa's Dion Dublin and a bikini-clad Rachel Stevens.

Against the odds, it turned out to be a night that changed the rest of my life.

A few halls had decided to gather together to have a huge party, and after the city boys had continued to mutate and clung together in an overpowering cloud of Lynx Africa, I squeezed past them to get into the kitchen to polish off the remainder of my Asda own brand whiskey.

As I opened the door, I was greeted by the sight of a lone girl, pouring herself a drink out of that same bottle. A little tipsy, I assertively called out, "Hey, that's my bloody booze!" But my bravado vanished the second Victoria turned to face me.

She took my breath away. I was instantly transfixed by her big brown eyes and rouged cheekbones that highlighted a heart-shaped face, blessed with clear skin and punctuated by the cutest pinched nose. Sunkissed brown hair flowed down to her shoulders, which framed the top of her petite figure that still housed a couple of pounds of teenage puppy fat, that only helped her perfectly fill out an emerald green dress. A slim, well-maintained eyebrow kinked when she'd clocked who had requested her to put down the whiskey, but a cheeky smile that revealed a pair of gorgeous dimples instantly exonerated her from any blame.

"Sorry, is this yours?" she replied. I was ashamed to be quibbling with a girl this beautiful over a bottle of unbranded alcohol, so quickly changed my tack and grabbed the first thing alcoholic to hand.

"Errr, no sorry - I thought you had my - umm - blue WKD," I stammered as I realised that I had picked up probably the worst drink of all time to impress a girl with.

"Oh really - are you a big WKD drinker?" she giggled.

"Yeah, totally. All the time. Where I'm from, we, um, drink it by the pint before a night out."

I literally wanted to concuss myself to prevent me from saying anything else idiotic, but my bed was already made. To try and establish some authenticity, I cracked off the lid

21

and poured myself half a pint of the ungodly aqua-bleached liquid. An infusion of blueberries and tablespoons of sugar permeated the room, and I took an almighty gulp that I was pretty sure I would be seeing again in a nearby toilet bowl as soon as it had galvanized my stomach lining.

"Well, that might be the case, but that's my WKD. I was saving it to make Cheeky Vimtos in a bit." My humiliation was complete. "But seeing as you've already started, I might as well join you," came an unexpected end to a sentence I was all set to begin repressing to stave away embarrassing memories for years to come.

"Sure, OK!" I squeaked in surprise. Victoria proceeded to pour herself half a pint of WKD too, then added some port and lemonade - the Sainsbury's Basics kind. What a woman.

Completely forgetting about Ieuan, Matt and all her friends, we exchanged introductions and began chatting, leaning against the worktops. Ten minutes later we were cross-legged on top of them, laughing at each other's jokes and reliving tales from our sixth form proms. When stronger quantities of Cheeky Vimtos were poured, she revealed that had moved to the city from Berkshire to study geography, and, like me, only knew a few people from her halls so far. I was in the process of memorising every tiny detail on her immaculate face when our newly-found friends interrupted and ushered us outside and on our way to the union.

Having previously longed for Ieuan and Matt's company, on this night I just wanted to be beside Victoria - but I got nowhere near as the meatheads enveloped her as if she was a timid zebra surrounded by a pack of well-groomed hyenas slathered in Dax hair wax. Conversations about Sir Alex

Ferguson retiring or whether Juan Sebastian Veron was worth the £28 million he paid for him just didn't appeal. And after going through the motions and a bucket of southern fried chicken on the way home, I slunk off to bed.

The taste of stale WKD and pepperoni was still on my tongue as I tossed and turned, unable to think about anything except the girl who had somehow managed to force football out of my consciousness for the time being, when the kind of thing that only happens in movies, and certainly not to anyone like myself, happened: three soft taps on my door. I opened it and there she stood, with a butter-wouldn't-melt smile. Despite being forced to endure a sweatpit for the past few hours, she had someone emerged as radiant as she'd entered.

"Can I come in, Scott?" she whispered.

"Of course - what's up?" I responded, glad that I was wrapped in my duvet as her presence in my bedroom had instantly stimulated my downstairs juices.

"I need to get away from those rugby lads; they're absolute morons. One of them just dared another to drink his own piss, and thought it would then be sexy to chat to me with urine breath. How gross is that?"

"Vile. Fancy some chewing gum?" I offered, acutely aware that my state of dental hygiene needed masking if it was the one requirement she requested from those in her current company.

"Thanks. Who's that?" she said, pointing to my wall.

"Rachel Stevens - you know the one from S Club 7?"

"No not her, silly, I know her. There ain't no party like an S Club party!" she sniggered before proceeding to precisely recite the chorus and a verse to that particular song for good measure. Despite being obviously tipsy, she seemed unashamed of her love for cheesy pop music despite being 18, which, for someone as self-conscious as I was, made her all the more attractive. It was almost as if she was saying, 'take it or leave it,' and there was more chance of me breaking into my own a capella rendition of 'God Save The Queen' than opting for the latter.

"Sorry, got carried away there! Who's the football player?" she said, perching herself on the edge of my bed, chomping on her gum.

"Dion Dublin. He plays as a striker for the team I support, Aston Villa." I murmured, more concerned that there was a foxy female now teasing me by attempting to blow bubbles.

"Oh cool. Are they any good?"

After five minutes of introducing this gorgeous girl to the other love of my life, we were squashed up side by side on my single mattress as she slowly drifted off grasping my arm.

"I'm pleased I met you tonight, Scott," she muttered just before succumbing to sleep. "I think we're going to have some fun times together."

Her prediction was proven true, as by the time we had returned to Llandrindod and Berkshire for Christmas we were officially an item. We were still together three years later when we attended each other's graduations, and her talent and passion towards helping the environment quickly landed her a well-paying job with Wandsworth Council's recycling team. This meant we were packing our bags and moving to the gold-paved streets of London together as our lives began to properly dovetail.

Despite the big step change, we coped well. Seeing her thrive in her new role gave me the determination to make her proud of me too and within two months, I'd been offered a job with Underscore. As the years passed, we enjoyed bouncing around from apartment to apartment, immersing ourselves in all the bright lights had to offer, and by May 2008, when we had been together for six and a half years and finally accepted that Big Ben and red buses were now home, I did the decent thing. Having scratched and clawed enough disposable money as I could from modest salary, as well as borrowing a lot more from my parents, I purchased an engagement ring and got down on one knee on a random but nerve-wracking Thursday evening in our front room.

Little did I know, but her tearful, positive response would be the high point of our relationship. She rightfully craved a dream wedding, but as is the case with most twenty-somethings in London, rent strangled our finances and we were happy to accept that it could be quite a while until our special day arrived. After four years of penny-pinching, a nice little sum was building up in our joint bank account - partly thanks to sacrifices like stopping my frequent trips to Villa Park and selling my beloved collection of Subbuteo and Panini sticker albums. I genuinely believed it was worth the sacrifices to help someone who would eternally make my life complete on that perfect wedding day.

But that girl started to stray away from her old self. Snobbery began to consume her and she suddenly opted to look down on those she deemed unworthy of her company, including the majority of her childhood friends, some mutual acquaintances we had made in Cardiff, and even Dav, Ieuan and Matt. Her work colleagues filled the vacancies and jealousy influenced her to become materialistic. I was soon fulfilling demands for designer handbags and shoes for Christmas presents. While I was tucked up at home watching Champions League games on the telly with a cup of tea and a packet of Wotsits, she would regularly whirlwind through the doorway at gone 11pm, insisting that she'd had to go for a few drinks at some swanky cocktail bar in Mayfair for a co-worker's birthday, which conveniently always had no signal to inform me of her whereabouts. As much as it ate away at me, I wasn't brave enough to bring up the fact that I suspected that she was having a fling elsewhere, as I simply didn't want to know the answer.

Victoria's transformation from the wholesome, lively girl I had stumbled across in that kitchen into an egotistical, annoying bore was complete when one day she uncharacteristically quit her job after her tardiness led to her being questioned and selfishly decided that she was going to take an indefinite amount of time off to figure out her next step. Having put up with a lot, I suddenly decided to confront her and arguments raged for days as she began to dip into our wedding fund to fuel her trips to her new mates Dolce and Gabbana and Michael Kors and our sex life had became as passionless as an Old Trafford crowd.

Her lack of employment ensured I remained shackled to Underscore to keep a roof over our heads, despite my craving for something more creative. But regardless of the tough days, I was determined to do what was necessary as I was engaged to someone I truly cared about and simply put it down to a phase she was going through. After all, we were still in our mid-20s.

However, by the time we turned 30, caring about environmental issues had been the latest skin that she had shed as my fiancée decided to join London's ever-growing crew of self-employed party planners. Zoning out and attempting to name Wales' starting line-up from famous matches became a daily ritual as she gossiped about what had happened on this hen-door or at that baby shower, even if the occasional income helped my wife-to-be contribute to the albatross around our necks that was our hefty rent.

As well as Victoria's new-found passion of planning weddings, we had arrived at a time of our lives where all our friends were getting hitched, despite being engaged for a decade less than us. The invitation to Sarah and Craig's wedding, which I still clasped in my hand as I resisted the urge to sob uncontrollably into the tissue paper and lace it was made up of, would be the latest in a long line that had needed RSVPing to, setting off a chain of events that lasted for months. Buying new suits, talking about the weather with whichever poor soul was sat next to me on our dinner table and listening to the same old best man speeches plagiarised from the internet were my three particular wedding bugbears. I had even accidently learnt the words to Sing Hosanna after singing it so many times.

Having been with the same woman - or, more to the point, two different versions of her - for 14 years I knew it was pretty pointless suggesting I missed this particular wedding to go and watch a game of football abroad, especially as Victoria's interest in the beautiful game hadn't gotten much further than our chat underneath the Dion Dublin poster all those years ago. But you don't get if you don't ask, right?

"Oh no, you'll have to tell Sarah and Craig that I won't be able to go," I said, putting on my fake-disappointment voice and hoping that over the near decade and half we had been a couple that she was still yet to discover I possessed such a cadence.

"Why's that?" Victoria said, finally distracted enough from her toenail painting to look at me once again with a screwed up face, seemingly delighted at the chance to step on more dreams.

"Well, it's funny, as this afternoon Matt managed to get us all tickets to Wales' first game of Euro 2016 in France."

"Well, you'll have to tell him you can't go - you can't miss Craig's wedding, he'll be gutted! You guys have been friends for years." This was completely wrong; we had initially gotten on politely as two men forced by their partners to spend time in each other's company do to try and make the double-date nights or cheese and wine evenings cordial affairs. However after he decided to stop drinking alcohol as a lifestyle choice the awkwardness between two blokes with nothing in common and without the safety net of booze meant that we now both loathed being forced into these situations. Him trying to come up with excuses would be just as futile with Sarah as my current attempt.

"Nah, I'm sure he'll be fine with it," I responded confidently.

"Well, what about me? I can't go alone. I mean, what bridesmaid goes to a wedding alone? The sad ones, that's who. I don't want to be one of those losers with no-one to dance with, so you'll have to be there." Her big brown eyes were almost filling with tears as she pictured that scene and it shattered my heart a little to see the girl who years ago had possessed such confidence in herself as she belted out S Club 7 songs had slowly become so self-conscious.

"You'll be fine! All your friends will be there and you'll have a great time without me," I said, knowing that this was as fruitless as trying to get tickets for the finals myself.

"Please don't spoil this day for me, Scott."

And with those eight words I knew I could kiss watching Ashley Williams lead his side out in Bordeaux goodbye.

***

"Just spoil it for her," came an unhelpful response from Dav. Once again we were sat in a random pub in London - the Hagen and Hyde in Balham, to be precise - as Dav had decided many years before that whenever we met up for a beer we should always go somewhere different - yet they all seemed to be similar versions of the gastropub scene sweeping the city with their dim lighting, unnecessarily loud background music and shabby-chiq décor. This initially quaint idea when Dav lived back in Wales became problematic when he decided to join me and take his plumbing business to the capital; a smart move as he was soon earning twice as much from each job, but still managing to leave his wallet at home with alarming regularity.

I secretly admired Dav - not just because he was my best friend of nearly 30 years, but because he was never afraid to take a chance like that. With university never in reach, or interest, for him it would have been easy to remain in Llandrindod with his long-time friends. After two years of regularly bombing over the border in clapped out old vans which were spluttering write-offs by the time he pulled up outside my flat, he decided to move down too.

I drew the line at him living on the same street as Victoria and I, scuppering his original plan, but as Victoria slowly morphed into an airhead it was reassuring to know that Dav would provide a slice of the good old days, listen to my latest issue and dish out some typically undiplomatic advice.

"I can't spoil this for her, mate, god knows how long she'd keep me in the doghouse for. She would never let it slide. Plus she is going to be a bridesmaid, so it is kind of a big deal."

"Always the bridesmaid and never the bride…" he smirked, waiting for me to take the bait.

"Shut up, Dav - we're getting married eventually."

"Eventually! When you two started going out, Joe Ledley hadn't even come close to growing his first strand of facial hair."

I normally didn't take kindly to jokes about my elongated engagement, but today I just didn't have to heart to come back and make a crude retort about Dav's taste in women going hand in hand with his trips to the clinic for a week's worth of penicillin.

Perhaps surprised to get away with making such a comment, Dav leant closer towards me so I could hear him above the non-descript electronic dance music that provided an out-of-sorts soundtrack to our quiet Tuesday night. With a hush to his voice he said: "There is one way to get around all this - you could leave her."

He was stirring the pot rather unsubtly as I sensed immediately that this had been his agenda for the evening all along. He and Victoria hadn't been friends for years; they had initially got along back in Cardiff, as Dav would visit once a month. Like most boisterous teenagers, this involved him binge drinking, stumbling home via Chip Alley and causing carnage back at the halls, such as the time he cracked a television screen attempting to invent indoor golf with a broom taking the place of a six-iron.

Borderline acceptable when you're at that age, but when the tomfoolery continued into his 20s in the apartment I shared with my girlfriend, a more refined version of Victoria quickly grew fed up, with the tipping point coming when Dav sat on a post-pub pizza he'd put down temporarily on the sofa and then proceeding to leave smears of orangey tomato stains all over the front room wherever his backside made contact with anything. Understandably words were exchanged, but things would never be the same again when Victoria proclaimed him as a waste of space, Dav labelled her a controlling bitch, and both of them told me in no uncertain terms that I could do better.

"Yeah right, mate. Like I'm going to listen to someone with your relationship track record and throw away a 14-year relationship because I can't watch a game of football."

"It's not just a game of football - it's *the* game of football we have been waiting all our lives for! It's history in the making. All you've got to do is grow a pair and say the magic words: Victoria, we're done. Or if you don't want the confrontation, maybe send her a text?" I'll even type it out for you!" he laughed.

Out of instinct I joined in. But deep down hearing my best friend reiterate the same nagging, private thoughts I'd had fairly regularly over the preceding years when I lay restlessly fretting about the future as Victoria slumbered peacefully, was a revelation. He had said the words that I couldn't force myself to utter - and, secretly, admonished myself for even possessing - as I refused to imagine what cutting the cord would be like.

"You're thinking about it, aren't you?" Dav said, surprised but almost pleased that the seed he had deliberately planted was beginning to lay down roots through my subconscious.

I was barely listening, though, as it was as if I had experienced an epiphany. I had reached a monumental crossroads in my life that I might not have got to had Wales not reached Euro 2016. If Gareth Bale hadn't have netted that late winner in Andorra in the first group game, or the team hadn't dug as deep as they did following Andy King's red card to grind out a 2-1 win against Cyprus, then I would not be thinking about telling my fiancée that 15 years had been quite enough. Was fate telling me that following the Welsh team to France was the best way to go?

I realised it was now or possibly never. I had to choose between Bordeaux with friends or boredom with my fiancée. Football or flowergirls. A fresh start or the same old feelings. The hard way, or the easy way. And deep down I knew exactly what route I was going to take.

CHAPTER 3

"Sing hosanna, sing hosanna

"Sing hosanna to the King of Kings"

Yeah you guessed it - I bottled it. On Saturday 11th June, I was stood in a quaint little church in the middle of the Cotswolds, holding an order of service next to a bunch of people I didn't know, lip-syncing a hymn. I wasn't amongst the 42,000 crammed inside the impressive Stade de Bordeaux, clutching a programme next to friends and strangers whom I hoped would become great acquaintances during the next 90 minutes, belting out Men of Harlech.

Once again it felt like I was so close to what I wanted, yet nowhere near, perfectly encapsulating my preceding 33 years. Stuck at the back of the church, due to a necessary last-minute dash for a nearby pub toilet, I hadn't even been able to catch a fleeting glimpse of Victoria, or indeed Sarah and Craig. Now, not only was I a plus-one at a wedding I had no desire to attend, but I couldn't even see it happen due to the array of appalling hats, which resembled row upon row of satellite dishes and television aerials overlooking an old terraced street and were obstructing my view.

If only the monstrosities masquerading as headwear did transmit signals. My mood had only worsened when, as I had feared for weeks, we arrived at the picturesque Gloucestershire village of Great Rissington and I had no phone reception. I would struggle to keep tabs on the Wales score throughout the day unless I found myself a television.

It was probably a blessing in disguise. On the journey down my phone was vibrating constantly as the lads bombarded me with picture messages of their antics from the previous night in Toulouse. Filled with fun and laughter, it had seemed to be the complete opposite of the abysmal TV footage of street battles between organised Russian hooligans and mainly innocent English fans in Marseille over the past few days, quickly casting a dark cloud over the competition. Victoria had revelled in lecturing me about how lucky I was to be going to the wedding instead of travelling with them to France.

However, it seemed as though my fellow Welsh fans were determined not to be tarred with the same brush. Any fears I had about the policing were allayed when I received a Snapchat of Dav with his arms wrapped around a local policeman, who was donning the infamous red, green and yellow bucket hat while Dav gurned away with a helmet perched on his giant cranium. Various videos also showed the scale of the Welsh support, who were endearing themselves to the locals by being friendly-natured, cordial and matching their choice of football shirt with the local wine on offer. They may have been tipsy, excitable and noisy, but compared to Marseille, the people of Bordeaux were delighted to welcome their temporary residents. It seemed as though the whole nation had gone over as one giant party - and I hadn't been invited. Unlike this bloody wedding.

When the final parps of the organ had sounded and we were allowed to sit down after enduring four verses and four choruses of that god-awful song, I glanced at my watch. It was 3.15pm. Sarah had been 45 minutes late because Victoria had been so upset with what the hairdresser had created on top of her head earlier that morning that she had burst into tears, ruining her make-up and the stylist had to start all over again. Only 45 minutes to go until Wales took to the field 738 miles away. I longed to know the line-up and what the boys' seats were like. With my attentions elsewhere, the majority of the service flashed by; 20 minutes later we were back outside in the small, walled grounds of the church.

While the rest of the guests formed a guard of honour for the happy couple outside the doors, I had whipped my phone out of my jacket pocket and wove around crumbling, illegible headstones in the overgrown graveyard, desperately trying to get a bar of signal, thinking no-one would miss me. Lo and behold, I got the tiniest smidge of 3G stood next to a statue of Jesus (it had to be a sign) allowing me to finally access Twitter and discover who the 11 players that would form the basis of quiz questions for decades to come would be. I was digesting the news that Danny Ward was filling in the large presence of the injured Wayne Hennessey in goal, and that Jonny Williams had been preferred to all of our striking options, when I heard a shrill, stern blast from behind me which startled me back into my surroundings.

"Scott - move yourself! You're right in the way there. What are you doing?" Victoria barked.

I swivelled around to be confronted with the sight of 100 people all looking disapprovingly - none more so than my fiancée, whose face was contorted with anger and embarrassment, looking like she would need that stylist again soon. Sarah and Craig were stood in the foreground with their eyes boring a hole through me and I quickly arrived at the correct conclusion: the photographer had been trying to get the traditional snap of them being doused in confetti, but ruining the background of his shot was a bloke in a grey suit, disrespectfully slumped on a figurine of a deity and shaking his head as the backlight of his phone shone brightly in his face.

"Oops - sorry!" I replied bashfully, but none of the 200-odd eyes fixed upon me seemed to have forgiveness in them. Blood rushed to my cheeks as I turned a crimson red through humiliation. I scuttled away as quickly as possible, forgetting that I was in a place of mourning and traipsing over the final resting places of many of the area's never-forgotten sons and daughters, which could only have continued to my onslaught of offense.

As the bride and groom got into their carriage drawn by two huge white horses - one of which I thought struck a remarkable resemblance to Slovakian defender Martin Skrtel, as it looked a little war-torn and irritated, they were waved away by my new army of haters, and as soon as they had disappeared into the countryside, the woman whom I had hoped to one day be sharing that magical moment with headed my way to give me both barrels.

"What the hell were you playing at? You can't go for a piss in a graveyard! What kind of animal are you?" she hissed. I was startled by such a ridiculous accusation.

"What? I went to the pub before the ceremony."

"Don't give me that, we all saw what you were doing, and for Christ's sake, Scott, do up your bloody fly."

I looked down and, sure enough, my trousers had been undone throughout the whole ceremony. When I had turned around to face everyone earlier, they had all caught a glimpse of my lucky red Welsh boxers peeking through my trouser fastening.

"Shit," I gasped, hurriedly zipping them back up. "They must have been like this for the last hour! I was not having a piss, I was checking the Wales team on my phone, that's all."

"What? Bloody football - whatever, I don't want to be seen with you right now; I've got to go. I'll see you at the reception, when hopefully I'll be in a better mood and a lot less embarrassed."

As Victoria rushed off to continue her bridesmaid duties, I stood among the gravestones in a daze. There's no other adjective in the English language more cutting than when your partner labels you as an embarrassment… hang on… Dave Edwards is starting ahead of Premier League-winner Andy King?

While trying to second guess Chris Coleman, I heard a cry from behind me, and knew instantly that it was Victoria. It wasn't a pleasurable scream, as I hadn't heard that for a while. No, this was a shriek of anguish. I turned to see her being comforted by three bridesmaids stood at arm's length and I soon realised why - she had stepped in a massive, fresh mound of horse shit, which had completely encased her right foot, condemning an expensive pair of heels to a Gloucestershire landfill site. At this point I did what anyone in my position would do; I removed my phone out of my pocket again, took a candid photograph and sent it to all my mates. Now who was the embarrassment?

Rather than weighing up the possibility of the existence of karma, I was more concerned about the time, still chuckling to myself as I revelled in schadenfreude and jumped into my silver Mondeo to instantly tune the radio to BBC 5 Live. The reception was at a rather grand stately home in a neighbouring village, so there wasn't too far to drive, but I was already running late so I sped away from the church as if I was an accomplice to a bank robbery. The locals must have thought I was auditioning for the next film in the Fast and the Furious franchise, as I ripped through their village and between the tall hedges that made up some country lanes, following a route I had already researched and practiced on Google Street View to ensure that no second was wasted.

However, there was an unusual soundtrack to my pedal-to-the-floor escapades: an orchestral number with a distinctive melody involving a triangle and a choir singing dramatically and beautifully. I'm not blessed with an encyclopaedic knowledge of Eastern European national anthems, but I suspected that this was either the Slovakian number or David Guetta had decided to go in a different musical direction with the tournament's official theme song.

I saw a road sign that stated the hall was just two miles away. But despite being so close, I took the opportunity to pull into a disused petrol station, yanked the handbrake up and switched off the engine. For just 90 seconds, I wanted to close my eyes and imagine that I was in Bordeaux, singing my heart out for my country.

The final beats of the triangle crackled through the car's speakers, followed by a short ripple of applause and cheering from the Slovak fans. Then, the one musical note that instantly causes the hairs to prickle on my arms, my eyes to widen and suddenly tighten again to prevent tears from sneaking out, and my throat to take a strong gulp. Every Welsh person knows that note and it stirs similar emotions in pretty much every one of us. Every time the brass section get the nod from the conductor and plays the first second of Mae Hen Wlad Fy Nhadau, tiny smatterings of the world stand frozen. In a heartbeat that note has the power to cast an immediate hush over the loudest pub and impose silence upon the world's largest stadiums; those who resonate with that calling stand to attention, ready to display their patriotism in the way they have been programmed to do so since birth - by the medium of song.

I am sure I am not the only one who doesn't know the proper pronunciation of the words of our glorious anthem, or be able to translate them, despite spending 12 years compulsorily learning the Welsh language at school, getting a A grade in my GCSEs, but being unable to understand Mr Bump's hijinks in a book written for a toddler. However, when offered the opportunity, I belt out my personal version with plenty of gusto, and today would be no different. I channelled my inner tenor and sang the verse still strapped into the driver's seat in the middle of nowhere, disturbing only a few birds scattered among the trees and hedgerows nearby.

"Gwlad, GWWWALLLLLLDDDDDD!" I roared as the chorus began, and I could hear the ferocity and passion of the huge contingent of 25,000 Welsh people savouring the moment inside the stadium. I imagined I was shoulder to shoulder with Dav, Ieuan and Matt; immediately, vivid memories flashed through my mind when this song had been the precursor to some great moments. The night we beat Italy in 2003, in front of 70,000 fans; or as an eight-year-old, stood on the terrace at Cardiff Arms Park at one of my first ever matches, witnessing Wales beat the then-world champions Germany 1-0.

As the final notes were drowned out by a huge rallying call from the Welsh fans to the 11 men they had pinned their hopes and dreams on, I opened my eyes and suddenly a river of tears streamed out of them. I was by no means sobbing nor was I upset, but I could only put their appearance down to a mixture of pride and regret. I knew I should have been there instead of clinging on to the thinnest strands of my relationship; it would have truly made me happy at this moment in time, and possibly forever. Instead, I had to switch on the ignition again and finish my journey to the reception.

I hurtled through a few more windy dirt tracks before pulling up outside a wonderful piece of Tudor architecture situated in the middle of immaculate greenery, but now was no time to admire the view. Our blue-shirted opponents had kicked off and just before I was about to switch off the radio, their star man, Marek Hamsik, was already causing havoc. Football on the radio always put you on edge as the action is described over-excitedly by a commentator whose voice fluctuates wildly, forcing you to believe the ball is always one kick away from ending up in the net. On this occasion, Hamsik had been depicted as slaloming his way past the entire Welsh team, and probably the entire 1958 World Cup side too, before scoring, but Ben Davies had miraculously cleared the ball off the line. I began to breathe again after my heart had stopped for the five seconds or so that we were on the brink.

Unable to take any more Chinese whispers, I had to find a television to see things unfold for myself. Already purple in the face from that early scare, I sprinted across the gravel courtyard into a reception fitted out with chandeliers, a grand staircase and royal red carpet, and spluttered out demands for directions to the nearest television. A perplexed and slightly scared receptionist pointed me towards a room just down the corridor. Opening the door of what turned out to be a bar with bookcases filled with literature on three sides, there was nobody to greet me but a TV that was quietly showing some period drama on ITV. Desperate times called for desperate measures, so I darted behind the pumps, located the remote control and changed the channel to BBC One.

I was greeted with a glorious image: my country in action at a major football championship, something I had waited my whole life to witness and it was more magnificent than I could ever have imagined. They looked resplendent in their red shirts. When paired with the Slovakians' blue strip against the green of the pitch and a peroxide blonde smudge that was Aaron Ramsey's new hairstyle, it was a kaleidoscope of colour worthy of a watercolour.

The only thing missing now was a cold pint in my hand, and as I had seemingly stumbled upon my own private lounge, I didn't hesitate in pouring myself one as Jonny Williams was chopped down in the Slovakian half. That could only mean one thing - Gareth Bale.

Bale had become a demigod after virtually single-handedly dragging Wales to the finals, scoring seven times in the qualifiers, including three matchwinners, and his post-match displays of delight became increasingly passionate as the holy grail got ever closer. It probably made the walking excuse that was Ryan Giggs, our last world-class player, feel slightly uncomfortable about his commitment to his country; like all of us, Bale was proud to be a Welshman, and never sulked about sacrificing a fortnight where he could have rested the most expensive feet in football history, soaking up rays next to the pool at his Madrid mansion. Instead, he was splashing around a wet field on the outskirts of Cardiff when international breaks came along, refusing to let his teammates down.

I stood transfixed as he stood in his customary wide-legged stance over the free-kick until the referee's whistle peeped. You could sense the Slovakians' fear; they had six men stood in a wall despite Bale trying his luck from 30 yards out, and the rest of their players were lined up on the edge of the area. None of this bothered the man with the number 11 on his back, and after taking six steps he wrapped his wand of a left foot around the ball and watched it sail into the net.

"YEEEESSSSSSSSSSSSSSSSSSSSSS! GET IN THERRRREEEE!" I bellowed, jumping out from behind the bar and bouncing around on the plush scarlet carpet with my fists clenched and my arms pumping up and down. "YESSSSS, YESSSS, YESSSSSSSSSS!!" I continued as I began embarking on a little jig in a circle before turning to face the screen and seeing all the Welsh players, substitutes and management in a giant huddle near the benches. That mass of people felt like it included the 25,000 in the stands and the millions watching at home also. I was in dreamland and completely oblivious of the presence of someone else in the room.

"Um, excuse me, sir - are you alright in here?" came a voice that caused me to jump out of my skin. Immediately panicking that it was Victoria again, but to my relief it was just an elderly member of staff with wispy white hair and a rather impressive moustache, dressed in a fetching black waistcoat and red shirt.

"Oh hello, I didn't see you there, mate; I was getting a bit excited, sorry."

"Don't worry, butt, I can't blame you." Butt? It couldn't be true…

"Are you Welsh, too?"

"Carmarthenshire born and bred. Great goal that wasn't it? I think I'll take my break now - you're not expecting any more Welsh lads are you?"

"Nope, I don't think so"

"Great." And with that my new best friend, Arthur, took a large set of keys out of his pocket, located the one he needed to lock the door, mopped up the overflowing pint I had forgotten was still being poured, and we settled down to watch the game in our own little corner of Wales on the wrong side of the border.

It was probably the most enjoyable experience I have had watching a game of football without being at the stadium. Arthur was such a delightful gentleman with some fascinating stories about following Wales right back to when he was a youngster in the fifties, including tales from the 1958 World Cup. I am normally not much of a conversationalist during games my teams are involved in and regularly shush those in my presence when they stray off-topic from what is transpiring in front of us. But this veteran was never in danger of being subjected to that disrespect - my ears were his as I soaked up every word.

"My one regret from that tournament was that I was never able to make it over to Sweden," he recalled. "Back then, of course, air travel was still relatively new and only for the wealthy, and growing up as the son of a miner, my father was nowhere near being able to take us on a boat either. I had to make do with radio reports and newspapers - and even then the information was scarce. A lot of people didn't even know Wales were in the thing."

"Are you going over to France this time for the other games?" I asked, slightly in awe.

"No, sadly not. I'm too old to be travelling long distances and getting involved in all that," he sighed wistfully. "I'll leave that to your generation. I'm just happy that I'm able to watch it on the telly, even though I'm not supposed to!" He gave mischievous wink and a smile. Arthur returned his eyes to the screen and seconds later leapt up from his chair alongside me, demanding a penalty from a referee slightly out of earshot hundreds of miles away as Jonny Williams was nearly decapitated by Skrtel's razor sharp elbow inside the area. As he settled back down, I asked: "As much as I'm enjoying your company, aren't you worried about getting sacked? I'm guessing your break was over a while ago."

"Me? No! I'm an old man, I've got my pension pot from a lifetime of posting letters looking after me. These handyman shifts are just for a bit of beer money and not to get grief from the wife. Mind you, it does help if you don't pay for it! Another one?" He pointed to his empty glass and I laughed and nodded in appreciation of his audacity.

"Haha she sounds like my missus - always something to moan about!"

"Oh no, don't get me wrong, I'm only teasing. My Bethany is a star, she is, Scott. I've known it since I met her in the village hall when we were 13-years-old. I wrote her a love letter a few days later asking her out and popped it through her letterbox. That was the first of probably millions of letters I've posted throughout the years, and it was the most significant."

Once again I was a captive audience sitting in the palm of Arthur's hand. Not only was he a patriotic Welshman who loved his football and beer, but he had been with his wife since his teens, and he was still talking in gushing terms about her all these years later. I sensed there was a life lesson or two to be learnt here.

"Yep, having the courage to write that letter was the greatest thing I've ever done. We were married by the time we were 18 - barely bickered since - and celebrated our golden wedding anniversary a couple of years ago. I can honestly say it's been bliss, it has. I pray to God that my time comes first because I'll be completely lost without her."

The rest of the first half passed me by as those words rattled around in my head. I couldn't help but see myself in Arthur, however his description of his childhood sweetheart was polar opposite to the pedestal I was currently putting Victoria on. Shit - Victoria! I had only nipped into the room to see the first 10 minutes or so, but the goal and Arthur's arrival had completely knocked me sideways and I'd forgotten that there was a dinner table I was probably expected to be at pretty soon.

I didn't want to be at that dinner table, nor did I want what I had been desperately trying to hold onto for the past few years. I wanted to be in Bordeaux, or locked in this room with Arthur, a free bar and a giant television. I wanted an argument-free relationship with someone who understood me fully and unconditionally, who looked out for my needs and would put me first occasionally. I wanted someone like Bethany, and that just wasn't Victoria.

Bale's goal was being shown over and over again during the half-time coverage and Arthur was smiling away. He looked so content with life - nonplussed about whether or not he kept his job after he unlocked the door because he could go home and continue his wonderful relationship with his soul mate.

"Can I ask you a question, Arthur?"

"Certainly."

"What would Bethany have said if you'd had a ticket to this game but you'd been invited to this wedding?"

Arthur paused, stroked his pointed chin and chuckled.

"That's difficult for me to answer, son, because she's never stopped me doing anything before, and vice-versa. We're very good about that. Life is too short for regrets; we're both 67 this year and I can honestly say we have none. We took every chance we had, spent money on memories rather than possessions and lived to tell the tale."

"But, hang on - you said you regretted not going to the World Cup in '58?"

"Haha be careful, smart arse," he chortled once again. "Of course I would have liked to have gone, but it wasn't an option. But, as for you, you could be over in France right now, but instead you're locked in a hotel room getting drunk with a pensioner and you need to ask yourself why."

He was right. Having once been my Bethany, it was suddenly blindingly evident that Victoria was now holding me back in all facets of my life, making me miss out on opportunities in my career and preventing me from living life with my friends. I felt myself suddenly teleported back to the same crossroads that I had first arrived at when Dav told me what I needed to hear back in London a few months back. But, still not entirely sure what to do, my heart still ruled my head.

The decision needed to be taken out of my hands. Having flirted with the notion that Wales' appearance at these Euros had been some sort of calling of fate to jump-start my life, I decided that it was time to put it to the test.

Chris Coleman and his players would inadvertently be the judge, jury and potentially executioners of my 14-year relationship.

My mind was made up. If we hung on and beat Slovakia, I was telling Victoria we were done. If we didn't, then I would go back, sit in the empty chair next to my vacant fiancée, and grovel for forgiveness about missing the three-course vegan meal that was probably being served right now. After suffering the backlash for years, we would eventually get married in a ridiculously expensive, garish ceremony and have a couple of kids as I worked hard every day to ensure they didn't turn out like their mother.

It felt like it was now or never. As the teams strode back out onto the pitch, there was suddenly so much more at stake. I took Arthur by surprise with a lusty "C'MONNN WALLLESSSSS!" as the biggest 45 minutes of my life got underway.

CHAPTER 4

I was completely on edge as soon as Wales kicked off the second half. The game of a lifetime had suddenly become the game of my life. I am normally not a gambler, especially when it comes to football; I can't stand it when people put a bet on a game then refuse to shut up about it for 90 minutes, worrying about the risk and the reward. Three points is usually quite enough for me.

But there was something much more important than cold hard cash riding on this match, and therefore I had instantly become a nervous wreck. Every time the red shirts poured over the halfway line, I sensed my body tingle with excitement in anticipation of what might happen in both the game and my private life; when the Slovakians won possession and headed in the other direction, a curtain of dread came over me. After they slammed the ball into the side netting early in the second half, it became too much to bear.

"Fancy something stronger, Arthur?" I enquired, getting up off my chair and wandering around to the other side of the bar.

"Well OK then, butt. How about some scotch?" he replied. "Try a drop of the Old Pulteney in the decanter, it will ease your nerves."

"How can you tell I'm nervous?" I said, attempting to keep a firm grip on the beautiful crystal vessel shuddering in my hand as I shakily poured a healthy measure of the amber liquid into two glasses.

"Calm down, man - we're winning, remember?" Like the whiskey as it washed down my throat, Arthur's words were soothing for a second or two, but the one-goal lead was a fragile one which soon vanished. An inspired substitution saw Ondrej Duda introduced to the fray, and seconds later he was at the bottom of ruck of bodies comprising of his celebratory teammates. He had snuck free in the area after Wales had switched off and struck the ball home to make it 1-1. Like a horror movie, anticipation forced my head into my hands before the shot had been taken and the sound of the crowd saw my neck sling in the direction of the floor.

"Bastards," slurred a now half-cut Arthur - the first swear word he had uttered all game. I returned my gaze to the television's top left corner; there were 29 minutes for Wales to recover, but they had been rocked. I gasped and winced as the rampant opposition peppered our goal in the aftermath, forcing me to knock more whiskey back. The clock was against me. It was no longer Wales v Slovakia: in my head it had become Scott v Victoria, and I was one swift kick of the ball with a figurative horse-manure-covered stiletto away from a lifetime of wondering 'if only.' If only Duda had forgotten to tie his laces and the substitution had been delayed. If only Jonny Williams had gotten that penalty. Or if only we had a decent striker on the pitch.

"Why is Coleman throwing him on?" I hissed when Hal Robson-Kanu was handed a chance from the bench. "He hasn't even got a club - Reading released him before the tournament!"

"Stranger things have happened - Barcelona might want him in a few weeks' time!" suggested Arthur, in hope rather than expectation. After all, this was a player who had scored precisely twice for Wales in six years, half of his tally in his previous two seasons in club football, and now he was expected to buck those trends when my relationship was hanging in the balance. It was almost as if Victoria had thrown him off the bench herself.

"Sure thing - if he gets signed by Barcelona, then I'll call my three children Hal, Robson and Kanu." I sneered.

"You think your missus will let you have three goes at it?" Arthur laughed, the alcohol eroding away at his gentlemanly manner and exposing the cruder side of his personality. I laughed, too, otherwise I would probably have cried: Victoria had once mentioned she had wanted to name our first born Shakira after her favourite musician - be it a boy or a girl.

I didn't fancy siring a tribute to a Colombian pop star destined for an eternity of bullying, so my hopes were now pinned on the much-maligned double-barrelled hitman. He did, however, manage to produce a glorious cross that Ramsey squandered with a poor header, causing me to thump the armrest of my chair in frustration. The Welsh fans located in the ground reacted much more positively and a hearty cry of the national anthem boomed around the stadium.

At that point my phone vibrated and I discovered a text from Dav saying, 'Incase you're listening to some boring drivel (Vic or speeches) we're drawing 1-1. 20 to go, Robson-Kanu on lol.' Everything seemed a bit hopeless, my life destined to meander along the same course plotted years ago.

I topped up my tumbler for the final 10 minutes, sensing it would take the edge of the wrath about to be unleashed upon me by my darling muse. I went to hand Arthur his glass, but he had obviously reached his limit and was now quietly dozing, wheezing slightly as the game passed him by. He knew best, and resigned to my fate I sat drunk and lifeless as everything washed over me; I was barely paying attention when Joe Ledley stroked a fine pass into a dangerous area for Ramsey, who took a touch and prodded it towards Robson-Kanu inside the area, who wobbled a leg at the ball and made an unusual contact, but it was trickling past the goalkeeper.

My eyes widened, my legs pushed me into a standing position, my hands clasped together in prayer, followed by that glorious moment that every experienced football fan knows - the millisecond you realise that the ball is crossing the line, unchallenged.

"YYYYYEEEEESSSSSSSSSSSSSSSSSSSSSSSS!! OH MY GOD!! ARTHUR, Arthur wake up! He's done it - Mighty Hal has done it!!

A frightened Arthur looked as though he was on the brink of a heart-attack with the presence of a mentalist going berserk in front of him. But he was soon on his feet and we hugged tightly, jumped up and down together laughing hysterically as I gave him a big old kiss on his forehead. It wasn't the prettiest of goals, but it was beautiful in its importance.

"Wonderful, wonderful stuff!" Arthur said. "I told you - Barcelona!"

"I'll gladly call my first born Hal if we hang on and win this," I proclaimed. That would involve nine agonising minutes to endure, so I sat back down, strapped myself in and awaited the backlash from the Slovakians. My heart was soon having palpitations when a header found its way past Danny Ward, but thankfully it clipped the post. I clasped Arthur's arm when the fourth official's board went up showing three minutes and began to count down, both in my head and out loud: 180 life-altering ticks.

"Blow the bloody whistle, ref," I immediately called out as I hit zero, joining in with the piercing whistling from the red sea of Welsh fans. I could picture Dav's face matching his shirt as he attempted to do the same, but he had never perfected that particular skill, showering people in jets of spit every time he tried. The only blast that counted would come from the referee, and a few seconds later he did just that.

"Brilliant!! Wow, what a game!" said Arthur, standing up in adulation of what the 11 heroes with the dragon on their chests had pulled off. He clapped his hands before turning to me. Just as I had been in Zenica nine months earlier, I was sat emotionless, stiff as a board - but there were very different emotions running through my head. The implications I had placed upon myself had dawned on me, and despite getting the result I had craved, I realised that I now had to cash in my winnings. It was time to finally tell Victoria it was over, but I wasn't sure if I could actually throw away all of the hopes and dreams I had possessed my entire adult life on the back of a football match. Dying for some guidance, I looked up at wise-old Arthur, who got down on his knees and embraced me. My bottom lip quivered and showered in fear and elation, I burst into tears.

"When I said you had to ask yourself why you were here and not there, I didn't mean Bordeaux, Scott," Arthur whispered gently into my ear. "I meant the dining room. You could have left here at any moment, but if you're having more fun with a random stranger you've known for 90 minutes than someone you've said you'll spend the rest of your life with, you need to fix that, butt. Now, I don't know what the answer to this is, but please take a leaf out of my book - go make some memories, and make sure they're happy ones. Promise me that?"

I looked into his serious eyes and nodded. That was exactly the pep talk I had needed. Arthur pulled his arms from around me, stood back and withdrew the key from his pocket. Staggering over to the door, he tipsily fumbled it into the lock and a small click signified that I was now free, in more ways than one. Thanks to Hal Robson Kanu, the route through that door offered a new start and a real shot at happiness.

Every step I took back along the majestic corridor, through the reception and towards the dining room, seemed to be in slow motion; it was almost as if I could hear a giant thud every time my shoes touched down on the plush carpet. What was I going to say? How would she take it? If I had been nervous at the start of the second half of the game that had forced me down this path, then that paled in insignificance as to what awaited me. I wished I was having a celebratory drink with Arthur right now, not having the most difficult, but necessary, conversation of my life.

Finally, I reached the doors of the dining room, but all was hushed inside before a ripple of applause and light laughter ensued. Damn - the speeches were going on. I was hardly going to stride in there and cause a scene having missed the whole of the meal, so I sat down on a chair by the side of the door and pondered what I was going to say whilst studying the table plan. The door crept open a couple of minutes later and whilst the waiters and waitresses tiptoed through carrying towering stacks of gravy-stained plates, I peeked inside to see if I could see Victoria on the table titled 'Ross and Rachel.' Sarah and Craig had named them after their favourite TV couples, which made me sigh with contempt. Wales' all-time worst XI would be better than that - imagine asking someone what table they were on and hearing the reply "Jermaine Easter" or "Daniel Nardiello". The aficionados on my short guest list would lap it up.

However, Victoria wasn't to be seen on "Ross and Rachel," or indeed "Peter and Katie" next door. I could also see "Alfie and Kat," but there was no luck there either, so instead of sitting outside stewing that there wasn't a "Tim and Dawn" table, I got up and walked outside for some fresh air to try to compose some sort of break-up script that would let Victoria down gently.

But all that went out of the window when I was an unexpected witness to something truly quite shocking. Stood next to a spiral staircase, leaning against the building's cream facade was Victoria in her jade green dress, but she was being held in a suited man's arms, who was tenderly kissing her neck as she ran her fingers through his slick, black hair. A virtually empty bottle of Bollinger had been knocked over on the floor, and you could hear the sticky fizz of the bubbles evaporating as the champagne oozed across the patio. She was definitely feeling the passion, as she had her eyes closed and head tilted backwards, completely oblivious that her fiancée was stood no less than 10 yards away. In fact, a referee could have paced out the yardage and sprayed vanishing foam across her bare feet and she still wouldn't have noticed - her equine-faecal stained shoes probably slung into a farmer's field on the way to the reception.

It should have been my worst nightmare, but, in fact, this was a glorious dream. I should have been tamping and exploding into a fit of rage, charging towards this mystery man and punching his lights out. But I felt none of that; I just stood there like a voyeur, watching it unfold. I knew this was my get out of jail free card and, more importantly, that finishing with Victoria was the right thing to do.

It took about 15 seconds for her to finally catch a glimpse out of the corner of her eye of a creepy bloke enthralled by their tonsil-tennis, and she frantically pushed her partner in crime away before it dawned on her that I was stood there. She froze.

"Hi, Vic," I casually said. "Enjoying the wedding?"

"Scott, oh, it's really not what it looks like," came the most pathetic attempt at a cover up in the history of lying. I glanced at the man - the smoking gun - and hoped that he was trembling in fear that he was about to take a hiding, but in a slight blow to my ego he wasn't - he just looked a little drunk and confused, and quickly managed to blur into the background of this particular domestic row. He had his sleeves rolled up showing off two tattooed forearms, which immediately sent an alarm bell ringing in my head to not try and get too macho.

"Come off it, Victoria, I'm not a moron. It's exactly what it looks like. What have you got to say for yourself?"

"I'm... I'm so sorry, Scott. I've just had a bit too much to drink." She began to walk towards me, reaching for my arm, but by now I was merely playing a role that I had been forced to watch so many times on the TV, ironically by the woman stood in front of me with crocodile tears forming in her eyes and lipstick smeared across her chin and cheeks.

"No, Victoria, don't touch me. How could you treat me like this? Fourteen years and you've flushed it all away." I was trying to stifle the laughter which threatened my Oscar-winning performance - maybe I should have been the lead in the nativity play that formed the basis of mine and Dav's friendship back in primary school.

"Please, Scott, let's talk up in our room about this. I can explain everything."

"Sorry, Victoria - I'm too embarrassed for this right now." I was satisfied with that particular dig, even if it wasn't the slightest bit true. "I'm not staying here tonight, so you can have the room to yourself - or maybe invite your friend along?" I added the last part for emphasis, pointing to the black haired bloke who was now trying to sneak back into the hotel. I wasn't going to risk starting a fight with him, mainly because I was happy he had snogged the face off my wife-to-be, as it had done me a massive favour, and as my previous two fights had seen me floored by a bouncer in a Swansea nightclub and punched in the back of a head on O'Connell's Street in Dublin, by a drunk Irish fan who mistook me as an Englishman, despite wearing a Wales flag as a cape.

"No, Scott, please stay. I'm begging you, baby." She was virtually in hysterics now. Her face was bright red and gloops of mascara were now dripping down the side of her face, reforming inside those dimples that I had been so hypnotised by.

"Nope, I'm not staying - and I don't mean tonight."

"What! No! Please, Scott, please stop. Where are you going?"

"I don't know, and, to be honest, I don't really care."

I knew exactly where I was going. I was going to the place in the world where I most wanted to be right now. I was following Arthur's instructions, and I was off to France to make some memories.

Well, eventually anyway - first I had to actually find my way out of this black hole in the Cotswolds. There was more chance of me passing a pre-match fitness test than a breathalyzer, and sleeping in the car would have been a bit of a anti-climax after my heroics with Victoria, so I wandered down the gravel path that snaked its way back onto the main road, leaving my now ex-fiancée a bawling mess in the middle of the car park. The further I got away from her as I turned corner after corner, I felt freer. No longer did I have to feel like a stranger in my own home, my money was mine to spend how I pleased, and my future already seemed to have so many more opportunities than the dead end I had previously accepted.

After a mile or so, I reached a long stretch of road and called a taxi to whisk me away to the next village or town. The driver duly obliged, and 10 minutes later I was dropped off in a nameless settlement outside a small, homely hotel called The Commodore, where I booked myself a room. With my overnight bag now at the mercy of whatever heinous act of revenge Victoria had in mind, I took the key and headed straight for a bar which looked like it hadn't been decorated since the Terry Yorath days. There were no chandeliers here. In fact, there were barely any lights. But it was more my setting, and inside, I perched among a bunch of chairs and tables that looked as though they'd been borrowed from a local scouts group. A group of around 10 men huddled together, staring at a TV positioned in a corner of ceiling and wall so high, their necks craned back at acute angles.

Having been so engrossed in breaking up with my girlfriend of 14 years, I had completely forgotten that there was an international football tournament taking place, and this wasn't any run-of-the-mill group game - this was England v Russia. I could tell by the mood in the room, which still lingered with the smell of smoke deeply-rooted in the soft furnishings a decade after the smoking ban, that England weren't leading. There were no 'ENG-GER-

LUNDDD' chants or over-zealous demands to engrave their name into the trophy now. There were 37 minutes on the clock and the game was locked at 0-0.

My arrival had not caused anyone to bat an eyelid, much like Victoria and that random bloke that had led me here. Left to my own devices, I pulled up a stool at the bar, away from the crowd. England were looking good, but couldn't find a way to break the deadlock. There were a few oohs and ahhs from the fellow punters watching the game, and a few angry groans when Wayne Rooney hit a post. But eventually their persistence paid off and they were up dancing around in celebration when an absolute rip-snorter of a free-kick by Eric Dier crashed into the net with 15 minutes to go.

I had been half-heartedly cheering on the Russians in my head, but I was still doing cartwheels trying to process the day's events, rather than focussing on despising the enemy in white. Regardless of how England got on, my mind was already turning to five days' time and their next game - against Wales. I just had to be there; with the lads while I reassembled the pieces of my life.

As the game edged into injury-time, the group of Englishmen were beginning the celebrations early. My vision was becoming more and more hazy and I could feel a piercing pain in my forehead that you only get when you have been drinking all day and not touched any food. I thought about calling it a night at 10pm, but before I could finish off my last dregs of Carlsberg and stagger upstairs, I just about made out a desperate cross, pumped into the England box, and a Russian player looping a header into the net. 1-1!

The sight of pint glasses being swept onto the floor and some vulgar Anglo-Saxon lexicon being screamed at the television brought me out in a grin and led me to order just one more pint and a packet of bacon fries to cap off the perfect day. A graphic came on the screen that showed Wales sitting on top of the group ahead of England. I snapped it on my phone and was sending it to Dav, proclaiming to enjoy it whilst it lasted, when one of the crowd, who was wearing a red 1966 replica shirt despite being about my age, joined me at the bar.

"Jesus - how shit was that?" he slurred in my direction. The smell of alcohol on his breath could have put a nun over the legal limit.

"Not the best, but it's not a bad result. Huge game now against the Welsh isn't it next week?" I replied diplomatically, hiding my allegiance pretty well, seeing as I was desperate to wave my photo of the group table in his bleary-eyed face.

"I don't know why I even bother," he said wistfully. "I was looking forward to the Wales game and getting one over those sheep shaggers, but if those overpaid tossers can't be arsed to put in the effort, then why should I spend hundreds of pounds travelling to France to watch them stroll around wishing they were on their holidays?"

"Valid point," I remarked, glossing over a lazy stereotype. I completely disagree that top international players have no desire to add medals to their collection and achieve eternal fame, to instead sit on a non-descript beach somewhere in the Caribbean, but on this occasion, I could not face the a debate with an intoxicated, obnoxious England fan, so I politely added: "Did you get tickets?"

"Yeah, but I might get rid of them. Spend my money on something more enjoyable, like putting up a new fence, or taking my wife shopping."

"Really?" My ears had pricked up.

"Yeah, I've got them on me, actually; was going to offer them to my mate when he arrives later, but he's late and I'm not going to trek over there with him to watch that crap." Supping the head off his pint, he struggled to retrieve his wallet out of his tight-fitting jeans, which were more suited to someone a decade younger without a beer gut, but when he did, he revealed two tickets to the England v Wales game.

"See, what a shame, but I'm not wasting my money on Hodgson and his bunch of muppets."

"Well, if you don't want them, I'll take them off your hands?" I enquired.

"You really want them after watching that?"

At that moment I had a thought that I might be more successful with my request if I put my morals to one side. As much as it sickened me, I said: "Yeah, well, my son really wants to go, so it would be nice to take him to his first tournament game, sing a bit of Three Lions, see his favourite player, Rooney, and get an easy win against those Taffs," I said through gritted teeth, ashamed of myself and relieved that everyone else I knew couldn't hear me. Upon returning to my room, I should have washed my mouth out with soap, but desperate times called for desperate measures.

"You have to start them somewhere, haven't you? Well, if you want them, you can have them, and as it's for your boy, I'll even do it at face value. Saves me going to the cashpoint to pay for all these beers and breakfast when I check out tomorrow, doesn't it?"

"Excellent. Cheers, mate. Where is the nearest one?"

For the umpteenth time that day I couldn't believe my luck; I was on a roll. Directed to a convenience store a few shops down the street, I sprinted there and withdrew £200 from a cash machine tucked between crates of fruit and Mr Kipling cakes. With the notes tightly balled up in my fist, I returned to the hotel and thankfully the bloke hadn't wandered off; he was perched at the bar with his head being propped up with one of his hands. Was I taking advantage of his drunkenness? I justified my actions by virtue of his sheep-shagger comment.

"I really appreciate this, thanks a lot!" I said, exchanging cold hard cash for the hardest tickets in the world for a Welshman to find. What felt like electricity shot through my hands when I could feel them placed into my sweaty palm. I finally had Wales v England tickets in my possession.

"No worries, fella, anything for a fellow England fan!"

"Yeah… sure thing. Cheers!"

Holding on to my precious goods as if they were as delicate as a butterfly's wings, I scarpered up the squeaky stairs and dived into room 28 on the first floor. I placed the tickets on my bed and just stared at them: the holograms, the stadium map, the tournament logo - how did this happen?! I had tickets that were rarer than Owain Fon Williams caps to see my team in Euro 2016, and against England of all opponents. I did a little jig and flung myself on the bed beside them, gazing their way as loving as I used to admire Victoria's beauty all those years ago.

But suddenly a horrific thought crept into my intoxicated head. If those guys were staying in the same hotel, what if England '66 bloke's mate had found out he'd flogged his chance of a ticket away, and they came for me trying to get a refund? Surely this good fortune was going to have a cruel twist to it eventually?

I couldn't take that chance. I grabbed the tickets, stuffed them into my wallet, strolled quickly but casually down the flight of stairs and checked out. A confused and concerned receptionist took £50 for a room that I had spent about 50 seconds in, and when I saw a man in an England Euro 96 shirt with GASCOIGNE 8 on the back stroll through the front door, I legged it down the street as far as my legs would take me, which was actually a fair old distance in my drunken state.

Eventually I found a B&B with their lights still on, and, to my relief, they had a vacancy. A few minutes later, my tickets were stored safely under my pillow before my head crumpled against it and I began to doze off after the most incredible few hours of my life. A day that began with me feeling exasperated had ended with me emasculated and exhilarated thanks to three points, two tickets and one Hal Robson-Kanu.

CHAPTER 5

"Wahhheyyy! Here he is!" came a familiar loud bellow about 50 metres away as a rotund man leapt out of his seat and jogged down the pavement to embrace me.

"Haha it's bloody good to see you again!" I replied to Dav, who was a little worse for wear after an afternoon of drinking in the French sunshine.

"I thought you could do with a cwtch, mate, seeing as there's now a vacancy for that in your life."

"Thanks, mate, I appreciate it. Get us a beer in; it's been a long journey."

"Sorry, bud, it's your round. You've got my ticket, yeah?"

Here I was - finally in France, or Lens to be more specific, on a beautiful sunny Wednesday. I had wanted to be here earlier, but having driven back from the Cotswolds on the Sunday - thankfully avoiding Victoria when I had gone to pick up the car - common sense prevailed and I was back in the office on Monday and Tuesday trying to focus on the Quavers promotion, but with little luck as Saturday's goals bubbled away in my head over and over again.

As five o'clock on Tuesday afternoon struck, finally my Euro 2016 adventure could begin. The night dragged by and I slept as erratically as a kid on Christmas Eve. I even turned up to St Pancras station an hour before my train departed, such were my excitement levels. I stepped on board the Eurostar with a bag containing only a few items of clothing, a toothbrush, my passport and those two precious match tickets, proudly donning my red shirt with BALE 11 on the back and the official competition patches on the sleeves.

A couple of hours later, I was strolling along the cobbled pavements of the tranquil city of Lille, in the postage stamp corner of the country. All was calm; old men sat outside cafés drinking coffee and chatting, and a tram gracefully swept down one of the streets. Sleek brick buildings faced each other from opposite sides to form warren-like passageways. It was classy; you could instantly sense elegance all around you. It didn't seem as though there was a football tournament, or, indeed, fan anywhere in sight.

But soon enough I began to hear them. 'Ain't nobody, like Joe Ledley,' came from some Welsh fans tucked away in the back of a bar. Then, 'Jamie Vardy's having a party…' swept up a bit further down the road. Those chants chipped away at the decadence, helping to replace it with tension. The French authorities had been concerned that English, Welsh and Russian fans were all congregating on Lille, as Russia were playing Slovakia there that afternoon before the Battle of Britain 24 hours later in nearby Lens. I had already read about isolated incidents of scuffling fans and seen some grainy cameraphone footage of the obligatory chairs being tossed around the place. Travelling fans had been advised to avoid being isolated, and an alcohol ban had been imposed on both cities.

When I had come across Dav, though, he, Ieuan and Matt were sat outside a restaurant, tucking into beers, burgers and chips. After Dav had finally stopped squeezing the air out of my lungs and I'd greeted the others with a rather more appropriate handshake, I took them up on their lack of culture.

"You come all the way to France and you order burgers? Come on, guys, live a little!"

"What are you talking about? These are French fries!" Dav replied. "Can't get any more cultural than that; the clue is in the name."

"Sure, mate. Anyone want a beer?"

"Don't worry, pal, I'll get you one. I think you need it," said Ieuan, who instantly waved over a waitress. "Can I get a beer for my friend, please? He's just left his fiancée and he's a bit down in the dumps."

"Oh, you poor man!" she said in an Eastern European accent, touching me softly on the shoulder. "Are you OK?" She was probably in her mid-20s; a real looker with her black hair tied up in a bun, held in place by a pencil - something I'd always had a strange attraction towards, but only a psychologist would be able to tell me why.

"Yes, I'm better than I've been for a long time, thank you," was my awkward response. "Cheers for your concern though."

"If you like, I give you phone number?" she continued in her broken English, completely throwing me off guard. It had been a long time since a girl had ever offered me her number before, especially this sudden. Just like those dodgy emails from African princes, it was surely far too good to be true, and by the smirk etched on Dav's poor excuse for a poker face I was pretty certain my instincts were spot on.

"Ummm, yeah go on then, why not?" I played along, keen to hear the punchline.

"Great! Give me your phone," said the waitress. I obliged and she tapped it a few times, and then came out with, "How do you spell Samaritans?"

The three lads howled with laughter, with Dav's booming chortle echoing down the street. "Ahh you fell for that one hook, line and sinker, Scott!" he said. "Thank you so much, Jolanta, you've made my day!"

"Happy to help," she grinned, pleased that she had pulled off her lines so well. "I'll get you that beer, Scott." And she toddled back to the bar.

"I knew it was a joke all along," I muttered. It hadn't been one of their better attempts.

"Yeah, right! You couldn't give her your phone quick enough!" said Ieuan.

"It took us at least 10 attempts to teach her how to say Samaritans correctly," added Matt. "I don't think she has any clue what they are."

"Well, thanks for that anyway, lads, that was quite the welcome," I smiled. It had been a brilliant way to break the ice - Dav had obviously filled the other two in on the state of my love life, and the last thing I wanted was to play the role of vibe assassin, bumming everyone out with my tales of woe.

"So you're doing OK then, butt?" asked Ieuan, as Jolanta returned with my pint of lager.

"Thanks. Yeah, I'm great actually. It needed to be done, and as soon as it had happened I felt a lot better. I mean, it did help that I caught her getting off with another bloke. But, yeah, I'm fine about it."

"It wasn't Gary Davies from Year 12 again was it?" piped up Dav. We all laughed and toasted our beers; it was great to be back amongst friends again. The next few hours flew by and Jolanta was back and forth refilling our chalices as the cold beers flowed in the afternoon sunshine. The other three recalled their time in Bordeaux, which had ended rather messily with Dav dancing around in a fountain with a few other Welsh fans, forgetting that he had his wallet in his pocket and ruining around 100 euros' worth of notes. They seemed like they were having a great time watching big games on warm summer days. Being self-employed meant Dav could take as long as he wanted off work; Matt had booked the whole of the group stage off; and Ieuan was a freelance travel writer, using this trip as the basis of a future piece about travelling around France. They were in it for the long haul, and I was determined to find a way to be too.

We quickly worked our way through the topic of the smouldering wreckage that was Victoria and I. The only contact I had had from her was on the Sunday - a text stating that seeing as I had driven home without her, she was going to occupy Sarah and Craig's house while they went on honeymoon and things simmered down. However, I was soon to find out that that wasn't the most dramatic recent break-ups within the group, as Ieuan drunkenly revealed that back on his trip to Lanzarote, he had persuaded whatever-her-name-was - he gets around and it's hard to keep track of names - to indulge in a spot of late-night skinny-dipping. Of course, their beach-strewn clothes were pinched whilst they were frolicking in the sea and while he found it hilarious, she took a much dimmer view and sent him packing back to the hotel, completely naked, to get some replacements. Exhausted from sun, sangria and sea sex, the sight of a bed had promptly sent him to sleep as soon as he crashed through the hotel room door, leaving her nude and unaccompanied on the beach. Thankfully some Spanish police found her wandering home wrapped in a binbag to cover her modesty, and after fending off accusations of being a lady of the night, she was returned to the hotel where she was greeted by the sight of Ieu's sand-covered arse perched precariously at the foot of their bed, snoring away. He wasn't asleep for much longer, and they enjoyed an awkward, silence-filled flight home as singletons.

After the hilarity had calmed down, Dav proclaimed: "Right, forget women, it's football that matters for a month." For once, he was right. Conversation quickly turned to the tournament so far and most agreed that Germany's name was already on the trophy after cruising to victory in their opening game, France had been lucky to win theirs with a last-gasp winner and probably wouldn't go far. We all laughed at England. But Matt, our group's resident football geek, was still tipping Poland to win the whole thing.

"Jesus, you're such a football hipster, Matt; you're always going for the outsiders because it's a cool thing to say," argued Dav.

"They're the dark horses, trust me."

"Dark horses? Black Beauty has more chance of winning the bloody cup than the Poles!"

"Have you not seen Lewandowski, Dav?" came back Matt. "Best striker in Europe if you ask me. And that Milik who scored against Northern Ireland is a great little player."

"Never heard of him so he must be shit," replied Dav, with an eloquent and well-constructed piece of punditry that Robbie Savage would have been proud of.

"How do you not know him - I thought you were collecting the Panini stickers this year so you could swot up on all the teams?" laughed Matt. "You've even brought it over here with you - I saw it in your suitcase last night!"

"Well maybe I haven't got him yet. I still need to find someone to swap with."

"And you thought you would find someone in the hotel?" I giggled.

"I hope so - got loads of bloody swaps. And it's bloody expensive; there's nearly 700 to collect and it's 50p for five stickers. I've only got Jazz Richards, Ledley and David Cotterill so far for us, too."

We then went in search of a decent bar to watch our gracious hosts as they played Albania and, sure enough, we found ourselves crammed into a petite place opposite a large cathedral which Matt took a shine to, running over to take a closer look.

"What are you doing butt?" shouted Ieuan.

"Oh nothing, just wanted to check out the Cathedral Notre-Dame de la Treille. It was in the official tournament guide that I have been reading."

"You really are a nerd," Dav commented emphatically, and we entered the bar which was filled with French fans in good spirits. Draped in tricolours, wearing berets and in fine voice, they welcomed our presence and invited us to sit alongside them and back Les Bleus as we knocked back Kronenbourg with the locals.

"I really hope eet is a France-Wales final," said one Gallic friend we chatted to following the 2-0 win for France. He was wearing a rather fetching blue, white and red curly wig as well as the gorgeous, classic World Cup winning shirt from 1998, rightfully with Zidane 10 printed on the reverse.

"I hope you're right, too!" I slurred, the effects of the day's booze now beginning to take its toll.

"You Welsh have been great guests," the Lille native continued. "The Russians 'av been terrible. Fighting, destroying our city. I actually feel sorry for zee English!"

"Don't worry - we'll look after our fine neighbours!" joked Dav. We had heard stories and seen on Twitter that the Russians - aggrieved after their loss that afternoon to Slovakia - had returned to the city centre, intent on taking out their frustration on any folks donning the cross of St George. However, they had come across an unexpected sight - a united kingdom of sorts. Putting their differences to one side, the Welsh supporters were merrily mixing with their English brethren over a pints in plastic cups, and when some Russian hooligans had tried to start something, the two tribes came together to fend off their attackers and send them retreating, chanting defiantly, "We're England and Wales, we're England and Wales; fuck off Russia, we're England and Wales!"

Watching the footage made me proud. Yes, we desperately wanted to beat England, and it would be so sweet to virtually dump Roy Hodgson and his boys out of the competition with a win the following day, but we were all here to mingle with every nationality we encountered, including the old enemy. We wanted beer, not fear, and build a reputation as popular newcomers at the table of this feast of football.

When the sun was firmly down and the stars had come out to play, we decided to navigate back through the winding streets to our hotel at around 1am. As we did, Dav felt the urge to shift some of the alcohol that was stretching his bladder to breaking point, and waddled in front of us to try and find a side alley.

"So what do you think the team will be tomorrow then?" asked Matt as we left Dav to catch us up.

"Well, I think Hennessey will be back, and I hope Ledley starts from the beginning," I responded. "It will also be interesting to see what Coleman does up front."

"Yeah, I guess you have to start Robson-Kanu now, he's got to have a bit of confidence," added Ieuan. "But I do like Vokes, I think he offers..."

"AAAARGHHHHH, FUCKING RUN BOYS!!" came a frightened howl a few metres behind us. We turned and Dav was hurtling back in the opposite direction, having lost a battered old Adidas trainer in the process of escaping as fast as his stumpy legs could carry him, which was about as quick as James Collins trying to keep up with Thierry Henry in his pomp.

Startled and guessing that he had encountered some of Lille's more unsavoury temporary residents, we began to chase after him - we didn't fancy any sort of battering from some Russian nutters looking for some easy prey. However, when I passed the alley Dav had shot out of, I noticed something wasn't right, and slowed down as the others disappeared into darkness.

"Boys, boys! Chill out! They're not Russians - they're Slovakians!"

Sure enough, there were five incredible specimens of men who all seemed to possess arms that Hulk Hogan would have admired. They had the body shape of a set square but they weren't wearing ominous black shirts, instead they were proudly displaying 'Hamsik 17' on their backs. Upon hearing Dav's squeals most had stopped urinating against a wall, bewildered by the commotion.

"Did he think we were Russian?" one of them called out. "Don't worry, Welshmen, we come in peace!" He collected Dav's discarded trainer and held it in front of him as proof of his intentions.

"Congratulations on the win tonight, lads!" said Matt, accepting the shoe and shaking one of the burly fivesome's hands, completely forgetting what had been gripped in it a few seconds earlier.

"Beer?" suggested the one closest to me, pointing to a box of bottles that they had seemingly just purchased from another premises brazenly, but thankfully, ignoring the alcohol ban.

"Sure thing!" I said, and we were soon toasting our opponents from a few days earlier as Dav sheepishly slunk back towards us from the abyss, his sock soaking up the rivers of warm yellow liquid that trickled back down the road before he was reunited with his shoe.

"Didn't you spot the Hamsik shirts, Cinderella?" asked Ieuan.

"Nope, I haven't got him in my sticker book yet, either," Dave retorted shamefully.

***

Unsurprisingly I was the first one to rise the next morning. An hour had been spent flicking through my phone, cramming all the essential matchday information into my head. Chris Coleman had slapped down any interest in mind games, with the English media typically stirring the pot suggesting that Gareth Bale's theory that the Welsh as a nation are more passionate than the English was disrespectful, even if correct. We would also be wearing our garish black, grey and psychedelic green change strip, which was only beaten in the fashion victim stakes by England's mismatch of white shirts and shorts splattered with various shades of blue and finished off with red socks, which I was adamant were purely designed to prevent us wearing red ourselves.

Having read every article and digested all the opinion pieces, the three men sharing a grotty old room in what had to be Lille's smallest hotel were still tucked up in their single beds, snoozing away almost in perfect time with each other. I yanked open the curtains and was greeted by a dull, drizzly morning, which I hoped was not an omen.

"Right, wake up, lads - it's Wales England today, if you had forgotten!" I called out loudly, trying to disturb the trio of tired travellers.

"Bugger off, mate, 10 more minutes," muttered Ieuan.

"Nope, get up and get these on," I replied, tossing them their Wales shirts which had been hung pride of place on a single rail drilled into a small alcove, which I assumed was the wardrobe advertised on the hotel's website. I was donning my brand new Euro 2016 version; Ieuan had the one we wore in the qualifiers with the pinstripes and green trim; Matt choosing a retro number that dated back from the mid 1990s; and Dav, obviously, in the skin-tight Lycra version from the Mark Hughes era, which took him a good couple of minutes to squeeze around his big-boned frame when he finally arose from his bed with the promise of a cooked breakfast. Unfortunately he was to be left disappointed as we were only offered a continental version instead. But after lining our stomachs with as many croissants, pain au chocolat and crepes that we could get our hands on, we strolled back across the cobbled streets into town and caught an early train into Lens to see what this part of France had to offer. After gliding through the French countryside for the best part of half an hour, we straight away arrived at the conclusion: not a lot.

Lens, while classified as a city, is basically just a small town, with a lot of faceless streets filled with run-down terraced houses. It must have been one of the most obscure places to hold a game of this magnitude - the standout fixture of the entire group stage - and Matt had taken great delight in boring us numerous times that the whole of the 'city's' population could fit inside its stadium. With this in mind, the locals, anticipating the biggest influx of Brits to hit these shores since the Second World War, had barricaded themselves into their homes, boarded up the windows and were prepared to ride out the storm. Lens was a ghost town, not one welcoming visitors anticipating a footballing festival.

Another invasion had taken place, too - the English had already occupied all the pubs that we encountered, with their flags of St George draped outside each one, marking their territory, and furrowed brows greeted us as we considered joining in regardless. Police loitered around each venue and the air of tension had become a fog. Having enjoyed soaking up the cosmopolitan nature of an international football tournament the night before and sharing stories and beers with French and Slovakians, this instead had the feel of a Premier League away day following Villa to somewhere like Manchester City or West Ham.

We eventually settled on a dingy old place that had the air of a Royal British Legion hall about it, but thankfully this one wasn't marked with a Union Jack outside. As time went by, more Welsh fans began to pop their heads around the doorway looking for a bolt hole with their own kind. Whilst the English inside were pleasant enough to begin with, as the weather improved and the temperature got warmer, those clad in white seemed to get a bit more boisterous, virtually in correlation to their levels of thirst.

"Shall we head down to the stadium, lads?" I said after we had worked our way around a round.

"Not a good idea, mate," said Matt. "Haven't you heard? The only booze they are selling in the grounds and fanparks is 0.5%!"

"What?"

"Yep, that's it. Basically you're paying eight euros for a pint of shandy."

"And it tastes grim," added Dav.

"You seemed to quite like it if I recall from Toulouse, Dav!" chirped Ieuan mischievously. "He didn't realise, Scott, that it was only 0.5%, so we kept quiet, and after four or so pints he was swaying all over the shop, slurring. But it couldn't have been the booze affecting him! It was all in his head, he was basically drinking placebo pints!"

"It tasted pretty strong to me," said Dav, who once again had found himself playing the role of court jester. "I reckon it was spiked." That old chestnut.

"Mate, there was probably more alcohol in your piss from the night before," added Matt as we piled on the laughter. Paying that much for effectively non-alcoholic beer would have killed Dav, who, with his fountain escapades and sticker collection, was burning through cash just days into the tournament.

We stayed put for a while longer, but at 12pm I was once again directing traffic as I ushered everyone through the crowds of tanked-up England fans as we made the half-hour trek to the State Bollaert-Delelis, which, just like most other crap away days traipsing around England following your club team, was situated on the outskirts of town in the middle of an industrial estate, eliminating any chance of an atmosphere whatsoever.

It wasn't the thriving, enjoyable experience that the other lads had described from their time in Toulouse, or what I had always pictured when I dreamt of being a part of a European Championships or World Cup. With no pubs or a fanzone of any description outside the ground, Dav and I separated from Ieuan and Matt, who had seats in another stand, and we trudged through the large car park, through two cordons of very passive security checks and entered the turnstiles. I was underwhelmed; this wasn't what I had seen on the television during the first week of the tournament. But as soon as we had pushed our way through the hundreds of supporters of both teams milling around the bare, concrete-lined concourses and stomped up to our seats, the occasion finally hit me.

The view was spectacular. Housed inside a very British-looking ground, with its four separate stands, was something resembling a painting of a famous battleground. On my right was a vast army of thousands of white shirted warriors, proudly displaying their country's flag wherever it could be attached. As I then turned to my left, everyone was dripping in red and there were twice the number of flags, all displaying the proud dragon, readying himself for battle and desperate not to be slayed by St George once again. On the white half of each flag's background was the names of settlements from every corner of the country - Menai Bridge, Flint, Cwmbran, Swansea, Aberteifi, Aberystwyth - and their battle cry was deafening. The PA announcer attempted to drown them out by playing each team's pop anthem, but when Baddiel and Skinner's 'Three Lions' came over the speakers, the Welsh fans cheekily changed the words to "England's going home" before breaking into an energetic dance routine to Kernkraft 400's bass-Eurotrance hit 'Zombie Nation,' which had been adopted as our song following the goalless draw in Belgium back in the qualifiers.

Joining in with the thousands around me, that was the moment it dawned on me that I had made it; this was it. I had wanted to be here ever since the draw back in December, and I had done whatever had needed to be done to get here - including finally dumping my fiancée. I was minutes away from witnessing something I had never thought possible: Wales in action in a tournament game for the first time. At that moment in time, there was nowhere else in the universe I would rather be, and after missing the Slovakia game that feeling meant so much more to me. I couldn't help but think of Arthur; I genuinely wished he was here to see what his kick up the arse had helped me to achieve. I was as happy as I had been in years.

By now the sunrays were beaming down onto the pitch, and I had to use my hand as a visor to continue my evaluation of the ground. It seemed that my stand, and the one opposite that ran adjacent to the length of the pitch that Ieuan and Matt had seats in, had no rules on segregation, and so the red and white shirts had blended into a fetching hot pink in some areas. Myself and Dav seemed to be on the edge of a large group of Welsh fans, but next to a smattering of teenage girls draped in the English flag, scoffing chips, and a few neutrals. It seemed there was very little chance of a punch-up following the first goal.

As the two teams warmed up either side of the halfway line, Wales seemed to be free of pressure. Many of the squad cracked the odd smile and jokes, whilst their English counterparts seemed to be limply going through the motions. I was a mixture of both: enjoying the fact that we had nothing to lose, but also desperate for a victory that would live forever in Welsh football folklore.

The teams left the field to rowdy roars, which were ramped up to Richter Scale-altering levels when they re-emerged 10 minutes later. Hundreds of kids faffed around the pitch performing some shambolic dance routine involving giants shirts representing both teams, which had seemingly been put together by the choreography team of Strictly buffoons Ann Widdecombe and John Sergeant.

There was only one piece of pre-match entertainment I was interested in. "Are you ready, mate?" I said to Dav. Knowing exactly what I was referring to, he looked me square in the eyes, with the intensity of someone set to go to war and simply responded, "Ready". We tightly locked our arms around each other and stood as still as statues during the funeral-like dirge that is the uninspiring 'God Save The Queen.' Then, it was our turn. Loud and proud, we belted out 'Mae Hen Wlad Fy Nhadau,' leaving no decibel inside of our lungs. It seemed as though our 15,000-or-so compatriots did the same thing during one of the most passionate renditions of our anthem that I had ever witnessed.

A huge eruption greeted the end of the pre-match protocols and eventually Aaron Ramsey and Gareth Bale were kicking-off. But the pride of seeing 11 Welshmen in action at Euro 2016 was quickly replaced by a different emotion - fear. Straight away we looked jittery and England capitalised right from the off, looking to put in dangerous through-balls and winning corners. They should have gone ahead on seven minutes, when a sweeping counter-attack saw Adam Lallana square for Raheem Sterling who seemed destined to score in front of the red wall occupying the stand in front of him, but somehow he managed to put the ball into them after skying over the bar.

"Nooooooo!" shouted Dav as he buried his face into my arm, unable to witness what he presumed would be the ball hitting the net.

"Don't worry, mate, he's missed it!" I replied with a face crumpled into a grimace, stroking his hair as if he was a six-year-old at his first game, not someone approaching his mid-30s and a veteran of many Wales matches. But my nerves continued to be frayed as the half went on and we struggled to cope. England were pushing us to the limit, and myself and Dav were emitting exasperations usually saved for rollercoasters as Wayne Hennessey saved a Gary Cahill header, and, when his hands weren't enough, Ben Davies got away with a cheeky handball in the area unpunished. The half ticked past 40 minutes and Wales were seemingly on the ropes.

"We've just got to keep it goalless until half-time and then Coleman can shake them up a bit," I offered as encouragement.

"Totally agree, mate, but I can't see it staying that way," was the glum reply to my left as Wayne Rooney brought down Hal Robson-Kanu 35 yards from goal.

"Haha shoot, Gareth!" I shouted, cupping my palms together to create a makeshift megaphone to gain the galactico's attention. "We might as well have at least one attempt this half!"

A few fans around me laughed; it was way too far out for Bale to replicate his exploits from the Slovakia game. He was surely going to clip it into the area for one of the big men.

Think again. We had one of the world's great players on our team, with magic in his boots. Hoisting up his socks, he had seemingly cast a spell over the stadium, as every eye was locked on the winger with the immaculate man bun. There was an air of anticipation, that something incredible was going to happen, and after he took five steps forward - THWACK! It almost didn't seem real. I watched the ball fizz over the three-man, white-shirted wall and disappear out of view for a split-second. Craning my neck to see where it had gone, I then saw the body of Joe Hart skidding along the turf in desperation - and was that the ball, behind him?!

"YYYYYYYYYYYEESSSSSSSSSSSSSSSS!" answered all those in red, exploding into united celebration, fists pumping and feet bouncing. Whilst pogoing on the spot, Dav gave me an almighty embrace that I can only liken to a boa constrictor squeezing the life out of its prey. If he was indeed going to be my new cwtching partner, then he had got off to an impressive start.

"OHHHH MYYY GOODDDDD, SCOTTTT! OHHH MY GODDD!"

"I KNOW, I KNOW! WHERE DID THAT COME FROM?"

Suddenly, a random bald-headed giant next to me, who hadn't acknowledged us before kick-off, joined in with our man hug, and we quickly found ourselves in the middle of a tame mosh pit as around eight or nine supporters got to know each other a little more intimately. It was pandemonium, and it was magnificent. Wales 1, England 0.

"I told you it wouldn't be goalless at half-time," quipped Dav. We were in dreamland.

Minutes later the half-time whistle blew but hardly anyone noticed as the crowd heartily burst into a rendition of their new favourite song, the anthem of the tournament: "Don't take me home, please don't take me home, I just don't wanna go to work." The stands were literally shaking from the Welsh fans bopping up and down and wringing every last drop from the moment; the euphoria flowing from all directions was a joy for the senses. The sun was directly facing us, turning us a little pinker than I had expected when I pulled those curtains open hours earlier, but I had a sense that the warm feeling I had all over wasn't anything to do with UV rays.

The half-time lull provided those in red with time to reflect on what we had. We were leading against the English, and if the scoreline stayed this way, we would be guaranteed a spot in the knockout stages and Hodgson's side faced elimination. We simply just had to hang on for 45 minutes. We had started with nothing to lose, but now we had something.

By the time the teams had re-entered the field of play, the jubilation had died right down and nervous energy was abound. Cranking up the ante, England added Daniel Sturridge and Jamie Vardy to their attack and as soon as the referee had put his whistle to his mouth, Welsh fingernails were slid into theirs. Chants were few and far between and the English capitalised by drilling out their national anthem one more time, unopposed. Even Dav, probably one of the gobbiest football fans I know, remained silent.

Our nervousness seemed to transmit itself to the players, who began slowly again. And 11 minutes after the restart the inevitable happened: Sturridge clipped a cross into a melee of players at the back post and Vardy swept the ball in from suspiciously close range. "OFFSIDE!! HAS TO BE?" Dav, I and everyone in our vicinity screamed as one, but the assistant referee was unmoved and rat-faced Vardy, with his hand wrapped in that needless cast, was allowed to run off to celebrate his goal. I looked and Dav and we had the same body language - hands on heads but a resigned look on our faces. It had been on the cards.

Back level again, the fear failed to disappear. Simply not allowing England to win and sealing a last 16 place in the process guaranteed a happy night out in Lille. But we looked a long way from doing that - 35 minutes to be precise. Like the historical colonisers that they are, England continued to bully us, shot after shot repelled. As each attack broke down, confidence was building on the pitch and in the stands. Defensive desperation was being replaced by resoluteness as players put their bodies on the line to protect their point, and at times it seemed their country. This, in turn, lifted the crowd, who began to harmonise again, urging their team to raise themselves for one final push. With five minutes to go, a Welshman was shown on the big screen with tears streaming down his cheeks, drawing laughter from the English support at the other end. When those in red noticed, they roared as one in support of him, encouraging him on to let all his emotions out. I turned to Dav and we had a little joke about it, but when out of view of each other, we both gulped hard as we tried not to imitate the latest internet meme. I could understand what that bloke was going through; it meant the world just being here, in the moment, watching our tiny nation on the verge of making it to the knockout stages. We had been put through the wringer for 86 minutes, and we were agonisingly close.

The fourth official's board went up and indicated three minutes of added time to be played. 180 seconds. 179…

"We're nearly there, Dav - nearly!"

"C'MON WALES!!" he screamed at the players with all his might, looking to give them one last injection of encouragement. Wales were in the England half and looking comfortable.

"Just keep the ball, lads, keep it!" I added. More seconds were being shaved off, but then we handed possession back to England, who shot up the other end. Sturridge found himself with the ball in the final third, faced with the prospect of finding a way through 11 exhausted Welshmen. Lacking in options, he played it to Vardy, who was fortunate to see a poor pass spin to Dele Alli. Once again, they rode their luck as a heavy touch seemed to allow Chris Gunter to clear, but Sturridge somehow managed to bundle the defender over, control the ball and at the last possible moment toe-poked it past Hennessey and into the net. I felt like I had been kicked in the teeth, the gut and the groin all at the same time, but it hurt more than that.

This time there was no shouting or screaming from Dav or I - just stunned silence, the same kind you have when you hear a loved one has passed away. At the other end of the scale, and stadium, the English fans went wild as the Liverpool man sought out the nearest television camera to perform his stupid dance celebration; more concerned with promoting Brand Sturridge than savouring his late winner with his teammate. The Welsh players were on the floor - the knockout blow had finally been landed, right before the final bell.

All our hopes and dreams, mere fantasy 90 minutes earlier, had been seconds away from reality. Now, they had been crushed. Once again, we had battled hard but England had won the war. Dav patted me on the shoulder but I couldn't look at him, just in case he was on the verge of breaking down like me; I didn't fancy my tearful face being the next to be broadcast for the rest of the world's amusement.

In the final second Bale had a header that flashed just wide, but I knew it was never going in. Someone had forgotten to put an extra 10p in the luck meter and we'd fallen ever so short. The English cheers that greeted the full-time whistle felt like 10,000 little daggers. I waited behind to applaud the bewildered Welsh lads for their fantastic efforts, and then attempted to make a quick getaway.

It was painful to see the English being such sore winners - some of whom were goading the crestfallen Welsh as we exited the stadium together. A few people were arguing about whether Vardy had been offside as they'd missed the replay, but the repeated chants of "Fuck off Wales!" boiled away at my insides. During the slow, funeral procession-like exit from the ground, I saw two lads who looked just as suicidal as myself in Ieuan and Matt. They had been amongst a group of English fans in another unsegregated area and had to sit there enduring their wild celebrations right in front of them. We were all hurting, and just wanted to get back to Lille.

Everywhere we went, we just couldn't move for over-zealous English fans. We passed many of them still drinking in pubs having not attended the game, and the police had to intervene in some minor scuffles after more baiting. It was pissing me off, too. Sure, if we had been victorious, then yes, we would have been singing loudly and proudly. But it would have been about the wonderful heroes in our team, not antagonising the opposition.

The train back to Lille was no better, and eventually, by the time we got back there, I was done.

"Boys - I think I'm just going to go home now, I need to get out of here. I can't be doing with this tonight. My night is ruined already."

"Yeah, I don't even fancy a beer, and I'm skint as hell. I need to get back home; this has been the worst day of my life," added Dav.

We left Ieuan and Matt to continue their trip without us, not knowing when we would see them again. Two hours later Dav and I were sat on a coach back to London beaten men, licking our wounds and trying to get our heads down for the long jaunt home. Just as we pulled out of the bus station, a group of lager-filled lads taking up the back seats started chanting, "EN-GER-LAAAND, EN-GER-LAANND, EN-GER-LAAAND", and my nightmare experience at Euro 2016 had its exclamation mark.

CHAPTER 6

Usually a place resembling a war-torn country in the heart of London, the sight of Victoria Coach Station was a very welcome one at around 6am the next morning. The back-seated, fake Burberry-wearing chavs' bodies, and possibly livers, eventually gave up on them about 20 minutes before we arrived at Calais and we finally got some peace and quiet. However, when they were woken and forced through passport control, they proceeded to spend the entire ferry crossing at the bar, meaning that when back in England, they were wide awake and singing anti-Wales songs all the way to London. Thankfully, a swift taxi ride home meant I got through my front door soon after the conclusion of the journey from hell, but even the sanctum of my own home would have an unwelcome guest.

In the near-darkness of the poorly-lit flat, I nearly tripped over a wayward handbag dumped in the middle of the passageway towards my bedroom, and littered all around it were strewn credit cards, various sets of keys, make-up and about seven packets of tissues. One high heel was on one side of the room, and the other was resting haphazardly on the sofa opposite an empty bottle of wine and a rather lonely, lipstick-tattooed glass. My darling fiancée was home.

From the snores emanating from the bedroom, I guessed she was struggling after a heavy night out; she only made dog-like snarls after such sessions. My mind then turned to the theory that she might not actually be alone, such were the unfeminine-like noises coming from that direction, but I couldn't see any evidence of a third party. Not wanting to wake her, I pulled myself lengthways onto the sofa, kicked off my own shoes and finally managed to get about four hours' worth of sleep.

When I awoke, nothing had changed. Everything was where it had been found upon my arrival, and Victoria was still growling away. I didn't really know how to approach the situation; after all we surely couldn't both keep living under the same roof now we had broken up, and I had no intention of changing that. Having been the one who had paid the majority of the rent all of these years, and having contributed to our joint bank account the most, I felt I was in the stronger position, but I didn't want to bring money into it. I actually liked my quaint little apartment and its location, and didn't particularly want to leave it behind. Conversations were going to have to be had; therefore, I boiled the kettle, made a cup of tea for me and a coffee for Victoria, and opened the door of the bedroom, where thankfully there was no male presence.

I gently popped the cup down on the bedside cabinet and gave Victoria, who had her mouth wide open as her head lay on a drool-puddled pillow, a gentle wake-up wobble.

"Morning, Vic. I've made you a coffee."

She grunted at first, rolling over to avoid facing me. But then when she actually realised that she wasn't alone as she had expected, she quickly reversed her position to look straight at me.

"What the bloody hell are you doing here?" she said forcefully, before what seemed to be a headrush caused her to flop her face back to the pillow as her hangover bode her a good morning.

"Last time I checked, I still paid rent to live here," I added. "I got back early this morning and was sleeping on the sofa. The front room is a state."

"Piss off, Scott, I live here too and I can do what I like."

"Well, we need to talk about that, don't we?" I hoped to take advantage of her weakened alcohol-induced state.

"There's nothing to talk about. I'm staying right here for now. I've got nowhere else to go."

"And where do you think I'm going to stay?"

"Dav's, seeing as you spend so much time round there anyway. Quite frankly, I couldn't care where you stay, you can go to hell after what you did to me."

"What *I* did to you? What are you talking about?" I said, raising my voice a little out of sheer surprise of her audacity. "If I remember correctly, I caught you cheating on me with someone else, not the other way around."

"I've said that was a drunken mistake, but you were the one that finished things between us," she retorted as the colour began to return to her dehydrated cheeks. "You kicked me to the curb and left me high and dry at that wedding. You even took the car with you the next day; how was I supposed to get home?"

"Don't make me out to be the bad guy here," I said angrily. "This is all your fault."

"Piss off, Scott - it's all on you," was the forceful response, filled with venom. "We could have talked things through, but you didn't want to. You should have thought of all of the consequences before you made the decision. Now I don't want to talk about this. I'm staying here - end of story."

"Oh, we'll see about that." I shouted. At this point, for some unknown reason, an image of Daniel Sturridge celebrating with his stupid dance popped into my head, almost to taunt me and rile me up further.

"Both our names are on the contract, so there's nothing you can do about it. Now bugger off back to France and enjoy your beloved football with your idiotic friends, and leave me in peace."

At this point I knew I had hit a dead end - I was too angry to string a coherent argument in my favour. After all these years of living together, she knew exactly how to fluster me, so instead of reacting verbally, I let my actions do the talking. I made a statement by picking up the mug of coffee from the bedroom cabinet, striding back into the kitchen and pouring it down the sink. It didn't make me feel any better.

"Get out, Scott, you idiot. Come back for your stuff another time," came a furious squeal from the bedroom.

I had to get out of there; things had taken a turn for the worse and I needed to think everything through. I grabbed my suitcase again, stuffed a few clothes in it that had been drying in the front room, and slammed the door firmly shut, hoping to worsen Victoria's headache. My mind was all over the shop, so I knew there was one place I could go to try and sort things out: about a half hour later, I had found my way to Dav's front door, still seething.

I rapped my knuckles harder than usual against his front door, but I guessed he would have been fast asleep, if he had been half as tired as me on the coach home a few hours earlier. A couple of phonecalls later - not to mention some shouting through the letterbox - his silhouette finally appeared through the frosted glass in the doorframe and he let me inside his flat, which was looking particularly hideous. (If Victoria had been on a year-long binge then the flat I found this morning might have begun to look like Dav's den.) Empty squashed beer cans covered the table in the front room, and an assortment of ketchup-coated plates and stained mugs were scattered on any available ledge. Random Everton posters were placed slapdash-style over random spots in the room, hiding dark damp patches, which were forming in the brickwork behind. Old newspapers and magazines were slung on the floor and a mouldy old beanbag was set up in front of one of the chairs, which Dav claimed was his lucky online FIFA seat.

"So what are you doing here - missing me already?" he yawned.

"It's Victoria - she's kicked me out of the flat and is refusing to leave."

"Ahh bugger. So you'll be needing somewhere to stay for a while, then?"

"Yeah, mate. Is that alright?"

"Of course, bud, just buy me some breakfast at Spoons, yeah?"

I could always rely on Dav. I thought it would be best to leave Victoria well alone, so with three days off work stuck round my best mate's place, there was only one thing for it. A trip to the supermarket later and we had two crates of Carling in Dav's fridge, a feast of football to watch from our sofa-bound positions. There would be eight games during that time, so we settled in and began with an impressive Italy beating Sweden, before an entertaining 2-2 draw between the Czechs and Croatia. By the time Spain had dismantled Turkey 3-0, we had both dozed off with a few hours' of booze in our system, still feeling the effects of the coach journey from hell. But the next day, after another Wetherspoons visit, we flew through Belgium sweeping past Ireland and draws between Iceland and Hungary as well as Portugal and Austria. Nine hours of football over two days was beginning to take its toll, and every time I took my gaze away from the action, I could see little white footballs flashing around; it even felt like Clive Tyldesley was giving a running commentary on my bowel movements during the gaps between games.

Therefore, when I awoke to my phone blaring out the Manics' official Euro 2016 theme song for the Welsh team, I looked down to find an unknown number ringing me. Rubbing the sleep from the corners of my eyes, I answered it in a semi-conscious state and instantly regretted making the day's first decision a wrong one.

"Hello, who's this?" I murmured.

"Scott - it's Graham. How are you?"

"Graham?" I said, before realising the only Graham in the world who had my phone number was my boss. "Oh, Graham - morning, I'm good thanks. You?" I quickly recovered, regretting that I hadn't previously saved his number as a contact, even though he did rarely ring me at home.

"Sorry it's so early, Scott, but I really need your help today. It's the Quavers campaign; they're unhappy with what we've given them and I really need you to save the day for us. They're threatening to pull the plug unless we give them something new urgently, so can you come in this morning and sort something out?"

Normally I would have been desperately backpeddling to find a way to get out of working on a day off, especially a Sunday - it is the day of rest after all. But having been cooped up in Dav's flat for the majority of the previous 48 hours, it seemed like a good way to get outside and into Graham's good books. After all, if I was the saviour of this particular project, then my newly-gained respect from management could finally begin my ascent to the top of Underscore. Well, it was worth a go at least, and it would take my mind off Victoria for a while.

"Sure thing, Graham, I'll be there right away." I said, and I could sense the relieved tone of his goodbye as we ended the call. A quick shower later and I was back outside sucking on fresh air, heading for Soho.

While hurtling through London's tube tunnels, I began to get excited - not the same levels as the England game, or even watching Villa attack the Holte End, but my heart was fluttering all the same. I felt as though this was my chance to show Graham and everyone at Underscore that I was ready to make the next step within the company - an upwards one. I felt as though I was the striker who comes off the sub's bench to save the day and score a last minute winner, like Daniel Sturridge... it still hurt.

Even though it was a Sunday, Oxford Circus station was once again heaving with people, as was Carnaby Street, but I managed to dodge and weave my way through the crowds lugging large shopping bags to the office. I got inside, buzzing to get down to work and save the Quavers campaign, but as I opened the office door, I was only greeted with stillness and silence. Every swivel chair was unoccupied and all desks unattended.

I didn't mind too much - it was better to crack on redesigning a campaign from scratch, without unwanted distractions or idle chit-chat - but I did find it frustrating that I had seemed to be the only member of the team Graham contacted. Maybe he felt that I was the only man for the job?

I walked over to my desk, ready to make a start on things, but was halted by the sight of Jamie Vardy's ratty face sneering at me. Revelling in my misery, my colleagues, in the name of banter, had taped a photo of the England's team celebrations to my computer screen. I wouldn't have minded so much if there were some real football fans in the office, but the people I had the pleasure of working with were those that come out of the woodwork every two years when an international tournament is on. They begin the group stage wondering where Beckham and Owen are, before, after one win, digging the £5 JJB Sports fake England shirt out from the back of a drawer and claim to know everything there is about our beautiful game. They watch the games in pubs, taking up valuable table space better filled by us full-time supporters, before getting bored after 20 minutes and start conversations with fellow-fleeting fans that are more suited to a Slug and Lettuce or Pizza Express rather than the Bedford Inn. Then, when England ultimately get knocked-out, they shrug their shoulders, proclaim they were always shit and jump off the bandwagon quicker than you can say "beaten on penalties".

I took a little bit of pleasure in screwing up the image into a ball and belting it Saunders-style across the room. As my ancient computer always took an eternity to start, I opted to brave the break room which had been uninhabited since Friday - evident by the rock-hard used teabags shrivelling up on the side of the sink and the stench of gone-off milk. Avoiding these potential pitfalls, I tried to locate my Ian Rush mug, but the face of the moustachioed maestro wasn't in a cupboard, the mutating pile of washing up or the crowded dish drainer. When I eventually found it, I was livid as swept into the corner of the worktop were five or six large shards of bone china.

My property had been smashed up in anger, celebration, jealousy or playfulness. It didn't matter which one, my adjective of choice was "gutted"; I had been bought that mug at my first ever game in the early 90s by Dav's dad, and

I was sadly very attached to it, unlike the handle that lay amongst the red, white and green mosaic pieces. While I sifted through them, desperately looking for something to salvage, I heard the slamming of a nearby door and some quick foot-stepping pitter-pattering across the beige carpet, getting louder as they made their way into my direction.

"Ahh, Scott, there you are," said Graham, who was dressed in a yellow Ralph Lauren polo shirt and some hideous tartan trousers, indicating he had come straight from the golf course. "Oh, you've seen your mug - yes terrible accident that, but Benjamin has said that he will get you a new one." I despised Benjamin enough as it was; every morning he turned up to work with an empty briefcase bar a couple of pieces of paper and a cup of Costa coffee. He deliberately copied Graham's mannerisms, which he once claimed was a mirroring technique that he had read about in one of the many life-coaching books he left lying around his desk, which also had some tatty old St George's cross bunting draped over it. Yep, he was one of them.

"Right, let's get to work, shall we?" my superior leader commanded. I knew that the "we" really only meant me.

"Did they say what they wanted?" I asked, attempting to avoid sifting through the vast amount of email chains sitting in a virtual world high up above us in the stratosphere, ready to be beamed back down to Earth as soon as I sat back down.

"No, they left it open-ended - just said they wanted something with the wow factor," was the unhelpful response. "I'll leave you to steer this ship, see if you can get some quick wins and seize that low-hanging fruit. I'll be at my desk if you need me."

Still annoyed at the poster and broken mug, I slunk off to my computer and began to bash out a few designs. There's only so much you can do with a bag of crisps, but still desperate to seize my opportunity, I spent the next four hours photographing stacks of Quavers, editing those images, painstakingly cutting them out on Photoshop and creating what I thought was a masterpiece of an exploding packet of crisps. In the absence of the marketing team, I came up with my own strapline: "'Save a packet with £1 Quavers". Admittedly it could have done with a bit more fine-tuning, but I was fairly pleased with my efforts, and emailed over the work to Graham before heading to his office for an evaluation, hopefully some praise and a slap on the back.

But before I could even open my mouth, as I opened his door, he was staring at his screen with a screwed up face, making a low-pitched humming sound. He couldn't have been a particularly successful poker player over the years - he might as well have scribbled his thoughts on his face as his expressions led him to be read like a book.

"Oh dear, Scott - I don't think they're going to like this. It's not really on-brand is it?"

"Why's that?"

"Why would anyone want to see anything exploding in this day and age?"

"Well, it's only a packet of crisps. I don't think any terrorist organisation would be thinking that the snack food aisle is the perfect place for their next bomb attack."

"You just don't know, Scott - you have to be so careful with these things."

"I think you're looking a little bit too much into it literally, Graham. I'm just trying to make it impactful. Kids would love that - after all, they're the ones who are going to be pestering their mums to buy Quavers."

"I don't think you've achieved impactful, though," he said, shaking his head without moving his eyes away from the screen.

"Why don't you just show it to them? We need to get a bit more of a steer as to what they want."

"Hmm. No, I don't want to take the risk. We need to get our ducks in a row - back to the drawing board, I think. But not today." He got up and patted me on the shoulders as he opened his door to show me out. I thought to myself that finally, despite not impressing him with my artistry, my commitment to the cause had impressed him, however, his next comment felt like he was only touching my back so he could line up where to stick the knife in.

"Go home and get some rest. I think we'll all need it. I think a deep-dive is in order tomorrow, where we can throw all the Lego bricks onto the floor and see where they land. It'll probably be a late night to nail this."

"Late night?" I stammered, stopping in my tracks.

"Yes - why have you got somewhere more important to be, Scott?"

"It's Wales v Russia!" I blurted out, panicking.

"Oh what, the football? I thought you guys were out after we beat you?" Graham said, with a patronising smile that I so desperately wanted to wipe off his jowly face.

"No, we can still qualify. We have to win tomorrow and we'll be through to the knockout stages."

"Well, I'm sure you will and then you'll be able to watch that game, but I need you here until the end of play tomorrow for this. This campaign is too important, we need to drill down and get it right."

By now the horror had overcome me and I could feel sweat building on my forehead. Now my heart was racing at Wales v England speed.

"Please, Graham, I need to see this game. I have to leave at 6pm at the latest tomorrow. Is there anything you can do?"

"Sorry, Scott, not going to happen" he said flippantly, before returning to his office to put a full stop on the conversation. His total disregard and lack of understanding was staggering - he only cared about Underscore, but I couldn't care less. I could feel the blood bubbling inside me, and suddenly all I could picture was my Ian Rush mug shattered in the corner of the break room. I imagined everyone in the office throwing it around in triumphant celebration of England's win, laughing manically as Graham stuck the photo on my computer, dressed in a fancy dress suit of armour and an England jester hat.

My mind was racing. That daydream was replaced by one where I was sat at my desk reading a text from Dav proclaiming, 'This is the best day of my life - Wales 5-0 Russia!' which then triggered those raw memories of missing out in Toulouse the week before, whilst the other three, and indeed the whole Welsh nation, had the time of their lives.

Then Arthur's words of wisdom came flooding back - 'Go and make memories, and make sure they're happy' - followed by Victoria's angry expression as she forced me out of the flat. By now I was seething, and when I finally blacked in again, Graham was about to lock up.

As soon as I saw his smug face, clearly enjoying his abuse of power after stomping on another meaningless minion's dream to only help seal the commission that would find its way into his bank balance and not mine. The lid finally came off the pressure cooker, and I couldn't stop the words from falling out of my mouth.

"There is a way I can watch it Graham," I bristled before pausing, but realised I was at the point of no return and allowed the trickle to become a flood. "I have worked at this place for nearly 12 years and I have never been handed an ounce of respect from you, or anyone that works here. I have been underpaid, undervalued, unsupported and unhappy but I have kept plugging away in the hope that someday it might all turn around. But I've come to the realisation that with you in charge, brown-nosers like Benjamin and the other morons that work here, this place is dying on its arse. And speaking of arses - you're the biggest one here. I have put up with your arrogance, your bully-boy tactics, your wanky corporate speak and your crappy George from Asda pinstripe suits for all these years, but I can't take any of it anymore. I'm done with you, and all of this, so you won't be seeing me tomorrow or ever again, because I quit."

It had felt like an out-of-body experience, but suddenly I was back in the office, staring at his bulbous face. It had been a speech that had been rattling around in the back of my head for a good few years, but I never thought I would actually utter it out loud, but when backed into a corner faced with the prospect of missing my team reach the knockout stages of the Euros, I had passionately lashed out like a scared animal.

Rather than being shocked or offended though, Graham was smiling, almost laughing. "Oh, really? That's what you think! I think you'll find that you signed a contract that includes a four-week notice period Scott. So, yes, I will be seeing you tomorrow, and you'll be seeing me, and you definitely won't be seeing your precious football."

Only one thing could dignify a response that supercilious: "Stick your four weeks up your arse, you... you arse!" I shouted and stormed out. I jogged down the spiral staircase - pausing halfway when I realised that I needed to empty my desk but remembering it was only filled with stolen company stationery - and continued to the bottom step before flinging open the double doors to the car park with glee. What had I just done?

As I strolled back through Soho's windy streets, I was in a trance, or was it a state of shock? Why had I been so impulsive? I had thrown my toys out of the pram just because I couldn't watch a game of football, and now I had no source of income. Smart move, Scott.

I came across a little square, a tiny green carpet surrounded by black railings and tall buildings blocking out the summer sunlight. It was all a blur, and I felt the need to sit down before my knees buckled as the weight of the world on my shoulders finally became too much to carry.

In the space of a few days, I had lost my fiancée, the England game, my flat and now my job. It had all happened so quickly, and only now the magnitude of it all was dawning on me. As I looked back at those four things, one stood out above the rest. Why did I care so much about football that I ranked a defeat alongside three life-changing moments, all of which I could actually control?

Wales qualifying for Euro 2016 had ruined my life. Had this had been a normal summer with Bale, Ramsey and co sat on a beach somewhere, then everything would have worked out perfectly. The Slovakia game wouldn't have clashed with the wedding that played host to the termination of my relationship; the trip to France for the England game wouldn't have seen me return home to be kicked out of my flat; and I would have been content with slogging through work until late on Monday evening as long as there wasn't the Russia match to watch on TV. If my Ian Rush mug and been in my hand, I would have smashed it too. Football had been responsible for so much joy in my life, possibly even the single biggest contributing factor, but now it was the cause of all my recent suffering. It was time to let it go.

Whilst pigeons pecked away at leftover crumbs around my feet, I decided there and then that I couldn't let a sport dictate my life anymore, and it was time to push it into the background. It was just a stupid hobby; a pastime to whittle away the weekends and give me something to talk about with random men I was forced into conversation with at parties or conferences. I couldn't affect results, players were just human beings like the rest of us, and clubs wouldn't care a jot if I decided to stop going to matches. It was meaningless.

A shell of my former self, I began a sombre journey back to Dav's flat. So many questions were running through my head: Where was my money going to come from? Would I ever find love again? How long could I stick sleeping on Dav's fumigation-requiring sofa? Could I find a new hobby - one that didn't involve a ball? I thought through some potential options: maybe starting a collection of some kind? I had been a train fanatic as a child, perhaps I could build a massive model railway? Or maybe I could do something intellectual, like learn some languages, or get into politics? The whole country, including myself, was seemingly going mad for the Great British Bake Off - was that my calling?

After three tries of knocking on the door, a trouserless Dav finally stirred from his evening nap and let me in with a grunt of acknowledgment. I walked into his pigsty of a front room, unsurprisingly uncleaned from the weekend's session, or indeed the one before that, and I spotted his Euro 2016 wallchart pinned to the wall; each scoreline scrawled into the little boxes, except the Wales England section which had been left blank as neither of us had the heart to accept the result. This schedule had been dictating my summer and now it was time to take back control. I grabbed a handful of it and tore it off the wall in rage, leaving only a few rags of newspaper dangling from the brass pins still pressed into the wall.

"What the bloody hell are you doing?" shouted Dav. "You've wrecked it!"

"No, this tournament has wrecked my life. I've lost my missus because of it, I've lost my home, and now I've lost my job," I sputtered angrily, on the verge of tears or some sort of nervous breakdown.

"You what? What have you done?" Dav put his arm around my shaking body and led me onto the sofa.

"I quit - I told Graham to shove his job because he wouldn't let me watch the Russia game."

"Well, you've always said he was a prick."

"Yeah, but he was a necessary prick. I have no income now."

"Well, it's a good job that you don't have a girlfriend and rent to worry about anymore, then, is it?" offered Dav, trying to cheer me up.

"What am I going to do, mate? I'm a mess." I was usually embarrassed to be like this around my mates, but not Dav. We had been friends for so long and knew each other so well, that he was perhaps the only person in the world I show my true emotions to.

"I tell you what we're going to do, mate. We need to get you out of here."

"Yeah, mate, that would help. This place is a dump."

"No, not here, and you could have tidied it up yourself by the way. No, we need to get out of London, we need to get out of England. We need to get away." Judging by the tone of his voice and the fact he had gone glassy-eyed, I knew where this was heading.

"No, Dav, I don't have any money now." However, my pleas fell upon deaf ears.

"You have something even more precious: free time! Just like me, Ieuan and Matt. We can now go and stay out in France and enjoy the rest of the tournament, without work to worry about!"

"Mate - I have no money."

"You have savings, right? And you don't have rent to pay at the moment. We can do it on the cheap, I'm sure. Let's just go to Toulouse for the game tomorrow and see where it takes us. Let's leave it up to fate."

There it was - that word again. Fate had seen me leave Victoria, and whilst it had been the right thing to do at that time, I wasn't sure right about now. Running away to another country did seem to be a good short-term solution to getting away from my troubles of not having anywhere to live and finding something to do with my newly-found spare time. It didn't, however, solve the issues of cutting football out of my life - but could I really see myself sticking little trees to felt-covered models of hills whilst the Flying Scotsman chugged around in circles on my little model railway, or spending my Saturday afternoons perfecting my focaccia? In a way, the only good things left in my life were my friends and football, keeping me from a life of celibacy as I practiced my new hobbies.

"OK, mate - let's do it. Find out where Ieuan and Matt are and let's head there immediately."

"That's the Scott I know and love!" Dav said giddily. He grabbed his red, yellow and green bucket hat and picked up his suitcase. "I'm ready to go now!" He was still in his boxers.

I laughed for the first time that day. A quick look on the internet brought up wallet-lightening flights to Toulouse, and a mere few hours after taking voluntary unemployment, my credit card was being swiped alongside my passport and we were boarding a plane to the south of France.

CHAPTER 7

I had started Sunday in London with an apartment and a job, and I was ending it in France with neither. This is what my life had become; a series of random events invariably linked to the affairs of the Welsh football team and their escapades at Euro 2016, and now we were approaching the final group game, if I was to continue basing my fortunes on theirs, then my life was about to become even more unpredictable.

If we lost to Russia, the following day would be our last in the tournament, and our summer soiree would be consigned to the history books as a fleeting fling. A draw would probably see us through, a win certainly so. But even then, we had no idea where our next game would be or when. It's the one time where the well-worn football cliché "one game at a time" actually genuinely applied.

Believing that this could well be the last chance we got to see Wales in action at major championships for another 58 years - and, in that case, my lifetime - I was determined to soak up every last moment and refused to miss out on anything. We landed in Toulouse around midnight and with no time to find or book a hotel at such short notice, we thought we would wing it and pull an all-nighter. It had been something Dav and I had done at a previous away game in Bulgaria a few years earlier, which resulted in us sleeping in a train station - me on a bench and Dav, somehow, in one of those photobooths you get your passport pictures from. The strip of snaps I managed to sneakily get of him fast asleep is one of my most cherished possessions from my travels over the years.

As our taxi pulled up in the city centre, there were plenty of French supporters still out drinking following their final group game - a 0-0 draw with Switzerland - which had seen them comfortably into the knockout stages. Ieuan and Matt were somewhere among them. They directed us to a small Mexican-themed bar, which was very out of character for the pair of them, and it was even more surprising that we found them, sipping brightly-coloured cocktails through psychedelic green straws and tucking into two massive plates of cheese-covered nachos.

"Mate, your life is spiralling out of control," was the first thing a tipsy Ieuan said to me. No hellos or fancy seeing you heres; it was almost as if we hadn't have left them in Lille, but I wouldn't have expected anything different.

"Cheers, Ieu, I'm fully aware of that. It's all good, though; there's something quite liberating about not quite knowing what the next few months will have in store for me."

"Getting to know all your fellow doleys in the queue at the job centre?" came a rare joke from Matt, who had obviously been underestimating the strength of the cocktails he had been necking all afternoon.

"Don't worry, mate, everything will be alright," said Dav, wrapping a big arm around my shoulders. "Forget about that stuff, like I said before - let's forget women, and now let's forget work. Focus on the football! Both of those will come and go, but Wales in an international tournament is like Daley's Comet: you only see it every so often."

"Hayley's, Dav," corrected Matt.

"Matt, what did I just say - no women!"

"Unbelievable" sighed Matt.

"So why have you chosen this place?" I asked.

"Well, we fancied mixing it up a little. We've been out here for nine days now and I'm getting a bit tired of the taste of lager," said Matt.

"Yeah, and this stunning girl in the street was handing out vouchers for buy one, get one free cocktails at this place all night," continued Ieuan, filling in the blanks and solving the mystery.

"Fair enough. I have no income anymore, so that suits me perfectly. Me and Dav will be happy to accept your free drinks, boys," I chuckled, and fortunately Matt took enough pity on us to head to the bar and order us a couple each to catch up. Knocking back his pick of poison, it didn't take us long to get a bit giddy, and with the music in the bar being cranked up gradually, more and more fans were slowly migrating to it, looking for a place to continue their evening's merriment. About 90 minutes after we had arrived, it was standing room only and the narrow thoroughfare through the bar had become a makeshift dancefloor. The same promo girl who had twisted Ieuan's arm earlier was soon fluttering her eyelashes at her naïve victim, convincing him that shots of vodka were the way forward. Before we knew it, we had abandoned our table and were mingling between an eclectic mix of people bopping away to some generic electronic dance music.

With none of us up-to-speed with the latest chart toppers or dance crazes, we decided to copy Joe Ledley's famous dance moves from when we had qualified in Bosnia, which went viral on the internet. Our fellow dancers were finding them hilarious and we were attracting plenty of attention, so much so that a little huddle had formed around us as we held a mini dance-off, with Dav getting a huge cheer when he performed his worm along the floor. As well as those French supporters still out into the small hours, we met some Swiss fans, a random German bloke, two Swedish brothers and a Spanish couple, and with this impromptu UN meeting taking place, I thought it was necessary to get a photo to capture a glorious moment showing what being a fan at international tournament football is all about.

As if I was Wayne Hennessey lining up a wall to defend a free-kick, I got everyone into position and, when they were all in the perfect place, I tapped the nearest person on the shoulder to ask if they wouldn't mind doing the honours. The shoulder, though, just so happened to belong to a gorgeous woman wearing a French shirt, who, when she turned around, flashed a smile at me.

"Hi - you OK to take photo?" I said slowly in my best French accent.

"Hi - yes that's no problem, but can I be in it, too?" came a reply in perfect English. She had short black hair and soothing brown eyes that almost hypnotically drew you in towards her oblong face, which culminated in a rounded chin. She was a natural beauty and seemed to be wearing little make-up, although a thick layer of rouge coated her soft, full lips.

"Of course. Sorry, I didn't know that you could speak English!"

"It's OK! Selfie?" Lifting the camera up, she took what can only be described as the worst group photo I had ever seen: it was literally me and her in it, with none of our continental chums in view. It wasn't even landscape.

"That is awful!" I laughed, and suddenly realised that could have come across as incredibly rude to someone I had just met, but thankfully she sensed the playful tone.

"OK, you try then!" she laughed and handed me my phone back. I proceeded to take one of the best pictures in my life, with 13 happy faces all squeezed into it, but there was one in particular that shone out.

"Look at that - first time!" I bragged proudly as I showed her the group shot. A few of the others included in it peered over my shoulder to try and get a look, but there was now only one person who was getting any attention from myself.

"It's good, but I think I prefer my photo," she said, and swiped her finger across my phone screen to take a second look at our portrait. Once again she gave me a cheeky smile, which lit up her face. Her thick, straight eyebrows rested almost nonchalantly above those hypnotic eyes, and I got the sense that she was completely at ease in my presence. I admired the photo again; she was incredibly photogenic.

"Haha, yeah, I think I do too, actually," I replied. Was she flirting with me? It seemed like it, and as a result my guard went up. After 13 years with Victoria, this had been my natural reaction to any female attention I had received, instantly dishing out a cold shoulder or blurting out the fact that I had a fiancée. However, that was no longer the case. For the first time since I began university all those years ago, I was in a bar, chatting to a girl and I could act upon it. My heart began to beat a bit faster and I could sense a tingle of adrenaline rush from my head to my toes. The guard was being lowered. But then - hang on, this was like the waitress in Lille again wasn't it? Had Ieuan and Matt set me up again? I looked towards their direction and they seemed pre-occupied; Ieuan was following his promo girl around like a little puppy and Matt was staggering around aimlessly. I thought I'd take the risk and just go for my best chat-up line.

"Can I get you a drink?"

"Sure - I'll have a beer please. I'll come with you."

We squeezed our way through the hoards of sweaty, grinding bodies pressed up against each other to the bar, where I ordered a pair of bottles of some random local lager, and passed one to her.

"So - I'm going to go out on the limb here, I'm guessing you're French?" I said, pointing to the badge on her shirt. It was a tight-fitting female version which offered a plunging neckline and was cut to hug her curves neatly. Like most guys, I'd always had a thing for girls wearing football shirts, but this was something else - if it had been a Wales shirt, it would have been perfection.

"Oui. And you are English?" Confused, I looked down at my attire and noticed that in my haste to get over to France, I hadn't even put on my Wales top for the journey over. I was wearing just a plain green polo shirt.

"Good god no! I'm Welsh!"

"Oh sorry! Well, you do all look the same," she smirked. She had a real je nais se quoi charm about her, and her playfulness seemed to shine through at every moment, immediately lifting my mood, which was a nice change to treading on eggshells around Victoria. We clinked the necks of our bottles together, took simultaneous swigs of what tasted like god-awful home brew, and continued our conversation.

"So are you here with anyone?" I enquired.

"Yes, well, some friends I watched the game with, but I think they might have left as they have work tomorrow. How about you?" Hoping she wasn't asking about my employment status, I pointed towards the other side of the room, where barely visible between the laser beams, dry ice and coloured spotlights were three idiots moonwalking into random people and bumping into tables. None of Michael Jackson's tracks were even being played, but to be fair, their moves were still better than the kids in the pre-match build-up at the England game.

"Please tell me you haven't spoken to any of them tonight?" I asked, half-joking but half-serious.

"No, not yet - they look like fun!" My heart skipped a beat. This wasn't a set-up; she was actually flirting with me of her own accord. It was time to step my game up, and those earlier spirit-laced cocktails were definitely having the desired effect.

"I don't suppose you want to dance? I guarantee I have better moves than those clowns over there."

She laughed, nodded and held my hand, leading me back into the middle of huddled masses. Contemporary dance beats continued to blast out of the oversized speakers, rendering any conversation inaudible as the bass thundered across the room, causing everything to vibrate. Having made some strong claims, I attempted to make do on my promise of being as good a raver as possible, but I could only fist-pump in the energetic style I'd learnt from years of nights out soundtracked by 1990s cult dancefloor hit 'No Limit.' In contrast, my new friend shook her hips perfectly in time to the rhythm, probably blissfully unaware of who 2Unlimited were. It was spellbinding to watch, and I couldn't take my eyes off her. It was then that I realised I didn't even know her name, so I leaned in closer.

"SO WHAT'S YOUR NAME?" I bellowed into her ear.

"WHAT?" she screamed back into mine.

"WHAT. IS. YOUR. NAME?"

"HELLO HELLO! WHAT HAVE WE HERE?" Dav had shimmied his way through the shadows over to us. "WHERE'S MY BEER, MATE?" A sense of dread washed over me; I really wanted him to disappear before he said something out of turn and forced this gorgeous girl to make a hasty exit. Unable to find out anything more about this seemingly incredible specimen I had just met, I also wanted to get away from this headache-inducing din. Plotting quickly, something that achieved both aims popped into my head, and I tapped the girl on the arm before putting two fingers up to my mouth in a v shape.

"Cigarette?" she asked, and I put a thumb up. She nodded and I pushed us back through the sea of bodies that was now dangerously overcrowding the bar; after plenty of 'pardons' and 'mercis', we escaped to the sanctuary of the front door.

"Do you actually smoke?" I asked when we were ironically back outside in fresh air, the double glazing protecting us from a lifetime of tinnitus.

"Sometimes - do you have any cigarettes?" she reacted. I hadn't thought this plan through.

"Errr, no, I don't actually. I can get some?" Once again she laughed. "Don't worry, I'm happy you wanted to come outside. It's a bit more personal out here." Initially I thought she meant to chat, but when her eyes locked onto mine, her brow furrowed slightly and her cheeky smile turned to a serious pout, I knew where this was leading to, and I was ecstatic. She instead shifted her vision towards my lips, and that was the signal for me to begin to slowly lean in towards her, catching a hint of her sweet vanilla scent, but a crash behind me caused us to break away and see what the commotion was.

"Ahh, what are you doing outside, Scott? Are you leaving already, you lightweight?" It was Dav - again - the most unwelcome distraction of them all, who had walked straight into a metal table and chairs as he stumbled through the door.

"No, mate, just nipped outside for a cigarette."

"Ohhh, what's going on here?" Dav grinned like the 10-year-old in a playground that I could still remember him being. He wagged his finger between the two of us. "Sorry to interrupt, I'll go back inside!" and proceeded to give me the most unsubtle of winks; it looked more like an invisible Joe Calzaghe had thrown a right hook directly into one side of his face. I was cringing inside - was Dav blowing my chances? He would be severely in my doghouse if that was the case.

"OK Dav, catch you in a bit, butt."

"Make sure you do, Scott - remember we've got to find a place to crash tonight."

"You need a place to stay?" said the mysterious French woman still stood directly in front of me. "Have you not got a hotel?"

"No, we were just going to stay out all night or sleep in the station," blurted Dav, piling on yet more embarrassment. This girl must have thought that she was dealing with two alcoholic tramps rather than visitors for a football tournament, but yet again she proved to be a one-in-a-million.

"Haha you guys are crazy. You can to sleep in my apartment if you like?"

"Oh my god, would that be alright? You would be a lifesaver!" I said. My chances of a late night kiss were definitely not over, despite Dav's appearance.

"Yeah, I'm sure I can trust you guys - you Welsh fans have made many friends in my country. I live around the corner, but I think I'm going to go now - it's getting late." She began to walk off.

"C'mon, Dav, let's go." I ordered, waving him towards us. "Nip in there and grab our bags."

"What about the other lads?" he asked.

"Leave them. They know where they're staying," I hissed, shooting Dav a look that said "Don't you dare ruin this for me, again." It was an expression that he had seen many times before, so he necked the final few mouthfuls of his drink, plonked the bottle on one of the disturbed tables and disappeared inside, returning with our bags a few minutes later and tossing one at me. He trailed behind the girl and I as we made the short walk to her apartment, which was only a couple of streets away.

"Here we are," she said as we stood outside an old, tall townhouse with windows neatly laid out in a pattern similar to a chessboard. Opening a squeaky metal gate, she led the way up a flight of stairs to the front door and let us inside. Navigating our way up two more narrow, concrete spiral staircases, she unlocked the door to her abode. It was a tiny, but cosy studio apartment, and I immediately worried about Dav's tornado-like presence in an area this small. Numerous paintings and artworks adorned the walls of the living room-stroke-kitchen, with the floorspace divided in two by the presence of a shutter, which led through to what I guessed to be a bedroom.

"Wow, this is a great place!" I truthfully proclaimed. "I love what you've done with it."

"Yeah it's nice. I only moved in here a few months ago, had to get from my old place." She turned to look at me again before adding, "my ex is what you British would call a wanker?" Me and Dav both laughed - our swear words used by foreigners is always funny. She strolled towards the kitchen, thoughtfully poured three glasses of water, and handed them to the two strangers she had pitied enough to find them a place to kip for the night.

"I'll get you some blankets," she said softly, almost with a motherly tone to her voice, and opened the shutter to enter the bedroom. The second she disappeared, Dav slapped me on the arm and whispered, "what's going on between you two?"

"I don't know, mate, I nearly kissed her earlier."

Dav looked as though he was going to explode, and lifted his arm up for a high five. "Nice one, butt! Do you think you have a shot?"

Leaving his arm in the air, I replied: "I don't know, she seems pretty keen. She's a lovely girl; funny, charming, gorgeous."

"I know - don't bottle it like you always do."

"What do you mean always do? This is the first time I've had this chance since Victoria."

"Yeah and look how long that took you," Dav added before performing that ridiculous wink again. Luckily this time the girl wasn't privy to it, as she re-emerged a few seconds later with a stack of neatly-folded blankets and pillows.

"There you go, Dav," she said, having already picked up our names in the short time she had known us. "I hope the sofa is OK?"

"Yeah this will be fine, thanks - cheers for having us once again," he said, stretching his legs out so they dangled over one of the arms and burying his face into the cushion.

"No problem." She then faced me. "As for you, Scott, you have a choice." I wasn't sure for certain but my eyes must have lit up, sensing the opportunity to spend the night cwtched up with a stunning foreign beauty in the south of France.

"Sure, what can I pick between?"

"You can either sleep on the floor in here, or share the sofa with him." pointing to Dav, who I was sure was stifling his laughter. She tossed me a pillow, and gave me a much more sensual wink than Dav's previous face spasm. She was teasing me! Inside I was a little bit gutted, but I also loved the audacity of her games.

"The floor will be fine thanks." I smiled ruefully.

"Let me just show you the bathroom," she said, gesturing me to follow her across the room. As I had done since the moment I had clasped eyes on her, I did what she said and made the six paces or so across the room. Turning a corner, I was greeted by a bathroom filled with green ceramics and a black and white tiled floor that was only large enough for one person to fit in, and she was occupying that space.

"Here it is," she said, but she wasn't pointing out any of this literal water closet's features. She moved towards me, and gave me a gentle kiss which lasted for just a second or two, before running her hand down my arm. Whispering towards the side of my face, she sighed, "see you in the morning Scott, sleep well." She brushed past me, pulled the sliding door, and then, when there was just enough room to poke her head through, she did.

"Oh, and as for my name - it's Colette," she added, before blowing a kiss in the same direction where I had been standing when she had put her lips against mine. I was stood still, stunned but grinning like the Cheshire cat that got the cream. The door slid shut and with that, I took residence on the hard, wooden floor for the night. Before I even began to be able to process another extraordinary 24 hours, I was fast asleep.

Six hours later my eyes managed to prise themselves open and I began to peer through the darkness attempting to identify where I was. It took a few seconds, but the jigsaw pieces of Toulouse, a Mexican bar, Colette, the walk home and the kiss completed a puzzle that made up an epic evening. I reached for my nearly-dead phone and admired the selfie she had taken of us when we first randomly met. Beer goggles weren't an issue; in fact, if anything she had improved in beauty from a few hours previously.

"Checking out your new girlfriend?" came a creepy croak from behind me, causing me to jump.

"How long have you been awake for?" I asked Dav, who was peering down over the edge of the sofa.

"You have no idea how uncomfortable this sofa is."

"I slept on a wooden floor, mate - I think I have an idea." At that moment, the shutter door slid open once again and rays of sunlight illuminated the room and once again through squinted eyes my dilated pupils could make out artwork and sculptures that covered almost every inch of the four sea blue walls.

"Morning - I thought I could hear voices. Did you sleep OK?" a dressing gown-clad Colette said. I had been right about her natural beauty from the previous night; the red lipstick was the only thing wiped from her perfect skin, and even though her hair had been scruffed up during the night, it still looked stylish.

"Yes, great thanks!" we chimed together.

"Would you like a cup of tea? I know you British!" She strolled across to the kitchen area in her bare feet. I leapt up and headed towards her; I was desperate to touch her again, but I wasn't sure if the effects of alcohol had caused her to make some decisions she was already regretting.

"Don't worry, I'll sort us all out, it's the least I can do."

"Merci!" she smiled, and sat in a chair watching me franticly open every cupboard, searching for the right ingredients and instruments to make three cuppas, which, when finally accomplished, we sat down and were belatedly able to have a sober, civilised conversation. Dav and I filled her in on our brief time in Toulouse, and she began to reveal a bit about herself too. She was an art student who worked as a nanny part-time, but she had originally trained to be a hairdresser. She had lived in Bristol for a year, allowing for her good grasp of English, and it was that Christmas in England that a friend bought her an art set as a present and she had become hooked. Returning to France, a couple of years later she had decided that being an artist was her life's calling and changed career paths. The artworks on the walls were mainly original Colettes, with a few famous ones interspersed that she used as inspiration. Despite not being an art critic, there was one that I recognised straight away.

"I know this one - it's a Lowry."

"Très bien!" she said with a sort-of stunned expression. "How do you know that?"

"Well it's a painting of people going to a football match in England back in the day, so of course I know it! Maybe you should paint your own version this afternoon - all those Welsh fans and Russia supporters heading into your brand new stadium."

"Don't paint the fighting though," Dav added.

"Haha, nice idea, Scott, but I'll probably just watch it in a bar. You Welsh fans seem like fun, it would be good to meet more of you." Ridiculously, I felt an instant twinge of jealousy when she mentioned meeting other people, especially my fellow countrymen. Now I had discovered her, I wanted to claim her all to myself, and I was concerned that if we left the apartment without her, there was a good chance I would never see her again in my life.

"Do you know where we might be able to get some tickets, Colette?" asked Dav.

"Hmm, I'm not sure. I'll text my friends who I was with last night; they seem to be pretty good at getting them." We began to tidy everything away and straighten up the flat, but a couple of minutes later a vibrating sound prompted a little squeal from our hostess.

"It's good news - they have one spare ticket!" she announced, and the bunfight was on. Dav and I immediately stared at each other, hoping for a sign that the opponent would be gracious enough to offer it to the other, but it was never happening. Following the short stand off, I said "we'll take it. We'll see if we can find another one later in the day."

"Great, I'll let them know you'll buy it."

"What are your plans for the day anyway, Colette?" I said, trying to hide my desperation. "If you have none, can we at least buy you breakfast? It's the least we can do to thank you for putting us up last night."

"Well, I do have to do some babysitting this afternoon, but I have time to eat now, if you want?" With food on offer, Dav didn't need telling twice, so after she got changed into a summery dress and heels, we were back out onto street level and we, well I, treated our new friend to a slap-up breakfast in a fancy café, opposite the bar we had met in, whilst that morning's sun was preparing to rise. We began to warm us up as we dined alfresco, watching the natives get on with their daily lives.

After finishing the final mouthfuls of an omelette, washed down with a coffee, Colette uttered the words I had been desperate for her not to. "OK guys, I must go. It's been lovely to meet you."

Dying to say something poetic that would convince her to call in sick and spend more time with me, I managed: "How will we get in touch about the spare ticket? Do you want my number and then you can give me a call?" It wasn't ideal, or indeed at all romantic, but with my phone as flat as the Emirates Stadium on matchday, it was the best I could hope for.

"Good idea," she replied and proceeded to tap it into her phone. "I'll be in touch later - au revoir!" And with that, she got up from her chair, gave us a little wave goodbye and made her way back towards her apartment. As the sound of her heels got fainter in the distance, I ran through my head any possessions I might have left behind, franticly trying to think of an excuse to return to her apartment, but there wasn't one.

"She's a bit special, isn't she?" said Dav.

"Yeah, mate, unreal."

"Did anything happen between you two last night?"

"We kissed, yeah."

"Tidy, mate. Fair play. Right, shall we find those two idiots?" Whilst we shared pretty much everything with each other, Dav and I never really went into the nitty gritty of our success, or lack of, with women - just the bare facts were enough. Dav managed to get hold of Ieuan and Matt, who were obviously still tucked up in bed at their hotel, so we strolled across the city centre, noticing an increasing number of red shirts along the way, before we managed to ditch our bags in yet another 'hotel,' which resembled a crack den.

"Right, so it's matchday, what shall we get up to?" asked Ieuan grinning. With our shirts, scarves and flags proudly on display, we went and found ourselves a spot in a nearby Irish pub and got stuck into four traditional full Englishes with a side of Guinness. Whist waiting for our phones to charge, we held a debrief of the previous night's events, and after filling the other two in about Colette, Ieuan embarked on a tale which started with Matt reluctantly leaving him at the bar alone to carry on chatting to the promo girl. When it finally closed, she asked if he would walk her home and it had only taken them about 10 steps before they had locked lips, and an invitation to stay the night. However, there was a caveat - she lived with her ex-fiancée, which he mentioned had been the first time Victoria had popped into my head for nearly 24 hours.

Hesitant, a steaming Ieuan had scrambled to find an alternative and proceeded to lead this girl on a crawl of hotels asking each receptionist if he could pay for a room for "about 45 minutes." Unwilling to take him up on his offer, he eventually walked her to her front door before the temptation got the better of him. Whilst in bed together, he had heard footsteps stomp across the landing and got freaked out - meaning he couldn't 'perform - and thus quietly slid his way out of the house, managing to avoid a beat down.

Plenty of laughter followed, before we ran through our individual favourite Sly Ieu stories. Before we knew it, our plates had been long cleared and we were slowly accruing beer glasses as the drinks flowed through us, and I had to nip to the gents. I sidled up to a urinal next to a fellow red-shirted fan, a bit older than me with bright white, fluffy hair and glasses. We exchanged pleasantries whilst keeping our sight at eye-level, and seeing as we had an unbreakable bond by the crest stitched into our jerseys, we felt the need to make small talk about the game.

"So where abouts are you sitting then, mate?" he asked.

"I'm not sure - not got a ticket yet!" I replied.

"Oh really. How many do you need? I have a spare pair if you're interested?"

Suddenly a thought flashed through my head. It was a little devious, but I was sure Dav wouldn't mind. Colette was going to watch the game in a bar, but if I bought her a ticket, maybe she would go to the game with me, and Dav could have her friends' spare?

Without hesitation, I replied, "mate, that would be amazing - how much are they?"

"150 euro each," was the reply, causing me to wince, and he obviously clocked it as he clarified. "That's face value, mate. I wouldn't rip a fellow Welshman off." He zipped up his fly and made his way to the sink, so I followed suit. Could I really justify paying 300 euros to take a girl I had only known a few hours to a game, just so I could see her again? It seemed like it was my only chance.

"OK, mate, I'll have them. Just give me 10 minutes to get some cash out, yeah?"

"Great stuff. I'm sat at a table by the big TV, come and give me a shout." After washing our hands, we shook them and I managed to sneak around the other side of the bar to avoid the lads' attention, withdraw the money from across the road, pay the Welshman and return to the table with two tickets tucked inside my convalescing wallet. Now all I needed was my phone to ring.

CHAPTER 8

One of the problems of living in this modern world of instant global communication is that a message can come at any time, from anywhere. While usually viewed as a technological miracle, in situations where you're desperate for a certain someone to get in touch, it can be agony. For the next few hours, every time my phone threatened to bleep or vibrate, it was being grasped by my sweaty palms as I was left frustrated by another pointless Facebook notification of a cat meme or someone inviting me to play Candy Crush.

I was beginning to panic slightly - not about the tickets, but that Colette had played her last scene in the story of my life. My mind was racing - how had I fallen so quickly for someone? I had quickly become besotted by her innocent enthusiasm and infectious charm; the same thing happened with Victoria all those years ago in university. Maybe the lack of contact was a blessing? Fat chance.

Not helped by the pints I was rapidly knocking back, misery was beginning to kick in and hope dissolving, until eventually there was a burst of electronic life next to me. The name I had been dying to see on my screen was finally there: Colette. Picking up, I tried to act as casual as possible.

"Hello, who's this?"

"Hi Scott, it's Colette." Despite a ropey connection, her sensuous French accent sounded so much sexier after spending hours on tenterhooks.

"Oh, hiya! How was your afternoon babysitting?"

"Yeah, not bad. Good to be finished though. My friend dropped that ticket off. Do you want to meet somewhere?" This was my opportunity; the goal was gaping. Pretending the clicking of wine glasses and smattering of loud conversation around us was making hearing difficult, I gestured to the other lads that I was popping outside to arrange the pickup.

Stepping out in daylight onto the street, I said: "Sure, but I've managed to get two tickets already from a bloke in the pub here."

"Oh," she replied, sounding pretty downbeat and a little annoyed. "You could have told me before I…"

Realising that I had made myself out to be an ignorant ticket-chasing knob, I quickly cut her off before she broke into a tirade, blurting out: "No, no, sorry that's not how it sounds! I still want your ticket, but I was just wondering if you would rather watch the game with me in the stadium than at a bar tonight? My treat."

The silence was like seeing a player on your team shoot from distance, and even when the ball is miles away, you just know it is going to fly into the net; however, it takes an age for you to find out as the world suddenly plays out in slow motion. Thankfully, this particular figurative effort thundered past the goalkeeper, probably hitting the crossbar on its way in for the full effect.

"Oh, wow, that would be incredible!" she screamed. "Are you sure?"

"I'm positive," I beamed, with the imaginary sound of a packed stadium roaring in delight at the wonderstrike I had just converted. "Shall I meet you at the stadium?"

"Sure thing! Hang on, is this a date?" she queried. I hadn't really thought of it like that, but I guessed that it probably sufficed, even if it was the most expensive date I had ever been on. Plus, if she wasn't happy with that arrangement, then at least I could sell the ticket. Best to be upfront and honest about it, right?

"Umm, yeah - is that cool with you?" I said, my face contorting with tension at the outcome.

"You don't sound convinced, but I'm counting it," she said coolly. "Text me the details and I'll meet you there an hour before kick-off. I'm so excited! Catch you in a bit."

I punched the air in celebration after executing the perfect plan. As well as scoring a date with Colette, I was about to look like the best friend ever. Returning indoors to my seat, Dav zoned in on my approach like a hawk surveying its prey, awaiting the verdict as to whether he was going to the crucial game or not.

"That was Colette, she's got the single ticket," I said a little forlornly to build up the mood. "Look, Dav, I've been thinking a lot about it, and you should take it. After all you did put me up for a few nights when Victoria kicked me out, and you might be doing so again when we get back. I'd like you to have it." I sat back and awaited the admiration, possibly some tears but definitely a huge bearhug for my generosity, sealing my place as the world's best best friend.

"Ahh tidy, cheers, mate. Yeah, that does sound fair," he mumbled before returning to his pint. "Any idea where the seat is?"

That was it; that was all the gratitude Dav could muster. Ieuan and Matt stared at me, gauging whether I would call out his lack of appreciation, but while I should have been angry, I couldn't be too righteous; after all I was bailing on my best mate to watch a massive Wales game with a girl I barely knew, especially with my previous track record of watching Wales with women.

Back in my teens, I once took an old flame called Gemma to a game, and despite it being a date, Dav insisted on accompanying us. We travelled down on an unglamorous bus to an unglamorous Ninian Park to watch an unglamorous game against Belarus. But as soon as play started, I was instantly engrossed and only spoke to Dav about players and tactics. For the whole 90 minutes I completely ignored poor Gemma, who cited my abandonment as a reason for our inevitable break up a few days later. It wasn't all bad, though - we actually won that game 2-1, but my other experience was thoroughly miserable. Victoria, back in her fun phase, insisted on coming with me to a World Cup qualifier against Slovakia at the Millennium Stadium, and I relented thinking she would see a good Wales performance and a win. Unfortunately, it turned out to be nothing of the sort - we got drubbed 5-1, our worst home loss for nearly a century - and as we made our way back onto Westgate Street afterwards, she naively proclaimed, "Well that was good, lots of goals to see!" which was met with scorn.

Checking my watch, it was now 7pm and only a couple of hours until kick-off. I urged the lads to finish their drinks and we began our walk north to the stadium, which was one of the more pleasant ones I have had in all my years of watching football. Unlike the monstrosity that was Len's out-of-town arena, the Stadium Municipal was situated on a small island in the centre of the city, steeped in history having hosted matches as far back as the 1938 World Cup. Filled with songs and beers, the Welsh fans were having a great time en route, seemingly determined to enjoy the occasion as a few hours from now we could be eliminated from the competition. Having been so preoccupied with Colette, I had hardly given the game any thought - but it hadn't needed it. I had woken up with the sense of confidence that we were not only going to reach the knockout stages on this particular summer's evening, but we were going to win the match too.

Our stroll through another attractive French city continued and we soon crossed a bridge onto the Ile du Grand Ramier that housed the ground. Welsh and Russian fans were mingling together beautifully, sharing jokes and even hip-flasks filled with who-knows-what, and the tension in the air had been left behind in Lens. The floodlights beamed like towering beacons in the distance, and the nostalgic smell of hot dogs and onions lingered. Nervous energy coursed through my veins, and it was fantastic. This -

nothing like my experience at the England game - this was what international tournament football was about. I remembered that I should have been in the Underscore office at this very moment, but instead I was once again in the one place I wanted to be in more than any other in the universe. And soon I would be alongside the one person I really wanted to share that moment with.

Having spent hours of my life waiting for women to show up late, it only made me want this perfect French woman even more, when I saw her already in situ outside the ground, looking stunning in a red top, a pair of tight low-cut jeans and tan coloured boots, accessorising her look with something that made me want to kiss her again right here, right now - a Wales scarf. She waved it above her head when she spotted us and, in an excellent cockney twang, shouted, "C'mon Wales!"

"Yeah, that's a London accent, but we'll let you off," I laughed. "Love the scarf." She giggled and opened her handbag, pulling out a ticket and making Dav's day.

"That'll be 50 euros please, Dav."

"No problem," he said, dusting the cobwebs off his wallet and pulling out some cash. "Thank you so much for sorting this out, Colette - you'll be my favourite person from Toulouse as long as I live." He promptly gave her one of his trademark bearhugs.

"Haha, don't worry about it. Get me a beer afterwards," she smiled, a little shaken up by the experience of having a giant oaf in a skintight Lycra top squeeze her tightly.

"Now, can you continue to perform magic and find Scott one?" asked Matt, while Ieuan stood gawping at the stunner in front of him, trying to roll his tongue back into his mouth.

She turned to me: "Oh, why, have you not got our tickets yet…" and I cut her off for the second time in a few hours, jumping in quickly to loudly say, "No, no I haven't got any tickets yet, we'll have to find some around here." A frown came over Dav and Matt's faces, whilst Ieuan continued to be a little giddy. I was determined not to let on that I had a pair of tickets tucked tightly inside my wallet pocket.

"Right, we'll catch you guys after the game," I said, and hurriedly began to escape from the scene. "I'll let you know if I get in." Colette followed and, with a shrug of his shoulders, Dav headed for his seat alone, a sure-fire certainty via the bar.

"I thought we had tickets?" said Colette, puzzled.

"No, don't worry, we do," I replied with a wink, which was quickly becoming our thing. "I didn't tell Dav I was going to watch it with you because he would have gotten jealous, and probably made you sit on your own."

"Oh, right, I see. Wow, ditching your friends for a girl you met last night, very naughty, Scott," she said, winking back. With the other three now among the thick throng of supporters slowly shuffling towards the turnstiles, I handed Colette her ticket and we followed suit.

"What is your favourite thing about watching football?" I asked, praying that her answer wasn't the players' legs or something similarly superficial that would see her added to the list of women I wouldn't be taking to another football match.

Without hesitation, she said: "I love the colour, the passion, the songs and the sounds. I used to love hearing the..." - she made a motion with her hands, not knowing the English word for turnstiles - "... clicking when I walk in, you don't get that anywhere else." The way she said it in her accent made it all the more poetic; romantic almost. What an answer! She continued: "Sorry, I can be more girly if you want - you'll have to obviously teach me the offside rule, oh and I rate the players' bums when they take corners," and let out a sarcastic bubblegum giggle, which had me laughing for real.

"I can deal with that, don't worry."

"Well, you won't have to, I am a real fan. This isn't particularly girly, but anyway" she said, once again opening her handbag, but this time pulling out a plastic bottle which was half filled with a thick red liquid. "Quick, help me finish this wine before it gets taken off me." Maybe it was God, or possibly a higher power such as Gary Speed, but someone somewhere was looking down on me whilst this girl personified perfection.

A couple of big swigs each saw off the illegal moonshine, and regardless of the strong, warm smell lingering on our tongues, we passed through security and into the oval arena about 20 minutes before the kick-off. You could tell it was an older stadium that had undergone redevelopment as it seemed very flat when you caught a first peek at the pitch, but when we found our row, the scene was breathtaking. The sun was setting overhead and the sky was a pallet of deep reds, bright yellows and sea blues. It hovered over a vast, wave-shaped roof that allowed the natural light to creep in, while four giant floodlights leant ominously over the stands, casting odd-shaped shadows on the immaculate green rectangle that would provide tonight's stage. And then there was the newly-dubbed Red Wall, all kitted out in scarlet, with their ever-expanding collection of flags paying homage to hometowns and heroes. Colette's eyes were darting, taking mental photographs of this superb scenery.

"Now this would be an amazing painting to hang on your wall." I said to her.

"That would be a challenge," she said, almost awestruck. "I said I liked the colours at a game, but this is another level - c'est magnifique."

She pulled out her phone and took a photo to capture the moment forever. After I filled her in on some of the less recognisable faces and recapped the bitter history between the two teams, stemming from the Euro 2004 play-offs that had me in floods of tears, the players made their grand entrance. With every seat occupied, Wales definitely had the advantage in terms of numbers in the ground, with huge swathes of red in all areas of the old venue, which would soon be rumbling to the sound of the anthems. Maybe it was the all-day drinking or the nip of whiskey outside, but with no Dav, I instinctively threw caution to the wind and stretched my left arm out, awkward-teenager-at-cinema style, and wrapped it around Colette's left shoulder. She laughed, and softly placed her head on my chest just as I began singing loudly, proudly, but making slightly more effort to remain in the right key. In the slight pause between the verse and chorus, I spotted she was staring right at me, still with her head on my left breast. I gave the gwlads extra gusto. What could be more perfect than a cwtch during the anthem? Once I had finally released my grip, and the noise from my compatriots around us had died down, she said: "I can't believe how passionate you are! Your heart was beating so fast."

"Haha, yeah, I get a little excited when I hear our anthem," I muttered, glossing over the fact that there had also been a stunning woman pushed right up against me, staring dotingly into my eyes, which was causing most of my palpitations. We remained standing for the Russian anthem and then it was go time: the flags, flagbearers, mascots and all the other paraphernalia was cleared off the pitch, and seconds later we were just left with what we had come to see.

The white-shirted Russians got us underway to the sounds of the wonderful Barry Horns brass band that provide the musical accompaniment to most Wales matches, but little did they know they were about to be completely overwhelmed. Just two minutes in and Gareth Bale found himself with the ball on the right, teasing and tormenting the concerned defenders in front of him. Ghosting into the area, he feigned to shoot before that deadly left foot swiped at the ball and got me off my seat. His shot was straight at Igor Akinfeev in the Russian goal, but he spilled it into Sam Vokes' path - he was destined to score.

I was punching the air in delight and forgetting I wasn't with Dav or the other lads; I nearly grabbed hold of Colette again in jubilation, but somehow the big striker was denied by Akinfeev, as well as the offside flag. I let out a high-pitched "AARRGHHHH!" in excitement and frustration, noticing she was virtually in hysterics at my antics.

"Sorry, I thought that was going in!" I said, much to the amusement of a few people around me, who were uninvited spectators to this particular date.

"Don't worry about it - be yourself. I'll only make a judgement after the game," Colette replied coyly, stimulating my self-confidence. She was right - given the circumstances I had to rein my emotions in a bit - after all I didn't want to scare her away or make her think I was some sort of psychopath if we conceded. As the game settled back down, a scenario ran through my head whereby we scored and I accidently clocked her square in the mouth whilst overcome with merriment, a sure-fire way to ensure I never saw her again, so I vowed to stay calm. That was until I watched something amazing unfolding.

With his newly-bleached blonde hair, it had been pretty easy to spot Aaron Ramsey in the opening two games, and he caught my eye as he switched a jog into an arcing sprint on the very edge of the Russian defence. Joe Allen also saw it and slid the perfect pass into his feet. The noise levels shot up, as 33,000 seats flipped backwards with everyone inside the stadium taking to their feet, cheering for their favourite in the now one-on-one duel that was the Welshman against Akinfeev. Like something from the wild west, both men waited for the other to draw first, but at the last second, Akinfeev dropped to the ground, and Ramsey showed fantastic composure to dink the ball over the giant.

"YESSSSSSSSSSSS!" I screamed when the ball rolled over the whitewash before nestling into the net. I punched the air aggressively with delight. After my premonition, I made sure I was well away from Colette, and instead grabbed the arm of some random bloke sat next to me, who virtually leapt into my arms, so I shook him like I was trying to get the last dollops out of a ketchup bottle. I felt a hand paw at me from behind, and when I turned around, I saw a bemused French girl half-heartedly twirling her scarf around.

With the celebrations dying down, I didn't quite know what to do to rectify what had been an awkward moment between the pair of us, as I left her to share in the jubilation that was a goal all alone. I offered up a high-five and instantly regretted it - I must have come across as not having any desire to touch her. I sat back down with an expression of grinning and grimacing - I had ruined a glorious moment and was already safe in the knowledge that any time I saw that goal replayed on TV, I would remember ditching Colette's embrace for that of a random middle-aged man.

Pockets of Welsh fans were partying in the stands, but I sat stewing at my idiocy for the next 10 minutes. What I needed was a second chance - which meant we had to score again. Against decent teams, such as Russia, Coleman would usually instruct his troops to sit back and defend their lead, so I miserably sat thinking that another goal would be a long time coming, if at all.

The game continued to resemble a table football match, with both sides attacking at a hundred miles an hour, pouring bodies forward. Bale was soon in the thick of the action again, this time buzzing around in the centre of the field, playing another cute pass, which afforded a red shirted player the Roman road to goal. Leaping out of my seat, my expectations crumbled when I spotted the number three on the back of that particular jersey; the opportunity had fallen to the rampaging Neil Taylor, who hadn't scored a goal for six years. My chance of redemption with Colette had fallen to a bloody left-back.

Holding out little hope, I clasped my hands over my eyes, immediately sliding my fingers apart so I could watch the inevitable unfold. Sure enough, Taylor - with so much time and space in the box that the nearest Russian defender could have well been over the border in Spain - blasted the ball straight at Akinfeev. My eyes were about to slam shut in despair, when fortunately the ball cannoned off the goalkeeper and back into the path of the defender, who proceeded to rifle it, on the volley, into the net.

"YOOUUUU BEAUTYYYY!" came an unfamiliar cry from myself, and like Taylor, I took my chance at the second time of asking. The ball was still trickling around in the goalmouth when I had grabbed hold of Colette, who had her hands in the air and was screaming in delight. I was about to shake her violently like the bloke next to me, when I remembered she wasn't as durable, so instead we hugged tenderly, shouting into each other's ears whilst the place around us blew up.

"Who are you calling a beauty?" she asked, hoping for a compliment, but now wasn't the time.

"Neil Taylor! Who did you think I was on about?" I replied, believing I was being incredibly suave and clever, but then realised that I was probably about to butcher another celebration. Thinking as quickly as our new goal machine had done seconds earlier, I took a leaf out of Dav's playbook: I gave her a big old smooch on the forehead, and she once again broke into a fit of giggles.

"Get off me - you're like a dog!" she cried, but I was pretty happy with that move. It had been the first time my lips had touched her since last night, and it was a baby step in the right direction toward doing it once again this evening - or maybe even if we got one more goal.

By now the stadium was swaying to the sounds of "Don't Take Me Home." A song sung at a football ground had never been so apt. I wanted to stay right here - at Euro 2016, in France, with Colette - and with no work to worry about, I could stay as long as my bank manager allowed, indeed attempting to drink all the beer. It was football of the champagne variety, though, that Wales were playing - and it was a privilege to watch. Even when Russia managed to capitalise on a rare error by Ashley Williams, which allowed Aleksandr Kokorin through on goal, the safe hands of Wayne Hennessey made a fine stop to keep his sheet clean. Soon after, Colette had been spellbound for the first time by the Bale Effect, as she jigged up and down as he dribbled 70 yards at full speed, sending defenders tumbling at his feet, before Vokes missed another good chance. The shots were raining down on the Russians, who were being forced into retreat. But as they received the release of the peep of the half-time whistle, a mighty rendition of "WALES! WALES!" carried our red shirted heroes off the field. Forty-five minutes from glory, and a spot in the last 16.

"So, what do you think?" I asked my guest.

"Wales are incredible" she said. "I never knew they were this good!"

"Nor did I," I replied, shaking my head - and it was true. That first half was as good as I had ever seen us play, ever. It was a joy to behold, and we looked dangerous every time we crossed the halfway line. Just like the nervous energy had transferred from us supporters to the players at the England game, it seemed their confidence was crossing over into the stands; we were lapping it up. Russia were done for; there was no chance we weren't going through now. It was a matter of when, not if, we got a third goal.

As the two sides re-emerged, the contrast between them was vast: Wales virtually floated back into position, while our opponents had seemingly spent the last 15 minutes packing their suitcases, knowing the game was up. Upon resumption, Bale and Ramsey continued as though they were mates playing keep-ball in Bute Park; the latter nearly dinked the white sphere over Akinfeev again, only to watch it roll wide. The pair, however, would get it right midway through the second half when, in an almost identical move, Bale this time caressed the ball into the net after the hapless defence suffered from another bout of rigamortis.

Strangely, I did the same. As soon as the ball left Bale's left boot, Colette was in my arms celebrating. Before I even had a chance to make my move, she was kissing me once again. Thousands of fans were screaming around us, but in my head everything went silent. The fans, Bale, even Ramsey's hairstyle; it was all blocked out and it was all about that particular moment. I've celebrated some great Welsh moments down the years, but none were as good as this one. Just don't tell Dav.

The kiss probably lasted no more than five seconds. But once we had come up for air, she screamed, "WALES! WALES!" Only her accent gave any clue that she was Gallic rather than from Gwent, and we just beamed at each other for the next few minutes. I was speechless - I had gone from rock bottom to the top of the world in just over 24 hours - and I wondered how she must be feeling. Twenty-four hours ago, Wales were just another team making up the numbers in the Euros, and now here she was snogging some guy from that country, screaming out his team's name.

With the result and a spot in the knockout stages secure, it was sheer bliss to sit back for the final 20 minutes and just let the occasion sink in by osmosis. We sang the whole back catalogue of songs, ole'd every pass, and shook our heads in disbelief every time we caught another stunned nearby fans' teary eye. Then, with five minutes to go, came a rumble from the other side of the stadium - were they singing "We Are Top Of The League?" It got more pronounced, and soon the Red Wall were bouncing as they chanted it. I grabbed my phone and checked the England score - they were drawing with Slovakia! The information spread like wildfire, and by the time the full-time whistle had finally put Russia out of their misery, the Welsh players and supporters united as one in their adulation of each other, 0-0 was announced as the final score in Saint Etienne: we had ended up top of the pile - handing us a much better chance of progressing even further in the tournament. To qualify for the last 16 was as much as we had dared to dream for. But now, who knew what could happen? Imaginations were beginning to run wild, but it was time to celebrate. Nights don't get much better than this, but there was one thing missing.

"Right, let's get out of here," I said to Colette, grabbing her hand.

"Don't you want to clap the players a bit more? Even I want to give Gareth a wave," chuckled Colette, now a fully paid-up member of the Bale fan club.

"Nope, there's something I've got to do," I replied, before pushing my way down the row of seats towards the exit and pulling my Franco-Welsh friend with me. With most fans staying behind to savour the moment, it was a pretty swift exit out of the ground. We were soon back at the spot where we had left the rest of the boys, and, a few minutes later, I saw the unmistakable figure of Dav and his bucket hat. We charged full pelt towards each other shouting "YESSSSSS!" before the inevitable crash, barely holding ourselves upright as we gripped our best mate tightly.

"THIS IS THE BEST DAY OF MY LIFE!" he bellowed.

"SAME HERE, MATE - UN-BLOODY-BELIEVABLE!" We were soon joined by Ieuan and Matt in a little huddle, but Colette was standing alone again. I waved her over, not expecting her to fancy diving head first into a pile of sweaty, boozed-up, ecstatic men, but dive she did. Linking our arms around each other's waists, we jumped around in a circle in a car park, singing "Don't take me home, please don't take me home…" and about a hundred other Welsh voices joined in. It seemed like the entire nation was staying firmly put for a bit longer yet.

The party was already in full swing, and we reflected on the night's memories that would survive a lifetime. As we strolled back over the bridge towards the city centre, lit up by stars and street lamps, Ieuan revealed that he had caught Matt wiping a tear from his eye during the latter stages, which Matt fiercely denied, and despite Dav being sat by himself, he had made numerous new friends, flicking through selfie after selfie of him with those who had enjoyed his company throughout the 90 minutes.

"So you two got in then, did you?" asked Matt to Colette and I.

"Yeah," she said casually, not trying to give our plan away. "Scott was great, he managed to get us tickets next to each other.

"Did you have fun?" Dav asked, almost with a hint a jealousy in his voice.

"Yeah, but I think he missed you, Dav; after the first goal he went and hugged the bloke next to him and left me all alone." Once again my face screwed up; in the aftermath of the display, the victory and finishing top of the group, that nightmare had decayed slightly, but now it was replaying in my head over and over again. With the lads laughing hard at my stupidity, I felt I had to leap to my defence: "Well, yeah, OK. But Colette got so involved that when Bale scored the third..."

"I gave him a high five," she interrupted, shooting me a stern look, as if to say that I literally should not be kissing and telling.

"That's it? Bloody hell, Colette, you could have got into it a bit more. You've just witnessed the greatest Welsh performance of all time." said Dav.

"I loved it! Now come on, join in - "We've got Gareth Bale, we've got Gareth Bale..." We all followed suit and paid tribute to our superstar. By the end of a long night trailing around Toulouse's bars once again, Colette had learnt, word for word, pretty much every Welsh song, while we had failed in our attempt to recite just two lines of Les Marseillais by the time the pub lights were switched back on and the barman began to usher the hoards of revelling Welsh supporters out on the narrow streets.

"Right, we're off back to the hotel - better start sorting out plans for the next game," said Matt, pulling the back of Ieuan's shirt to end his drunken pleas for a gaggle of French girls' phone numbers. "Are you two crashing with us tonight?"

I looked at Dav, but he had clocked where this was all going, saying: "I will take you up on that offer Matthew, merci beaucoup." All attentions then turned to me. I had been dancing with Colette all night, but there had been no offer of a nightcap, and I really didn't want to ask for fear of being shot down in front of all of my friends. I looked at her, hoping she would say something, and eventually she did.

"Jesus Scott, yes of course you're staying at mine tonight," she smiled. "Wave goodbye to your friends, and come with me." I resisted the urge to break out into a little dance there and then, and gave warm hugs to the rest of the group before going our separate ways, and grabbed her hand for the walk home.

"God, you British are the worst," said Colette as soon as we were out of the trio's earshot. "You are so polite all the time, and so tense when it comes to sex. What did you think we were going to do - what would you have done if I hadn't said anything?"

I laughed loudly at our nations' strange quirks and replied, "cried myself to sleep probably and lived a life of regret."

"I did enjoy watching you struggle to work out what to do when the first goal went in, though," she added. "You were too shy to even give me a hug!"

"I'm shy?" I laughed. "I'm not the one who was too nervous to tell my friends that you pretty much mounted me when the third goal went in."

"OK, we're even," Colette said. "It was a shame there wasn't a fourth goal - who knows what would have happened then?"

"I think we're about to do exactly that," I said, as charming as could be. I got a wink in return as we bundled towards her front door; our hands round each other's waists, climbing up the labyrinth of stairs and into her apartment. With no prying eyes focused upon us except each other's, she pulled across the sliding door and led me into her bedroom, capping off possibly my best day ever in the perfect way.

CHAPTER 9

As I stirred in the morning with the happiest hangover of my life, bright sunshine had crept through the blinds and my ears picked up the quiet hum of rush-hour traffic mixed with birdsong. A dainty, well-manicured hand was resting upon my chest, with the remainder of Colette's naked body pressed up against me. My left arm was numb from being lain on all night by my bed sharer, as the pair of us had drifted off to sleep after a post-sex cwtch.

She was still dozing, so I began to get some feeling back into my dead arm by combing it slowly through her immaculate hair, replaying an incredible evening back through my mind: Ramsey's goal, Taylor's goal, Bale's goal, everything that happened after that. My jobless, homeless life seemed complete with Wales in the knockout stages of the tournament and a beautiful French woman lying next to me in bed.

My hair-playing must have awoken her from her slumber as she began to mutter, yawn and eventually separate her eyelids. I leaned across and gave her a peck on the forehead and wished her good morning. Thankfully, she smiled back at me rather than turn away, and we kissed once again. Pulling herself closer towards me, she rested her head on my heart, just as she had during the anthem the day before. We lay together silently for a few minutes. It could have lasted a few hours and I wouldn't have minded as I didn't have a care in the world; that was until I felt a droplet fall onto my skin. Then I heard a sniff, followed by another, and I realised that Colette was quietly weeping.

"Hey, what's up?" I said, beginning to worry that she was having morning-after regrets about sleeping with me so soon after our initial meeting.

"How has this happened to us?" she sobbed. "How have we gotten so close this quickly?"

It echoed my thoughts from the day before which I had attempted to quickly bury - que sera sera and all that. I was following a path of fate which had led to this point of overwhelming magnificence, well until she had started crying.

"I'm really not sure, but aren't you glad we have?" I replied.

"Oh, Scott, I am. I have really enjoyed getting to know you, and the game yesterday was wonderful, but I think we both know this isn't a one-night thing, is it? That's the scary thing."

"What do you mean?" I asked, fearing the answer.

"Well, you're obviously going to be leaving - whether it's back to England or somewhere else in France. I can't come with you as I have to study, so this is as good as it's going to get between us, isn't it?"

I could feel my bottom lip tremble as I watched her battle to get her words out and simultaneously keep her emotions in. I slowly cupped the side of her head with my hand and gently pushed it back down to my chest so she couldn't see my face. Whilst trying to sooth her by caressing her damp cheek, I quickly tried to conjure up a solution. How could I have this girl every day I was in France? How could I remain in Toulouse and still follow the football? How could I avoid returning to Britain after the tournament? But no epiphany arrived; I knew we were doomed.

"Look, how about I stay here until the next game - it's on the weekend. We could enjoy the time we have left together and see if we can come up with something? You might get bored of me after four more days!"

Humour failed to lift the mood, and I felt her head shake horizontally against my chest. "No, that wouldn't work. We'll only get more attached and then things will harder. I'm sure your friends will want to head elsewhere today and continue their trip - you should go with them." Was that an instruction?

"But what if I don't want to? What if I'd rather stay here and spend the rest of the tournament in Toulouse with you? I don't say this often, but there are more important things to life than football, and I think you could be one of them."

"I wouldn't want you to miss out on anything, Scott; you're having too much fun," she said, glossing over my declaration. "I can see what Wales qualifying means to you -

that feeling will last longer than what you feel for me right now."

I wasn't so sure, but the right words were proving elusive. My perfect morning had quickly turned into a disaster, and that was before the final nail in the coffin - "I'm so sorry, Scott, I think it's for the best before we get too attached. You should go." Game over.

I clasped her hand a bit tighter, but my throat had swollen up and nothing else was coming out; instead I was using every muscle in my face to prevent the tears. I rolled out of bed as she buried her face in a pillow, silently putting on my scattered clothes, having been passionately pulled off my body mere hours before. As I sat on the edge of the bed after tying my laces, I couldn't simply accept my fate. I had to say something from the heart, even if it wasn't perfect, but that would be everlasting and memorable.

Softly straddling my fingertips along her arm, I whispered: "Colette - thank you for the last few days. I don't know what brought us together, but I only hope that it isn't also now pulling us apart. This is goodbye for now, but not farewell. If you ever want to see or speak to me again, you've got my number."

She turned her head to show me a smile, and I briefly kissed her one last time on the lips, before hastily making my exit. As I closed the door - metaphorically and literally - I felt strange; as if I should cry but I couldn't force any tears out. I then thought that I should see this for what it really was - a fling in a random European city - but I couldn't bring myself to do that either.

Repeating the walk from the day before back to Ieuan and Matt's hotel, I trudged through the streets with hunched shoulders before eventually pitching up outside their place again. I rang them to let me in, and remarkably they were up and about rather than stewing in their beds. It was Dav who came down to greet me, still on a high from the game as he leant on the doorframe

"Alright, mate, I am still buzzing! Has it sunk in yet? We qualified for the knockouts!"

"Yeah, it's amazing, isn't it?" I replied with a muted tone.

"What's up, butt, didn't get any action again after or what?"

"I don't want to talk about it at the moment, mate, if that's alright?"

"Ahh, I see where you're coming from. Understood - come on in." He opened the door wide enough for me to enter the building, and we marched up to the room where we found Matt running his finger across a French road atlas and Matt studying Dav's Euro 2016 sticker book.

"Morning, Scott - how are we?!" Matt said.

"Yeah alright, lads."

"Don't worry about him, boys," said Dav. "He's just sulking a little bit. He had a spot of the old brewer's droop last night and couldn't get anything going with Colette."

"What? No I didn't!" I shouted. "That's not what I meant at all, you idiot."

"Well, you can't blame me for thinking that!" defended Dav. "You'd had a skinfull last night, staggered back to hers and then came back here looking right moody. You're beginning to blend in with all the locals."

"Well, that definitely didn't happen. In fact, the complete opposite, actually," I accidentally divulged. The boys all looked at me in harmony with big silly grins wiped across their faces. "WAHHEYYY!" they cheered.

"Nice one, buddy," added Ieuan, offering a handshake. "That'll help you get over Victoria, if you weren't already."

"Cheers, boys. Right, what have you been working on, then?" I said, keen to change the topic.

"We've been looking into who we'll play in the next round and where," explained Matt. "By winning the group, it means that we'll probably play Albania, Northern Ireland or the Czech Republic in the next round. But we have to wait a couple of days to find out."

"OK, fingers crossed not Czech Republic," I analysed. "So where could we be playing?"

"Well, we know that for definite, mate, and it's perfect for you, Romeo," continued Ieuan excitedly. "That's because we're heading to the city of love, boyo. Paris here we come!"

You had to be kidding me. I had just found and lost an incredible woman, and now I was being dragged to Paris in the summertime to watch lovers gazing into each other's eyes, holding hands and rubbing their affection in my face for days on end. Was this karma evening itself out? After all, I had enjoyed nirvana-like highs the day before, so I guess whatever happened next had to be disappointing. In a selfish way, I wish that we hadn't won the group. It was magnificent and hilarious to see us sitting above England in the table, but now I was personally paying the price.

With no other choice, we picked up our bags and began our voyage to the French capital. As we navigated our way back through the streets of Toulouse, I felt a twinge of sadness to be leaving; I had thoroughly enjoyed my time there, minus the last couple of hours, and part of me really hoped that it wouldn't be the last time that I set foot in this part of south-west France.

"What time is the train?" I asked Matt, who had designed the trip to the nth degree so far. He was a master at planning, easily factoring in costs, times and routes to ensure we got the best deal. If his career in health and safety failed, he could be a valuable asset at Thomas Cook or London Euston's helpdesk.

"Nah, we're not getting the train, mate, it's a bus."

"What?" I choked, under the impression our trip would be a quick and comfortable one. "How long is that going to take?"

"It's not too bad - only eight-and-a-bit hours."

My mood hardly improved with that news, and for the first few hours that we weaved through the idyllic French countryside, I wasn't much company. The boys had sensed this and had stopped talking to me - and, in fact, to each other. After 12 days together there was nothing left to catch up on, and I think we were all enjoying listening to music rather than forcing conversation. The long journey north, though, did provide me with the opportunity to do a lot of thinking about what life was going to be like after the tournament. We now had no idea how far Chris Coleman could take his brilliant crop of players, who had already achieved our sole ambition to qualify from the group, and had done so in style. For my sake, I hoped that it would be a lengthy run, another two games or so if I was being greedy, just so I could prolong the inevitable when I got back to London. I would have to find a new place to live, a new job, and live like a monk for a few months to let my bleeding bank balance recover from this trip. And then there was Victoria, and Colette - it was all making my head spin. I was determined not to let it all get to me, though - after all I could suffer some sort of breakdown had I begun to delve too deeply, so I vowed that as long as Wales were in Euro 2016, I would only focus on that. It really was the only thing in my life that was going right, and if I was going to have to endure months of stress and worry after the competition's conclusion, I was going to have the time of my life and end this particular chapter on a high note.

That meant there was to be no moping around Paris aching over Colette. I was going to head there with the boys and soak up everything the city had to offer, a place that incredibly I had never visited despite being only a two-hour trip from my now-former doorstep. With that change of heart, I instantly began to look forward to experiencing a bit of culture on this trip, rather than just boozing the days away.

At around 9pm, we arrived in a city winding down for the day, and began looking for a place that would happily house four Welsh blokes for the next five nights. But with the city rammed with football fans from all over the continent, and money getting tighter than Dav's 2003 Lycra home shirt, there was only one thing for it: a hostel. A couple of Google searches and phonecalls later, and Matt had found us a place to stay for the unbelievable 12 euros each a night. If we had thought that the places we had stayed in (excluding Colette's quaint little flat) had been bad so far, then our latest abode was something else. Initially, it looked promising, and a nice reception area greeted us. But after we had swapped our money for a key to our room, we realised we had got exactly what we had paid for. Three flimsy-looking metal bunk beds were the room's only feature; there was no other furniture, or even curtains, in sight. Looking out into the Parisian night, there were bars across a window that provided our only porthole to the outside world. A tiny, yellow-tinted toilet was shoved away in what had previously been a walk-in wardrobe, and the nearest sink or shower was located further down the hallway, shared by the rest of this place's prisoners.

"It'll do," said Dav. "Shotgun top bunk." He began to ascend to the top of one of the beds and in doing so nearly pulled the whole structure down to the ground as he clung onto the ladder for dear life. "On second thoughts, I'll stick to the bottom."

"I wonder who has the pleasure of sharing with us guys?" Ieuan said, and began poking through the suitcase that was lying on one of the other beds.

"Ieu, leave it alone, mate!" said Matt, giving him a slap on the arm.

"What? I'm trying to find out if it's a football fan or not."

"Yeah, let's get out of here before Ieu starts trying on his clothes, it's like Alcatraz in here," I said, opening the door and promptly finding the detached doorknob gripped in my hand. A couple of attempts to free ourselves from our cell later and we were out and about, experiencing the delights of a warm Paris evening. The culture would have to wait until tomorrow as we were all starving. We located a bar and watched the final moments of Croatia beating Spain, and then discovered that the Czechs had lost their final game and were no longer capable of meeting us in the last 16. With the confusing third-place qualifying scenario, we scrawled away on a napkin, attempting to work out who on earth, or rather Europe, we would be facing next, with Northern Ireland or Turkey looking like the main candidates.

That night, fatigued from the journey and the effects from Toulouse's heavy celebrations, we decided to turn in early and get up at a reasonable time to do some exploring. With all my worries balled up and wedged firmly into the back of my mind, I fell asleep pretty easily and was only awoken in the middle of the night when a large man crashed through the door and collapsed in a heap in the middle of the floor, the doorknob bouncing around alongside him. He was wearing a Germany shirt, so I presumed that he had been out all night celebrating their win against Northern Ireland and was the room's other occupant. When I reawoke in the morning, he was still lying in the same position; and such was the size of him it took two of us to move him back into his bed before we went down for breakfast. In keeping with its prison-like feel, we were not surprised to find half a loaf of bread - but no toaster - and a box of cornflakes. Opting against the fine spread on offer, we began ticking off the sights on the banks of the Seine.

Over the next three days, we swapped our 'lads on tour' football trip for a cultural extravaganza. With our Wales shirts taking a breather in our bags, we climbed to the top of the beautiful Arc de Triomphe; strolled all the way down the Champs Elysees; ascended the steep hills to take in a different view of the city from Montmarte; got the briefest of glimpses at Mona Lisa in the Lourve; and spent some time relaxing on the lawns at Notre Dame. There were river cruises and stops in patisseries as we worked through intricate cake designs and Dav and co. even stepped out of their comfort zone and indulged in some French cuisine. The evenings were spent sipping away at red wine, rather than knocking back vats of fizzy lager. It all felt rather sophisticated: we were finally acting our age.

The same couldn't be said for the various fellow cellmates who had occupied our spare bed, lured in by the cheap costs. The German had been replaced by an Austrian, who we discovered the following morning had thrown up all over his bedsheets in the night - possibly due to alcohol or watching his team meekly exit the competition at the hands of Iceland. Either way, the room reeked and we quickly evacuated for the day. By this time, the group stage had concluded and we had discovered who our opponents were on Saturday: Northern Ireland. Another Battle of Britain clash, but this time with a real chance of a Welsh win against a group of fans similar to us, deprived of international tournament appearances and now keen to make the most of this unexpected chance. It also meant that spare tickets would be in short supply.

Sure enough, by Friday, the Green and White Army had begun descending on Paris, and one found his way into our dormitory whilst we were making a brief-as-possible pit stop ahead of a night on the town.

"Alright, fellas, no fighting now!" said a lad in his mid-20s with sandy blonde hair as soon as he entered the room, doorknob in hand.

"Hi, mate - no you'll be fine, we're all Celtic in here," Dav replied, getting up to shake his hand and introduce us all to Bryan. Sitting down on his bed, our new-found friend commented sarcastically, "lovely place, isn't it? Smells a bit funky, though?"

"Yeah, you might want to check down the side of the bed," I laughed. "Our Austrian friend may have had a bit too much to drink last night." Bryan immediately leapt off the bed and began to inspect it thoroughly.

"Ahh well, it won't matter when I'm back here steaming at god-knows what time o'clock in the morning, will it?" he joked. "So, what are you guys up to tonight? Room for one or two more?"

An hour later, we were in a nearby bar, toasting pints with Bryan and his friend Jim, who was slightly older than us and bald. The pair of friends proved to be excellent company; they had been travelling around France as well, so were in the same boat as us when it came to finances, tickets and how much they were enjoying being a part of the festivities. We supped Guinness all night, sharing stories of our tournament so far and what we had seen. They told us some amazing stories of Irish fans enjoying themselves, and showed us a video of their fans reuniting a lost boy with his father by lifting him up and chanting. It seemed refreshing that the Welsh and both sets of Irish supporters were helping to turn the tide on the negative press coverage concerning British football fans.

Within a few hours, the bar was packed with British supporters, including a few English fans; their sense of entitlement had foolishly seen them book travel and accommodation expecting to have won the group themselves, but, to be fair, they were taking the piss-taking in their stride. Those from Northern Ireland were even louder and rowdier than ourselves, and it seemed that every five minutes they were singing the song that was rivalling 'Don't Take Me Home' as Euro 2016's unofficial anthem. Wherever you went, you couldn't escape a shout of 'Will Grigg's on fire, your defence is terrified,' which would be repeated to death. As we lurched our way back to Alcatraz, you could hear it echoing around the empty streets; one lone burst would soon be sung by a choir, and indeed a hammered Bryan broke into a rendition at around 3am in the hostel, prompting cries of 'Shut up, you prick' from a number of rooms.

After packing in so much of what Paris had to offer in such a short space of time, it had seemed like forever since the final whistle had blown against Russia. But from the moment I sprung into consciousness again on that Saturday morning, I couldn't wait for the game to begin. The great thing about the terrible breakfast and facilities at our hostel was that you had no desire to spend any longer than necessary inside of it, so we were tucking into alfresco crepes and croque monsieurs by 10 in the morning, joined by Bryan, who was nursing a pint of tap water. Chatting about the game to the background sounds of buskers playing accordions, we were being cautious in making any bold predictions, and the pre-game amble was all very courteous: "It doesn't matter if we win or lose, it's been a great tournament." "Well, if we don't win I'm glad we've at least lost to you," and all that bullshit. We were merely being polite, as inside we all would have sacrificed our granny to see our team in the last eight at the expense of our British brethren.

We walked for about 45 minutes from our charming breakfast spot through a large statue-studded garden, bristling with Welsh and Irish fans with flags draped over their shoulders and face paint on. The sun was beaming as we continued to embrace the calm before the storm, and after crossing the river we made our way towards the Eiffel Tower. Shunning the lengthy queues to get into the fanzone, we decided to try and find a local bar. After skirting around the edges of the Tower's grounds, I spotted a red-shirted Welshman, equipped with a pint in hand, and waved the group down a little side street. Expecting to find a quiet bar with a few Welshman quietly sipping pints inside, as soon as we turned the corner we were engulfed by a crowd of about 300 people standing outside four or five restaurants, all having a whale of a time. Songs were being sung, beer was in high supply, and a single football was being whacked around in the air, resembling the Shrovetide game that soccer got its origins from, or Bobby Gould's Wimbledon side of the late 1980s. Clocking a free table near the action, we ordered some drinks and watched the ball get pelted into, and retrieved from, trees and thrown up on the balconies of those apartments overlooking the street, with bemused neighbours reluctantly throwing it back into the melee. A pair of rogue fans donning England shirts attempted to pass through the red and green masses and remarkably the fans parted as if instructed to by Moses. The pair were given a guard of honour for their team's lack of exploits so far. As I chuckled to myself, I felt as though they would have the last laugh, having dodged a bullet by avoiding another elimination at the hands of Portugal, and instead offered a safe passage through to the quarters by drawing Iceland.

Working his way through the rabble, Jim somehow managed to locate us, displaying a furrowed brow as he did. His two hopes at tickets had proven to be false leads, and now we were all faced with watching the game in the nearby fanzone alongside thousands of other ticketless supporters. Fretting, Ieuan and Dav did a sweep of all of the bars along the road, shouting out, "Anyone got any spare tickets?!" but it was no good. We still had a few hours to go until the 6pm kick-off.

"You might as well give up, lads," Jim said forlornly when the pair returned empty handed. "Soak up the atmosphere here instead and stop worrying about it."

"I can't," replied a defiant Dav. "I've got to be in the stadium. Done all three games so far, and I'll find a way to be at this one."

"Yeah, I'm with you on that," I chipped in. "I've missed one game already, and I'm not going to miss any more." By the looks of Ieuan and Matt's faces, they too had already decided that they would be amongst the 45,000 packed into the Parc de Princes, one of France's most iconic stadiums.

"Boys, I wish you the best of luck in finding some, and with the game," said Bryan. "I'm gonna stick here with Jim, but if you're about later, give me a call and we'll meet up after and discuss our famous win over you Welsh.". Dav and he swapped numbers and we washed down the final remnants of beer before jumping on the Metro. Whilst we hurtled through the underground tunnels, I pulled the lads together and said: "We're going to have to sound out a tout I think lads. Who's up for that?" I looked around and Dav was nodding, Ieuan was giving a face that said he wasn't sure but was keen, but straight-laced Matt was looking concerned.

"I don't know about that, Scott, we could easily be ripped off. I've heard plenty of stories about fans buying fakes and getting rejected at the turnstiles."

"Yeah, I know that. But what other chance have we got? Everyone else around there now will probably have a ticket. I'm up for taking the risk, and going as high as 150 euro?"

The other two nodded, but Matt was again reluctant: "It's a lot of money to throw away."

"Well, we're all in, mate. We don't want to leave you behind," Ieuan added. Eventually Matt relented: "OK then, I'm in. No more than 150 euro though."

Finding a tout proved to be as easy as getting through the Russian defence. As soon as we exited the Metro back into daylight, we spotted one shuffling around with a big thick beard, black coat and long, unwashed hair, muttering, "Tickets - buy or sell." Dav approached him, and asked him how much.

"170 euro, my friend," was the response.

"Nope, 150 is the highest we can go to."

"170 is the lowest I can go to."

"If you have four in a row all sat together, I'll give you 160 each. Can you do that?"

The tout smiled at Dav, and nodded his head. "OK, 160 each; you have a deal. I have to see my friend across the road and swap some tickets around."

"Great," said Dav. "I'll follow you."

Determined not to let his only opportunity at seeing the game slip out of sight, he man-to-man marked the tout through the crowds that were beginning to mingle around the streets in the stadium's shadow. Whilst that was going on, Matt was having second thoughts.

"I thought we were only going up to 150 euros?" he moaned. "I don't trust him, guys, he looks really shady."

"Have you ever seen a tout that doesn't look shady?" I asked him.

"Well no, but…"

"Have you got 160 euros?" enquired Ieuan.

"Not on me."

"What have you got, then?"

"About 20 probably." Ieu and I both sighed, and soon Matt was being frogmarched by Ieuan to the nearest cashpoint and forced to withdraw the adequate funds, seemingly with a metaphorical gun to his head. During this time, the tout and Dav returned with a bunch of tickets in hand.

"All sorted," said Dav proudly. "Where are those other two muppets?"

"Getting cash out," I replied. The three of us stood awkwardly at the top of the steps before Ieuan returned, literally pushing Matt through the crowds with a hand on his back, making sure he handed over his wad of notes. Before doing so, Matt had rubbed his finger across them, checked the holograms, looked at a photo of a similar ticket online, and tried to smudge off the ink.

"Stop messing around and just pay the man," demanded Ieuan impatiently. With his hand shaking as he did so, Matt relinquished his money and we all did likewise, and finally we were in possession of something that resembled match tickets.

"Pleasure doing business with you," said the tout ominously, now 640 euro richer. He scuttled off and quickly blended into the crowd, ready to take advantage of another desperate football fan.

"You boys better be right about this," said Matt, who saw all hope of getting that money back disappear before his eyes should he be in possession of a very expensive piece of white card.

"Look, we'll go into the stadium now and test out whether they work or not," I suggested. "That way we'll have time to find some more if these don't."

"I'm not spending any more money!" exclaimed Matt, and we all laughed at his current state. He was sweating profusely, and the damp patches under his arms were protruding through his retro Wales shirt. After asking a local policeman for directions, we were pointed down a couple of residential streets and soon we could see the imposing structure in front of us. It was a brutal looking building, made almost entirely of concrete with a series of razor-sharp ribs forming a unique outer shell of the stadium. It had been a ground that I had always wanted to visit, but Matt's negativity had made me nervous as to whether that would be possible today or not.

Locating our gate, we walked through the heightened security checks and towards the turnstiles. The moment of truth. I closed my eyes as I slipped the ticket into the reader and waited. A loud beep signalled that I had indeed bought a real ticket, and I pushed the stile with relief as it folded around and let me enter. Dav was next to follow successfully, and then Ieuan too met us on the other side. However, Matt was being refused entry. He pushed his ticket into the slot three times, wriggled it around a bit but still there was no joy. "FUCK!" he shouted out, and gave the turnstile a firm wrap with his knuckles. It was a little hard not to laugh at him, but we were also concerned. His shout had caused a steward to head his way, and we watched with bated breath as he inspected the dodgy ticket. A few seconds later, he pushed it into the slot and we all heard the beep. Matt thrust his way through the turnstile and sprinted our way before leaping on top of us in celebration.

"We're all in!" he exclaimed in triumph, his face beaming with delight.

"What did the steward do to make it work?" asked Dav, who was rubbing his face after receiving a sweaty armpit in it.

"Oh, nothing really. I was just putting it in the slot the wrong way up, so the barcode wasn't being read." We all burst into laughter, and his reaction to not being allowed entry would become the butt of all our jokes for the rest of the day.

With that literal hurdle overcome, we headed inside. With 90 minutes to kill and no chance of re-entry to get any real alcohol, we succumbed to the 0.5% Carlsberg that was being sold inside the stadium. It tasted foul, but Matt was relieved to shake off being the focal point of our taunts for a while as he kept asking Dav if he felt too drunk after his incident in Bordeaux.

Our seats were situated in the top of the two-tiered ground, which was a splendid-looking arena. It had tight, steep stands, similar to the Millennium Stadium, and there seemed to be not a bad seat in the whole place. The sun was once again shining directly into our eyes as we waited patiently for the game to get underway. The stands gradually filled, with swarms of green and red fluctuating all over the famous venue, and the sing-off began well before the teams had kicked off. The PA announcer played up to the Irish supporters by giving them Sash's 'Encore Une Fois' - the inspiration for 'Will Grigg's On Fire' - causing those from the Emerald Isle to dance around in the stands. We responded likewise with 'Zombie Nation' and there was a real party atmosphere all around us. The booze consumed in the day and the feel-good factor surrounding both teams had created a powder keg of enjoyment, and it was brilliant to finally be able to soak it all up flanked by my three best mates.

Bopping along to dance classics was all well and good, but there was only one song that mattered to us four. Unsurprisingly, an unchanged Wales XI entered the pitch for the pre-match protocols, amongst an avalanche of colour and sound. Northern Ireland were up first with their identical, but more emphatically sung, version of the English national anthem, which only riled up the Welsh fans, who are usually prickly after hearing that particular tune. It was a good effort by the Green and White Army, but 'Mae Hen Wlad Fyn Nhadau' was blasted out by the Welsh fans, led - in my head anyway - by four interlocked lads in the top tier. As the final line died down, we all moved towards each other and gave ourselves a pre-match huddle as we screamed, "C'MON WALES!"

That would be a phrase uttered often throughout the 90 minutes, but with a slightly more frustrated cadence. The Irish started the brighter, and the gentle giant that is Wayne Hennessey had to stretch all of his frame to push away an early blast by Stuart Dallas.

With their first real attack, Wales had us jumping for joy. Venturing forward again, Neil Taylor, as he did against Russia, found himself in the final third and he whipped in a cross for the towering Sam Vokes to head down into Aaron Ramsey's path, and our blonde bombshell got a toe onto it to prod it into the net.

"YESSSSSSSSsssssss…… ohhhhhhhh" was our cry as we climbed off each other's shoulders and pretended like our celebration had never happened, our joy curtailed by the sight of the linesman's flag. That would be as good as things got for Wales, who seemed to be suffering under their tag as favourites and playing some scrappy stuff. Northern Ireland meanwhile were stroking the ball around with freedom, and Hennessey had to make another acrobatic stop to tip over a fizzer from distance by Jamie Ward. The comfortable victory we had all expected would not be forthcoming.

171

As well as getting the better of us on the pitch, our opponents were taking us to school in the stands, too. We felt we had gone 1-0 up after the anthems, but the Irish were romping away with their support; the Will Grigg chant being sung so often and for such long periods of time that Dav was beginning to visibly shake with annoyance. When he finally snapped, he turned to the green masses situated probably 70 yards from him and screamed at the top of his lungs "SHUT THE FUCK UP WOULD YOU! HE'S NOT EVEN PLAYING!" Despite not hurling abuse at them, it was really grating on me, too - especially one fan constantly banging his drum to the beat of the song, which continued to thump around in my head following the end of the first-half and during the interval.

"I'm so sick of Will Grigg," I said.

"Who the hell is Will Grigg?" said Ieuan.

"He's on fire apparently," offered Dav.

"He plays for Wigan Athletic," answered Matt. "He has yet to play a second in the tournament and some journalists are saying that he's the star of it so far."

"We'll see what Gareth Bale has to say about that," I replied, with a splitting headache that the sunshine, lack of any recent alcohol, and that bloody drum had contributed to, as well as the stress of watching a poor Wales performance. The second half had kicked off again, but no-one had seemed to notice because there had been just as much going on during the 15 minute interval than after the restart. The relentless Northern Irish fans continued to drown out the Red Wall, who had by now been sung into submission.

We desperately needed something to lift us out of our Saturday afternoon siesta, and it came when Bale went down softly under a challenge in the middle of the pitch, about 30 yards from goal. It was almost as though he was teeing up the free-kick for himself in the perfect position, and soon the spread leg stance was on show again, followed by the tippy-tappy run-up and a cannon of a shot that headed goalwards before dipping violently. This time, though, Michael McGovern was able to do what Slovakia and England had failed to and beat the ball away from danger.

It was the only time since the disallowed goal that we had got out of our seats because of something that happened on the pitch. In fact, the game had been such a damp squib that Dav had gone to buy a bottle of Fanta during the first half. Looking at the big screen, there were around 15 minutes to go, and I just sensed this was going to be one of those days. Were we cruelly going to be denied a spot in the quarter-finals by a Northern Ireland winner from a corner in the last minute, or maybe even the disaster of a penalty shoot-out defeat? That seemed to be the likely option, as our opponents sat deeper and deeper in defence as Wales probed.

As 'Will Grigg's On Fire' boomed around the ground once again, Aaron Ramsey gave it to the only other man on the field who looked capable of doing it, and boy did Bale deliver. With one swish of his wonderful left foot, he sent a magnificent pass dangerously across the six-yard box, where the unfortunate Gareth McAuley - with Hal Robson-Kanu breathing down his collar - panicked and sliced the ball past McGovern into his own net.

I never usually celebrate own goals; I once suffered in ignominy of scoring one in similar circumstances during the dying seconds of a primary school semi-finals aged 10, bursting into immediate and uncontrollable tears. From that day, I vowed not to toast someone's misery, but this was the bloody knockout stages of Euro 2016, so I went wild. I grabbed Dav tightly by the collar and jumped up and down so much that I ripped his skin-tight shirt right off his back. He didn't seem to notice as he had been engulfed by the merged shape of Ieuan and Matt, his hat flying forward about seven or eight rows. Plastic pint glasses were being crushed under our feet and spilt Fanta fizzed down our row as relief, more than excitement, took over. As the 10 outfield players jogged back to their own half to restart the game, we sat down and assessed the damage.

"What the hell has happened to my shirt?" laughed Dav, tugging away at the strands flapping around him and displaying his vast gut for all around to admire.

"My shoes are orange!" came a cry from Ieuan, whose ice-white Stan Smith trainers were now coated in sticky pop.

Some neutral fans, presumably Parisians, looked on in disgust at the state of us, whilst the Welsh supporters around us found it hilarious and began taking photos of Dav. One guy in front of us turned around and shouted, "Anyone lost a hat?" and tossed it backwards when Dav laid claim to it.

The game was still going on, but now we had the goal it looked unlikely we were going to concede. As the final minutes ticked away, the boys were scraping and clawing for every ball, and the slight figure of Jonny Williams even managed to take out his namesake and captain Ashley as they both desperately smashed into each other making a tackle. The skipper courageously battled on despite constantly holding his damaged shoulder, telling Chris Coleman in no uncertain terms not to put James Collins on in his place, which was definitely the right call in my book; the mistake-in-boots that was Collins defending a one-goal lead with minutes between us and a quarter-final spot would have sent me over the edge in the dying stages.

As they ticked by Dav was clinging onto me for support. Crosses were being flung into our box, but they were constantly repelled by the excellent defence. A long-throw was blocked, then a corner conceded. McGovern came sprinting up for it out of his goal, but fittingly it was Bale who belted the ball to safety, and then… peep, peep, peep. It was over! Wales were in the last eight of the European Championships. The last eight!

All energy had been expunged in that breathless final few minutes, and rather than more boisterous rejoicing, it was just hugs and sighs of relief all round. The Welsh players seemingly had more to give than ourselves; they were jubilant, undertaking a lap of honour as they tried to applaud every Welsh man, woman and child in the stands, and we returned the favour, at which point a tear began to form in my eye. My tiny, wonderful little nation would be one of eight teams contesting to be European Champions.

Gareth Bale then took to the field alone, proceeding to have a kick-around with his daughter. I had never wanted to be a three-year-old girl before, but being able to stroke the ball around on the Parc de Princes turf and have the new prince of Welsh football give me a cuddle was the only way this moment was going to get any better.

CHAPTER 10

Football fans are easy targets for the media to get their claws stuck into, depicting them as booze-fuelled, foul-mouthed, far-right hooligans; but even the staunchest opponents of supporters would have had eaten their words if they had been outside the Parc des Princes. As I walked triumphantly down the concrete steps, I was the recipient of much back-patting by those in green. Outside the ground, you couldn't move for gracious handshakes, well-wishes and once back out on the Parisian streets and free to buy non-Carlsberg products again, opposition fans were arm-in-arm and sharing beers.

It was such a splendid sight that the four of us bought some cans from a local corner shop and proceeded to sit outside a stretch of bars situated by a roundabout and a small square. We enjoyed the moment alongside hundreds of other fans, many of whom were asking Dav to explain his shredded shirt. Soon enough, random sing-offs were the norm, and you couldn't have guessed who had actually won the match. The Irish were beaten but buoyant. They had plenty of cause to toast their side's achievements despite them coming to an end, and judging by their mood, they were definitely up to that particular task.

Cans consumed, we decided to get the Metro back towards the Eiffel Tower and many others did the same. The Will Grigg song roared through the carriages as we whizzed under streets and the Seine, but once we had reached our destination, a stern 'sshhh' from a policeman caused a group of drunken fans to obligingly shut it down straight away, no protests or questions asked. Paris was full of drunken fans, but rather than feeding the stereotype, they were being incredibly well-behaved while merry. If the Welsh weren't crowned Euro 2016's best supporters, then it had to be our Celtic cousins. We proceeded to the tower's grounds again and bartered with some traders to get some more lager at rock-bottom prices. We then sipped them perched on the steps of a museum, digesting what had happened to us: Wales were in the quarter-finals of Euro 2016. We couldn't stop smiling.

The night was long and enjoyable; we shared many a drink with Northern Irish fans, who were now keeping their dreams of lifting the trophy alive vicariously through Wales, and even the locals were wishing us well and suggesting that they hoped it would be a France vs Wales final. But strangely, there were no drunken antics or memorable stories to account for in years gone by from this particular night. It was almost as though we were in a dream - after all, getting to tournaments wasn't something that happened to our country, let alone the knockout stages, and definitely not the last eight. Nothing was mentioned between the four of us, but almost telepathically we had decided to save ourselves for future battles. Who knew how long this could go on for?

On that note, when we woke up on our final morning in Alcatraz and realised that the quarter-final was back in Lille, we had be sensible.

"Boys, is anyone else thinking that perhaps we should head back home today?" I asked everyone as we forced 13 euros' worth of cornflakes and bread and butter into our rumbling stomachs.

"Thank god," said Dav. "I was thinking that all last night. I need to sort my life out a bit."

"And then after a few days of home comforts, we'll meet up again and head to Lille?" I suggested.

"What home have you got?" sneered Dav, but of course we all laughed - banter and all that.

"I am well up for that," piped up Ieuan. "I never thought we'd get this far, so I only packed 12 pairs of pants. I've been out here now for 17 days. You do the maths."

"I better go back too and pop my head into the office and see what's been happening whilst I've been away," added Matt.

"Yeah, I'm sure all those health and safety experts have been going wild recreating Woodstock in your absence," I joked. That settled it, so we all packed our bags and to avoid paying the extortionate tournament-inflated Eurostar fares, we hopped on the next cross-Channel Megabus, getting in some useful shut-eye as we headed back to Blighty.

Once back in our homeland - albeit one that had distanced itself politically much further than the literal 21 miles separating it from the continental following the EU referendum a few days earlier - Ieuan and Matt headed west to God's country and I followed Dav back to his landfill-like apartment just in time for the Hungary-Belgium clash that would decide who had the honour of being cannon-fodder to Gareth Bale, Chris Coleman and co. in the quarters. Like Wales, the Hungarians had been one of the competition's surprise packages, but they were no match for a Belgian side oozing with quality as they tore them apart 4-0. However good they looked, though, we had faced them in the qualifying group to get to France and prevented them from scoring in both games, so despite the daunting task of keeping Eden Hazard and his fellow golden generation members in check, we still had a chance.

We would now be facing them the following Friday, which meant that I had the pleasure of kipping on Dav's sofa for five nights. After my first attempt, Monday morning broke with me flat out on the wooden floor as it seemed much better for my spine than having a cornucopia of coils dug into my back. Having endured bunk-beds, floors, sofas and bus seats for the majority of the last three weeks, I couldn't take anymore, and decided to text Victoria to see if we could sort out our living arrangements. A simple message, constructed over half-an-hour, said, "Hi, we need to talk about the flat," and was sent hoping to clarify that I was only interested in a bed to stay in, not someone to share it with.

Despite being unemployed, the tournament was still going on, so I was sticking to my pact. As Dav headed off in his van to try and claw back some much-needed funds for the weekend in Lille, left to my own devices I searched for tickets rather than jobs. My knowledge of UEFA's ticketing website was helping me come up trumps, and I was soon busily tapping refresh on my phone as the ticket portal opened for business ahead of Friday's festivities. Once in the queue, an agonising 20-minute wait watching a tiny virtual yellow bar flicker across a webpage ensued. I had to sit through a countdown clock before I actually reached the portal for tickets, but it was all worth it. I clicked on 'Wales v Belgium' and there they were - tickets available for Category Four - the cheapest possible at £38 each! However, when I went to select the quantity, I could only choose two at a time. Concerned that a phone call from Victoria could interrupt my progress and scupper my chances, almost as if she knew that she had the power to stop me being in attendance at Wales' joint-biggest game in their history, I made a snap decision and bought them anyway. I entered my card details as carefully as a surgeon performing brain surgery, and finally the confirmation email came through - not only were Wales in the quarter-finals, but I was too.

By the time Dav returned, he was greeted by a pair of Domino's finest 12-inch Mighty Meaty and Tandoori Chicken pizzas, and the news that I had got two tickets. I wasn't sure if he was more delighted with the food or the football, but we cracked open a couple of cold ones and tucked into our cheese and tomato-based treasure as we settled down to watch England join us as Britain's representatives in the last eight.

Iceland were seen as no real threat, and it only took our glorious neighbours four minutes to score via a Rooney penalty. However, the Scandinavians equalised just two minutes later, and Dav and I were choking on pepperoni and ground beef when Ragnar Sigurdsson pounced on a mistake to put them ahead on 18 minutes.

"There's no way they're holding on," I said to Dav.

"Nah, no chance," he replied with his mouth full, tossing another ravaged crust into a soggy cardboard box that was destined to remain with the rest of the overflowing recycling pile for a good few months, emitting greasy fumes. But hold on they did. They reached the first milestone of half-time easily enough, and then they made it to the hour mark.

"They might just do this, you know!" I said excitedly as soon as 60 minutes came up.

"No chance. England will find a way," returned Dav. However 75 minutes came and went, and it was looking like a lost cause. By 85 minutes they were devoid of any ideas, bamboozled and seemingly already imagining the horrid headlines plastered on both the front and back pages. It was only once we reached injury-time that Dav began to waver in his prediction. Of course Daniel Sturridge got a mention, but eventually the final whistle was blown and England had suffered yet more tournament failure and ignominy.

We exploded into fits of laughter, incredulous that the apparent creators and rulers of the game had been humbled by a bunch of part-timers in the knockout stages of an international tournament. Even more hilarious was the video footage soon uploaded onto Twitter of the entire Welsh squad boisterously celebrating the demise of the old enemy as they watched the game together in their hotel. An embarrassed Roy Hodgson resigned just minutes later, and my mind immediately flashed back to all those sneering, cocky faces that had been so unsporting as we exited the Stade Bollaert-Delelis in Lens just 11 days earlier. They were going home, and we would be crossing the Channel in the opposite direction. He who laughs last…

Perhaps still buzzing from the demise of Hodgson's England, the next day I decided to be a good friend and sort out Dav's life, partly in appreciation of his accommodation and also because I was staying indefinitely and couldn't stand the squalor any longer. I took boxes of mouldy cardboard, rusty tins and an alcoholic's collection of bottles to the recycling centre before hoovering, polishing and dusting the front room, restocking the cobweb-covered kitchen cabinets and Febrezing the stale stench out of the whole place. A solid morning's work done, as I filled in the scores on a new Euro 2016 wallchart to replace the one that took the brunt of the tantrum the week before, ironically I got a message on my phone from Victoria. It simply said: "Come round in a couple of hours and give me a hand with some of these boxes."

The mood suddenly changed. What the hell was she doing, boxing up all my stuff without me even there? God knows what state it was in; knowing her all my breakables would be going the same way as the Ian Rush mug back at Underscore. I was so upset that I was being forced out of the flat that I flat-out ignored her request and decided to not wait until the requested time. I slung my jacket on and rushed out of the flat, closing the door with an emphatic thump, and caught the bus to Clapham.

Raindrops trickled their way down the windows during the staccatoed journey through the hubbub of London life; people hunched under umbrellas and dodged puddles. The weather perfectly personified my mood, as I wondered whether this would be indeed the final time I ever saw Victoria. Part of me was desperate for that to be true; after all she had treated me like crap for a number of years, culminating at the wedding 17 days earlier, when I had emancipated myself from her controlling nature. But also, this was someone who I had shared all of my adult life with, and experienced some wonderful things alongside. Cutting her out completely was akin to slicing every treasured photograph of the pair of us in two, or diluting the good times by half.

But as the bus dropped me off at the top of our road and I began to hastily splash down the wet pavement, the sight of a sodden removal van parked outside our block of flats made me realise that I would not miss anything about her. Livid, I opened the outside door and hurtled up the steps to our apartment before bursting inside, met by the scene of towers of identical brown cardboard boxes, all taped up and Victoria's neat handwriting inked onto each one. At least it looked like she had packed up my stuff in an acceptable fashion.

"Vic?" I called out.

"Scott?" came a voice from the bedroom. "I didn't think you would be here so soon?" I stormed into the room and saw her on her hands and knees, pulling out crates from under the bed.

"Well, I thought I better had, seeing as you've already booked a removal truck," I remarked, pointing outside.

"Sorry, I just wanted to get most of it in there before you got here."

"How cruel are you?" I said, shaking with anger. "You didn't even want me to move my own stuff out? At least you had the decency not to just throw everything out of the window."

"What are you talking about?" she said confused. "Your stuff? I haven't touched it." Glancing around the room, she was right. My Wales calendar was hanging up, and my dragon-shaped alarm clock was sitting on my bedside cabinet. The DVD rack had been filtered through, but the Rocky collection and Alan Partridge box-sets had been left behind, and the Dion Dublin poster that had drawn Victoria and I together in the first place was still framed and on the wall, even if it was slightly at a crooked angle with boxes marked 'summer clothes' resting on it.

"I'm the one moving out - not you," she said to clarify the situation. "I'm going to head back to my parents' place in Berkshire and get away from London for a while. I need a change, so I'm going to leave all this in storage until I get my head right and work out what I want to do next. I just wanted you to come around and decide what we should do with a few bits and pieces that we bought together before I take off."

I was stunned. She lifted up a box from the floor and placed it carefully on the bed. Inside was a random assortment of items - from the mundane like an old stereo to sentimental things such as a photo frame of us at the top of the Rockefeller Centre in New York City and a grey hoodie of mine that she had been virtually sewn into during the winter months.

Taken aback by her sudden change of heart and having a raft of memories slung into my face, stirring up old emotions, I managed to say, "Honestly, Vic, you're welcome to have any of it. It's the least I can do."

"Are you sure?" she said, staring at me with a mixture of surprise and sadness in her eyes. I nodded and she sat down on the bed, evaluating her packing skills before breaking down into tears.

"Hey, come on, don't be like that," I said, sitting alongside her. I debated as to whether or not it would be crossing a newly-formed boundary to make physical contact, but seeing her with her head in her hands and elbows on her knees, it seemed like the only humane thing to do. I put an arm around her and rubbed her shoulders, and she turned her head into my armpit and sobbed away.

"I know... you're right. It's the right thing to do but... but I feel terrible," she wailed. "I've been such a bitch to you, Scott... I deserve all this."

Long-lost feelings meant it genuinely shattered me a little to see her so upset, but her remorsefulness helped my own grieving process all the same. Left to stew away for two and a half weeks, thinking about what had happened, she had belatedly realised the error of her ways. At that moment, any hatred or resentment I had towards her evaporated, and I only hoped that this would be the catalyst for her to return to the wonderful, beautiful girl she had been to me for so long - just now not with me. After a few minutes, the tears eventually stopped falling and we hugged.

"I'm so sorry, Scott, for everything," she said.

"Don't worry about it," I replied.

Drying her eyes, she said, "Can you give me a hand with these boxes, then?" She gave a rueful smile and I mirrored the expression. Together we began the process of shipping all of her stuff out of the apartment, down the stairs and into the van outside. It took a good half an hour, but eventually everything was loaded up.

"How about one last cup of tea?" she suggested. "I'm sure the driver will wait an hour or so longer - after all, he's getting paid for it."

"As long as you didn't pack the sugar and teabags," I joked, and she unleashed that gorgeous laugh that I had heard so infrequently over the past few years. We headed back upstairs and I poured us a couple of cups. We sat opposite each other at the kitchen table, dunking Rich Teas into them and chatting like the good old days. She had wanted to know how my adventures in France were going and what I had planned for the rest of the tournament. I finally got to find out how the rest of the wedding went, and we giggled at her stepping in horse shit and ruining her shoes, which had gotten accidently left in our hotel room and found by one of the chambermaids, who remarkably called Victoria to find out if she still wanted them. I informed her that I had left Underscore and she was pleased for me as she knew I hated working there. As she tipped the last crumb-laden swashes of tea into her mouth, I took a long look at her. She had obviously been through a tough few weeks, as she hadn't bothered to put on much makeup and her hair was frizzy and unkempt. However, she seemed relaxed, which I hoped was due to not feeling the need to conform to what her friendship group demanded of her. She was dressed in Primark, not Prada, and the whole picture reminded me of the girl who I had fallen in love with as a teenager. I hoped there and then that she would soon meet someone who would find this version of her, the one that I would reflectively cherish in the years to come, and she would make him as happy as she had made me for so long.

"Right, I best be going, then, Mum and Dad are expecting me," she said defiantly, tapping her mug down on the wooden surface. This was it.

"Send my regards to Roger and Cath."

"I shall indeed," she nodded. "Thanks for the tea, Scott. I'm so glad we had that chat."

"Me too, Vic," I replied, now also trying to hold it together. "Hopefully, one day soon, we can do this again sometime."

"Hopefully - we'll always be friends, Scott, don't ever forget that. I am truly sorry for the last few years, and I hope with time you forgive me."

"I already have, don't worry about it," I said, leaning out to hold her hand, which gripped the edge of the table. She glanced down at the last time we would ever do so, and we both let it linger for a couple of seconds longer than normal.

"Oh, that reminds me," she said suddenly, breaking the silence. "You best be having this back." She moved her hand away and proceeded to slide her engagement ring off her finger and place it into the palm of my hand before closing my fingers around it. "Thanks again for giving it to me; the night you did was one of the happiest of my life."

"No, Vic, I can't take this back - it's yours. Do what you like with it. What use is it to me?"

"It cost you a lot of money, I'm sure - money you barely had at the time and that I kept blowing. Speaking of, I've been thinking about our joint account and you should have all that, too. After all, you put the majority of it in there."

"Are you sure?" I stuttered, completely taken aback by this personality shift.

"Yeah, I'm positive," she smiled. "There's a few thousand in there which should tide you over for a while whilst you job hunt. But promise me one thing will you?"

"Yes, anything?" I agreed in a state of confusion

"I want you to sell that ring and spend whatever you get for it on tickets to the Euros. If Wales get to the final, I want you to be there. You deserve that more than anything, and it would truly make me happy to know I've made you happy one last time. I'll be expecting to see photos of you at every game they have left on Facebook over the coming weeks. Deal?"

I was amazed. "Deal," I laughed, and she held out her hand to shake on it, her dimples once again reminding of the girl I used to know.

"Right - goodbye, apartment!" she said, tears teetering again as she headed towards the stairs. "And goodbye to you for a while - but not forever, yeah?"

"There's no chance you're escaping that easy!" I said as an attempt at comedy through clenched teeth, and we had one last hug. With lumps in our throats and unable to say anything else, we just waved at each other and as she began her decent downstairs, and I closed the door.

***

Sunbeams streaked through the giant glass arched roof of St Pancras station on a warm Friday morning as an excited Ieuan and Matt practically skipped towards Dav and I around brunch time. Slung over our shoulders were four bags, all containing the necessary amount of clothing needed to see us through the final 10 days of the competition, if the glorious scenario of Ashley Williams leading the squad out at the Stade de France actually leapt from my dreams and into reality.

"What the hell have you done to your hair?" exclaimed Ieuan at Dav.

"Well, I thought I would have to do something in celebration of coming this far," said Dav proudly, taking off his bucket hat to show the full extent of his recent trip to the barbers. Taking inspiration from Aaron Ramsey, he had decided to bleach his hair peroxide blonde in honour of our midfield maestro; however, it had turned out more like Eminem's look of the late 1990s.

Trying to hold back the tears, Matt added, "Great work, butt, but you look more like Gordon Ramsey than Aaron Ramsey!"

"Gordon Ramsay? More like Gordon the Gopher!" yelled Ieuan, virtually in hysterics by now, but, to be fair to Dav, he was also finding these outdated pop-culture references amusing too.

"Alright, alright, calm yourselves and don't use up all your jokes straight away. I've got the drinks in," I said, passing over a cardboard tray of Café Nero's caffeine boosters.

"Cheers, Scott, but shouldn't you be saving what little money you have for important stuff, like tickets and travel?" joked Ieuan.

"Or rent perhaps? Or not..." came a chipper Matt, who alongside his fellow friend from our nation's capital had yet to be informed of Tuesday's cathartic showdown.

"Well, let's just say that all that has been sorted out. My attendance at the tournament is secure, so I thought I'd treat you all to some warm beverages in celebration, and if you're lucky, maybe something alcoholic later."

"You could have bought us all our Eurostar tickets instead," grunted Dav in typical fashion. After mocking his stinginess for the millionth time over the past few weeks, we headed to the platform where our red shirts began to blend into the crowd. Ieuan and Matt informed us that their train had been rammed with Wales supporters travelling to London to hop on the trans-Channel train to Lille too, desperate to see their team in action one last time. Back in my flat, I had wasted away the past two days just bouncing around alone, constantly fixated upon the Belgium game and immersing myself in any article, news report or social media post about the match. After all of that, I wasn't feeling particularly confident; our good recent record against them was nullified by their fine performances in the tournament since losing to Italy in their opening game; they had scored eight goals from their next three games without conceding and were showing just why many had tipped them to win the whole thing before a ball was kicked. Despite all that, this was going to be our biggest game in 58 years and a tough ask. Even if we went out, progressing as far as we ever had before in a major championships was something to be celebrated this weekend, before the world returned to normal and we went back to watching the big guns do battle for the prizes.

As we began our journey south towards the tunnel, I filled the guys in on what happened between Victoria and I, and how I had ended up with the flat, my savings back and possession of a diamond engagement ring. Having all witnessed first hand her transformation over the years, the three of them were stunned by this recent development.

"So, what are you going to do with the ring?" asked Matt.

"Sell it, I guess. I mean, it means nothing to either of us now," I replied. "Victoria even suggested that I get rid of it and use the money to go to a Wales game."

"Definitely do that!" said Ieuan. "You could probably get final tickets for whatever you get for it."

"Have you got it with you?" said Dav.

"Yep, in my wallet." I said. "The way the pound has slumped since Brexit, I thought it would be better selling it in Europe, whilst we're still allowed over there. So keep your eyes peeled for a jewellers, or one of those cash for gold places."

The two hours slipped past us faster than the whippet-like Craig Bellamy chasing a through-ball, and soon we were pulling up back in familiar territory in Lille. It was a very different scene from when my Euro 2016 experience had started a little over two weeks earlier: the weather was brighter, my mood was better, there wasn't an Englishman in sight and the bars were already packed with my compatriots tucking into lunchtime beers. It took all our collective strength not to dive in headfirst and join them, and instead we scuttled across the cobbled streets surrounding the station, trying to avoid all temptations and instead checked into our hotel. We all shared a sense that this could be the end of the road for Wales, and with that in mind, and also due to the fact that all the cheap accommodation had been booked up, we had traded in nights in Alcatraz for something a fraction more luxurious - two rooms that also included en-suite bathrooms - Dav was even delighted to see he had the use of a dressing gown if needed. If Wales were going out, we were going out in style.

Bags safely stored away in our rooms, we raced downstairs and back into the warm afternoon to get stuck into some beers. As soon as we spotted a group of lads doused in red, white and green we migrated towards them and swiftly sat outside on a table enjoying the cool, refreshing taste of Belgium's finest export since Eden Hazard - Stella Artois. Conversation was purely focused on the match ahead, and we discussed everything from whether Belgium would feel like they had home advantage as we were just 10 miles from their border to whether Sam Vokes, Jonny

Williams or Hal Robson-Kanu would get the nod from Chris Coleman to start. We had all been in Cardiff just over a year earlier when we had beaten them 1-0 on a night that set the stage for our adventures so far this summer, and we just hoped that a similar performance might see us squeak through to the semi-finals. Every time those two words crept into my conscience, suddenly the more daunting the game became.

As the last of my second Stella slipped down the neck of the bottle and into my mouth, I felt a vibration in my pocket. Pulling myself away from the chat briefly, I looked at my phone to see who had requested my attention. Once I had read the message it quickly became all theirs. A short, sweet and to-the-point message said, "Are you in Lille today? If so, do you want to meet up after the game? Come on Wales! Colette."

CHAPTER 11

Seeing that name again was bittersweet. On the one hand, I was doing cartwheels inside, knowing that she was thinking of me, my whereabouts, and hoped to be a part of it. But then again, could I handle any further disappointment in her presence? Being so engrossed in reaching the quarter-finals and everything that had happened with Victoria had distracted me from my all-encompassing obsession with Colette, and a near-fortnight of radio silence had seemed to secure her place in my life story as just a statistical notch on the bedpost. I wasn't happy with that, but now I had the chance to do something about it; however, I just didn't know what that was.

Not wanting to kill the vibe by throwing my relationship problems at the group when there was a full-blown discussion about whether our trips to these fine stadiums across the country would have been improved by the addition of a selection of pies, I slid my phone back into my pocket and tried to ignore it. I would give myself plenty of time to consider my options, compose a sensible response and act cool. Around 30 seconds later, I grabbed my phone again and hastily typed, "Hey! Yes I'm in Lille tonight, would be amazing to see you if you're here. Missed you!" I shook my head as the 'Message Sent' icon flashed up on my phone - it was sure to be the most desperate, pathetic text currently bouncing from satellite to satellite miles above our heads. I had been given the chance to see this extraordinary woman again and I simply couldn't pass it up, or mess around with it. I was dying to see her, even if I wouldn't allow myself to fully commit to that chain of thought.

I left my phone out on the table so I could keep an eye out for any responses, but, by now, I was a mere passenger in the feisty conversation, which had become a debate over which flavour their first pie of the season would be when club football returned in August. For the record, Dav opted for chicken balti, Matt cheese and onion, and Ieuan put the cat amongst the pigeons with the choice of a sausage roll, which was causing uproar.

"C'mon, Scott, you've got to be the adjudicator on this: is a sausage roll allowed at a football match?" asked Matt.

"What? Umm, yeah why not?" was my half-hearted response.

"It's just not a pie, is it?! Pies are traditional, sausage rolls belong in Greggs."

"It's all meat and pastry. What are you getting so het up about, butt?" chuckled Ieuan. "I just bloody love sausage rolls."

"On that bombshell - who's up for another beer?" I asked, already in motion and knowing full well that nobody was going to say no. As I waited at the bar, my phone buzzed in my sweaty hand and my heart skipped a beat - Colette had replied. "Brilliant, I'm on my way to Paris this weekend for the France game but I could come and see you tonight if you like?" Straight away I envisioned two scenarios: she turned up after a Wales win and the sheer thrill of seeing both caused me to spontaneously combust, or following a gallant defeat she helped lift me from my end-of-tournament gloom. Either way I was winning. "Wow, that sounds great! Yeah definitely, I'd love to see you after the game, let's make it happen" was hastily bashed out by my restless digits. As I handed over a crisp 20 euro note to the barmaid, an instant reply said "Cool, speak soon. Good luck!"

My pre-match nerves had vanished. It seemed like both Wales and I had nothing to lose now; two plucky underdogs punching above their weight, hoping to the end the night with a slightly brighter future and further challenges ahead. If our Euro 2016 flame was extinguished, then so be it. We couldn't have asked for anything more - the whole squad were coming home as heroes, and I was meeting up with a magical girl who had played her own starring role in my tournament memories. That word made me think of someone else: Arthur. I had given him my word that after making some tough decisions, I would go and create some happy memories, and now I realised that I had already accomplished that. Whatever the outcome on the field that evening, this was going to be a night that I would never forget.

I strolled back to the lads with four bottles expertly gripped by my claw-like hands, and they were now suggesting that "foreign imports" such as burgers and hot dogs meant that the humble pie was in danger of extinction at Britain's grounds. Unable to partake in this nonsense, I interrupted with, "So, guess who has been in touch?"

"Colette," said Dav nonchalantly, not even bothering to look at me when he said it. "I thought you were acting weird, thinking you were above our pie chat."

"She wants to meet after the game tonight."

"Go for it, mate," said Matt. "But only agree to it if we win. You'll be so devastated if we lose that you'll be the worst company ever."

"I won't!" I protested. "I'm not a sore loser."

"Come off it!" said Dav. "Remember when we lost to Russia in the play-off? I didn't hear from you for a week or so. The England game at the Millennium in the Speedo years? You walked out of the ground with 25 minutes to go. You couldn't handle the loss the other week to them, so you left the country on a Megabus and sulked around at home before your fiancée kicked you out."

"Yeah, at least you won't be bringing us lot down with you if you're with Colette," said Ieuan.

"Honestly - I won't be like that tonight," I laughed. "Whatever happens, it's been bloody brilliant so far. We could get spanked and I wouldn't care - it's been a blast."

"Sounds like you're ready to go home already," said Matt. "We've only just got here."

"DON'T TAKE ME HOME..." piped up Dav, and suddenly half the bar was in full song, almost as if they had all been on tenterhooks waiting for that particular call. The afternoon continued in that vein, with Welsh fans pulling up chairs next to us and sharing stories of memorable away days following the Red Dragons around the world. When it came to this particular one - the biggest of them all - the feeling was unanimous: we'd just wait and see what happened. Unlike our cousins to the east, there was no sense of entitlement about being in the quarter-finals, or an expectation to beat Belgium despite having done so in the qualifiers. It felt like we were the plus-one invited to a house party filled with unknowns, but by the end of the night we had become everyone's new best friend and the entertainment revolved around us. One elderly gentleman summed our predicament up perfectly when he was asked if we could make it to the semis: "We don't want to be greedy now do we?" It struck me as a very Welsh thing to say; centuries of English oppression naturally saw us become an afterthought on the world stage, which actually suited us perfectly. It's in a Welshman's nature not to make too much fuss or step on anyone's toes. Instead, we just concentrate on ourselves. Success does strange things to our countrymen; as soon as they get too big for their boots, the rugby team have gone from heroes to zeroes in a matter of months many times over previous decades. We were over the moon with our lot right now - it may have only been a quarter-final spot, but that was as good as our neighbours had done in a generation. Anything else would be a wonderful, but unexpected, bonus.

Belgian supporters had been pouring over the border into Lille all day and eventually began to take over our bar - all cordially, of course - and they light-heartedly poked fun at us for drinking Stella, before engaging in in-depth tactical discussions regarding the evening's entertainment. With that in mind, we finally gave up our seats about 90 minutes before kick-off and began walking to the Stade Pierre Mauroy, the battleship grey, spaceship-like arena on the city's outskirts. You couldn't move for fans in red and black shirts with Lukaku or Hazard printed on the back, but eventually they became scarcer as we left behind the quaint streets of the city centre and found ourselves walking down the side of dual carriageways. Spotting the error of our ways, and with the heavens about to open on us, we eventually flagged down a taxi to safely transport us to the stadium before someone - most probably Dav - drunkenly staggered into the path of an onrushing bus. The taxi dropped us off in the vicinity of the ground and Dav and I picked our tickets up from a collection point after queuing amongst a red river of Belgian fans.

Matt and Ieuan went about trying to find someone who would kindly sell them a couple, encouraging us to leave them to it. With time on our side, Dav and I sat on a bench sipping 0.5% Carlsberg out of plastic pint glasses, tucking into some frites and enjoying the calm before the storm.

Fed and watered, we sailed through security and began stamping our way up a myriad of concrete steps to our seats. The view from my perch felt oddly familiar, and when I looked around I realised why - it was like being in a mini Millennium Stadium. The stands were steep, the TV screens looked the same and there was even a retractable roof, although despite the rain pouring in it was left open, which was a shame as the atmosphere would evaporate into the atmosphere. There was a real buzz of anticipation - the

Belgians were confident of not just beating us but winning the whole thing, while we knew we were capable of frustrating them and just prayed that we would do it one more time. Five minutes before kick-off the Red Wall had fully formed, only this time it had a slightly different hue to it. We realised that it was, in fact, the opposition who had created this magnificent feat in co-ordination. Their geographical advantage, coupled with the fact that they expectantly supported the second-best team in the world according to the FIFA world rankings, something that was only just more trustworthy than world football's governing body itself, meant that they had probably snapped up around 80% of the 50,000 capacity, and they were making an almighty racket which echoed around the stands, amplifying when the two teams emerged from the tunnel. The mere sight of 11 Welshman strolling out onto the pitch caused Dav to squeeze my arm. It was exhilarating.

The weather had only helped things seem a little more Hollywood, adding to the background as the players lined up to sing their national anthems, hoping it wouldn't be for the last time this tournament. Our opponents had the honour of going first, and their elegant theme was juxtaposed by the ferocity with which their supporters sang every word. The Welsh fans respectfully waited their turn, but when that spine-tingling first note blasted out of the PA system, we were ready to match them - and boy did we give it a good go. When I turned to the man I held tightly next to me, I could see the veins straining out of his neck - I had never seen Dav this ramped up before. It in turn inspired me to give it a bit more oomph and despite our huge numerical disadvantage, we held our own. If this was to be the last time we sang those words pre-match, then we had done ourselves more than justice.

But in this game of vocal ping-pong, back came our Flemish friends and by the time play began they were once again in control of the volume, helping to fire up their 11 representatives in light-blue as they began much the better. Just five minutes in and Ben Davies was in the book after blocking Kevin De Bruyne, meaning he would miss the semi-final should we get through. But the way the opening stages were going that looked to be mission impossible. A couple of minutes later, Dav, I and the rest of the Cymru contingent's reactions resembled innocent bystanders to a traffic pile-up, as we winced, screamed and waited for the inevitable as Yannick Carrasco forced Wayne Hennessey into a save. The rebound, though, fell to Thomas Meunier, whose scuffed attempt was scraped off the line by Neil Taylor. That clearance fell to the spellbinding feet of Eden Hazard, who thumped the ball back towards goal, but some desperate defending saw it somehow deflect it over the bar. Three shots in about six seconds had been repelled, and the sound of 50,000 groans mixed with despair and relief must have been audible from miles around - the Welsh fans, boosted by that let-off, began to instigate some support for their side. Was that a sign of how lucky we would be tonight?

If it was, then it would be a false one, as just 12 minutes into the game our brief audible uprising was silenced. Belgium probed away in the final third, but with so many players back behind the ball, Wales looked comfortable, and with no way through, the Belgians were getting impatient. Hazard played the ball to the instantly recognisable Radja Nainggolan 30 yards out, and the Welsh defender almost dared him to shoot. After he let the ball roll across his body onto his right foot to line-up a first-time attempt, we awaited the ball sailing into the crowd. But seconds later, hands were on heads as the heavily tattooed midfielder with the blonde mohican instead blasted it past Hennessey's despairing dive and into the top corner to cue delirium for the majority in attendance.

It was admittedly a stunning strike; one that you could only sportingly applauded for its brilliance, but it really jolted a nation's hopes and expectation. It had taken just 12 minutes for us to fall behind against one of the tournament favourites who were in inspired form, and Chris Coleman would have to force his players up the proverbial mountain to get anything from this one. But we had to keep the faith - we couldn't allow ourselves to give up yet, and when a chorus of "Wales, Wales" started nearby, we jumped on it and helped it gather momentum, almost as a verbal pat on the backside to inform those in red that we were still behind them. Another goal for Belgium would probably have sealed it, so they dug deep and got stuck in, which resulted in a couple more yellow cards that seemed to halt the one-way traffic. The more Gareth Bale got on the ball, the more Wales grew into the game. On one foray forward, he slipped the ball into Aaron Ramsey's path, handing our own blonde bombshell the chance to create something. Ramsey, in turn, cut a delicious pass back into the path of... what? Neil Taylor again? What was he doing on the penalty spot?

Regardless of the spontaneous concerns in my head, the full-back made a great connection with his weaker right-foot and seemed set to score another crucial goal, but Thibaut Courtois in the Belgian goal managed to instinctively stick out a hand and beat it back down into the turf before it was cleared. "OOOOOFFFFFF!" was the cry all around us as arms held aloft in anticipation were forced to fall. But it was a sign that Wales had recovered, and it got Belgium a little worried. A few minutes later, we explored down the right side again and this time won a corner which Ramsey trotted over to take.

Corners are a funny thing in football - despite the fact that about one in 20 actually leads to a goal, they cause fans to roar with passion, stand to attention and then wait with bated breath, and that was exactly what we were doing now, sensing that this would be the time that something happened. Once the big men had lumbered forward to add their presence into a congested penalty area, Ramsey whipped in a delivery that was just begging to be attacked by someone, and fortunately for us it was the patched-up, unmarked Ashley Williams who had been allowed the length of the Severn Bridge to charge onto the end of it, and he gleefully bashed the ball into the net with his head.

He had barely made contact before Dav's blonde bonce had leapt on top of me, squealing in joy, and the noise from all around us was amazing - there was so much of it that it felt like you were underwater as my ears couldn't process it all. "GET IN THERE!" was all I could say, over and over again as Williams sped away to the Wales bench to start a large pile-on. It seemed all the players, subs and coaching staff wanted to be acting like us rabble in the stands as they darted around manically, punching the air and hugging the nearest person they could get their hands on. As well as proud Welshmen, they were fans, too. They were also in the privileged position of affecting what happened - and right now they were doing a damn good job of it.

The goal had changed the whole complexion of the game and we didn't want the half-time whistle to be blown. Bale burst forward all alone, drilling the ball towards goal, only to see his shot saved. Williams then got on the end of another corner kick but this time couldn't find the target. There was even a late opportunity for Hal Robson-Kanu, who, despite his new-found cult status, showed everyone why he didn't have a club to return to once the tournament ended when he fluffed a tame header straight at Courtois. Nevertheless, as the two teams jogged back to the changing rooms after 45 minutes enthralling minutes, a breathless Dav and I were delighted.

"If we can just pinch one, mate, it's on!" he said, jigging up and down like a kid after too much Coca Cola and Smarties.

"Calm down, mate. Long way to go yet," I said, trying to dampen his childlike expectations, just in case it all ended in tears. But despite my words, after being deflated by the early goal, I was all pumped up again inside, and I just had this sneaking feeling.

"One piece of magic could win this - and I know someone capable of doing that!" I blurted out, completely ignoring my previous statement as I pictured our number 11 rasping another free-kick into the net and setting a mouth-watering showdown with his club colleague Cristiano Ronaldo's Portugal in the semis.

"Who are you talking about - Robson-Kanu?" said Dav sarcastically, and we both laughed. However, when the game resumed, our facial expressions returned to a screwed up state. Riled from the grilling their manager had probably given them during the break, Belgium flew out of the traps and shots were raining down on the Welsh goal. Their superstar trio of Lukaku, De Bruyne and Hazard all flashed efforts just off target, and Wales once again had started slowly. The goal was coming, you just knew it, and it did - but it was beautiful.

There are moments in your life you will be able to visualise in ultra-HD detail for years to come; ones that stimulate your senses all over again and bring you back into that precise moment. You have the ability to replay exact conversations word-for-word, enjoy the smells in your nostrils again, and even sense the temperature on your skin. Only those special memories make hairs on arms stand to attention and eyes water when you recall them. For most people, these occur when reflecting on the birth of their children or perhaps their wedding day, but I don't have those to fall back on just yet. What I do have, though, is a goal; a goal so breathtakingly extraordinary and unexpected that it doesn't even matter that I wasn't the one in the red shirt that scored it. For years to come, when times get hard, I won't need to go to YouTube and type in "Hal Robson Kanu wondergoal", I can just close my eyes.

It goes like this: As with everything, Bale is involved. He is on the halfway line, his feet brushing the whitewash as he clips the ball left footed towards the rampaging Aaron Ramsey, who delicately collects it on another white line, this one marking the edge of the Belgian box. There is a collective "Go on!" from the fans around me, myself included, having been starved of attacking threat from our side since the interval. Under pressure from Toby Alderweireld, Ramsey gets the ball out of his feet and hooks it towards Hal Robson-Kanu, who is lurking around the penalty spot. He kills it with his right foot but has his back to goal, two Belgium defenders, Munier and Denayer, breathing down his neck. Neil Taylor, yet again, creeps into the box from the left-hand side, unmarked, and it looks as though Robson-Kanu has to simply pass to the full-back and keep the move alive. At this point, Marouane Fellaini also arrives at the scene, and the whole stadium and everyone around the world watching is expecting a lay-off to Taylor. But, magical goals aren't scored by accepting the easy.

In a fitting tribute to the recently deceased Johan Cruyff, Robson-Kanu opts to attempt the move that he made so famous, it is still taught to Welsh schoolchildren by their PE teachers 40 years later. He drags the ball backwards with his left foot and spins his burly frame 180 degrees to face the goal, sending all three unsuspecting defenders scurrying into the concourses for some watered down Danish lager. The speed of the turn almost sees Robson-Kanu slip over, but he doesn't. My mouth falls open - what a chance! - and with no defenders left to protect him, a stunned Courtois is afforded little time to set himself. With ice flowing through his veins the Welshman opens his body up, coolly caresses the ball into the net and makes himself famous. Thousands of fist-clenched hands shoot into the air around me as the Welsh fans go potty; their cheers are of incredible shock, higher pitched than normal. I jump up and down on the spot, spinning around for probably around 10 seconds. Dav is doing the same, furiously punching the air and completely beside himself. The final thing I can visualise before my senses become overloaded and I'm back in the room is me grabbing him and screaming "WHATTTTT AAAAAA GOOOAAAALLLL!!" over and over again, my vocal chords strained and voice croaky.

I will watch hundreds more games of football in years to come, but I am virtually assured I will never experience a moment like that. I am content with that. Once again, Hal Robson-Kanu had turned my life upside down, and it was the kind of goal that would do the same for him. Win or lose this game, he would never have to buy a pint in the country again, and if I bumped into him I'd offer to buy him a house if he so required. Maybe Arthur was right - perhaps Barcelona wasn't out of the question? That goal was majestic enough in its execution that you could have sworn Lionel Messi had pledged his allegiance to Wales due to a grandmother from Patagonia. It seemed almost a shame that the game had to continue after that moment of magic. It felt like it should have been the climax to the night's entertainment, like the mass explosion of gunpowder at the finale of fireworks, or a band saving their greatest anthem for their encore.

However, Wales supporters were so ecstatic, they were looking down on cloud nine; there was none of the nervous tension that had afflicted us during the second half of the England game. High on elation, there was no way we were letting go of that sensation just yet. Belgium were stunned, and desperate pot-shots from distance were met by howls of derision by us in the stands to wind them up more. The brass band sounds of the Barry Horns only added to the carnival-like fever that we were all feeling.

But old habits die hard, and once Robson Kanu's goal had become a memory and the reality of the present kicked in, fears enveloped me. Football can be so cruel; two goals now, or a heart-stopping penalty shootout exit, and not just the day, but the whole tournament would be ruined. I remembered my pain when Sturridge scored and said a silent prayer to any god that wasn't glued to the game to prevent me from feeling that way again. Our warriors in their red suits of armour were starting to show signs of fatigue and Ramsey was booked for handball which meant he would miss a potential semi-final. My pulse rate went off the charts when Davies made a tired foul on Lukaku, which should have seen him receive a second yellow, but luckily the referee disagreed. Then Williams stuck out a lazy leg which saw Nainggolan hurl himself screaming in agony to the floor. Despite the theatrics, it looked to be a penalty, but again the officials were lenient. I looked over to Dav, hypnotised by the action, and I noticed that he had his fingers firmly crossed by his side. It was stupid, but I desperately joined him, as it felt like we needed all the luck we could get.

As the game entered the final five minutes, the masses of Belgian fans implored their team to throw more caution to the wind, and it just felt once again that another goal was imminent. But maybe a god had taken pity on me, or the finger crossing had worked, because for the second time in 45 minutes, it did - for Wales.

Chris Gunter found himself on the right flank, and I screamed "GET IN THE BLOODY CORNER" in the hope we could shave some minutes off the clock. I doubt he heard me amongst the cacophony of noise from both sets of tense fans, but if he did, I'm glad he ignored my lack of footballing experience as he sent over an inviting cross into the area. Sam Vokes provided a timely *répondez, s'il vous plaît* given our surroundings. Using all of his might, he sprung into the air and with one blow of the ball with his forehead, it flew immaculately past a helpless Courtois, grazed the inside netting of the far post and Wales were in the semi-finals!

As soon as it hit the net, I screamed my head off like a seven-year-old girl at a boyband concert. If Vokes' jump for the goal was good, mine onto Dav was just as impressive - from a standing start I had flown through the air and on top of my best mate standing about a yard or two away from me, flinging my arms around his neck.

"OHHHH MYYYYY GODDDDDDDDD! OH MY GOD!" he bawled.

"WE'VE WON IT, MATE.... IT'S OVER.... IT'S OVER!!" I said, still hanging off him.

"I CAN'T BELIEVE IT!" he gushed, finally pushing me off and then using his hands to convey his disbelief by putting them on top of his head. A similar stance had been taken up by many of the thousands of beaming fans around us, some shaking their heads, others in tears of joy. Someone behind me shouted "MARK, GET ON THAT BLOODY TICKET SITE NOW!" and no-one wanted the celebrations to end as I high-fived, hugged and kissed randoms all around me for the final inconsequential few minutes. We did it all over again when the final whistle confirmed what we already knew: Wales were in the semi-finals of the European Championships.

With the second best team in the world beaten, our red-cladded superstars could finally display their true emotions, which once again were not dissimilar to ours. Some buried their faces in their shirts to hide the tears, others fell to the floor once they had realised the magnitude of their achievements. Their place in history was assured; Hennessey, Chester, Williams, Davies, Gunter, Allen, Ledley, King, Ramsey, Collins, Taylor, Bale, Robson-Kanu and Vokes had done something that a thousand players before them had failed to achieve when handed the honour of representing the land of their fathers - make it to a semi-final of a major tournament. They were now just one step away from the final, and then a 50/50 chance of winning the whole thing.

For us fans, it was time to take the handbrake off our wildest dreams. They had been so beautifully stupid just three weeks before that we hadn't dared to even contemplate winning Euro 2016 - forget pigs flying, for it would be likely and suitable to see sheep shooting through the skies. But suddenly those ambitions were so tantalisingly close to our outstretched fingertips that we could almost grab their woolly tails.

This could actually happen. Wales could be European Champions.

CHAPTER 12

It was a sight so glorious, full of triumph and wonderment, that I couldn't stop staring at the pitch as Wales bathed in their glory. It was similar to Zenica all those months ago, but so much better: that had been the start of the dream, and here was its latest chapter unfolding in front of us; the best part was that there were still a few more pages to write. The players linked hands and sprinted towards their jubilant supporters watching from the stands, before diving and skidding along the grass on their chests to emphatic cheers. It was almost as if they had won the whole thing already, but this moment didn't require a big shiny silver pot with red ribbons attached to it. It was special enough as it was.

I hugged Dav for probably the fifth time since full-time. We waited until the last of the squad had imprinted stud marks in the Lille turf, before we too exited a stadium that we would forever hold in our hearts. It was only when seeing other animated friends reunite outside that dread came over me - did Ieuan and Matt get in? If not, they would have regretted not being there for the rest of their lives, if they had missed out on our most glittering of golden moments, and I felt a tinge of guilt for being there if they had not. Thankfully, about 10 minutes after we returned to the same spot we had left them as mere quarter-finalists, they danced into view and their faces displayed all the hallmarks of a pair who had witnessed one of our nation's greatest nights of sporting history.

"Boys - how incredible was that?" croaked Ieuan, his voice sounding like a 13-year-old battling the effects of puberty.

"Just unbelievable. Unbelievable," I analysed so elegantly. It seemed to be the only adjective I could conjure up; I was so exhausted and enthused by the experience, my ability to string a coherent sentence together had gone the same way as Ieuan's vocal chords.

"That has to be the single greatest performance in our footballing history," added Matt. "Top of the tree - and we were there."

"How did you get tickets?" asked Dav.

"It was a close one," continued Matt as a speechless - in more ways than one - Ieuan gestured at him to tell the tale. "We didn't have anything by kick-off, as the touts were charging silly money, so we waited until five minutes in. The bastards were literally just about to tear them up and throw them in a bin, so we managed to get some for under £30 each! The moment we paid up, we heard a roar and entered the stadium a goal down, and we were sat right in the middle of all the Belgian fans. They were brilliant, though; we had good fun with them. They all shook our hands at the end."

"And then Matt cried," squeaked Ieuan, in the hopes of trying to stitch his mate up, but it backfired.

"I don't blame you at all, mate," I said. "I was close to tears myself. We've been through so many lows of supporting this team over the past two decades, but now we're finally reaping the rewards. Let's enjoy it while it lasts."

"Speaking of, mate, shouldn't you be meeting your bird?" said Dav, and it took a couple of seconds to register what he was talking about, before realising that he meant Colette - the icing on top of a Wales-3-Belgium-1-shaped cake.

"Christ! How did I forget?" I spluttered, and instantly ripped my phone from my jeans pocket and looked at it for the first time in a couple of hours. It was rammed with notifications: missed calls from friends back home, Facebook photos of people watching the game on giant screens in Cardiff; there was even a text from my mum which stated, "This football is going well - even I'm watching it!" But eventually, in amongst all these unnecessary distractions, was what I was looking for: "Wow what a win! Do you still want to celebrate together? I'm at a bar called La Capsule, let me know."

I didn't need a second invitation and hastily bashed out, "Sure thing, I'll be there right away, celebratory drinks are on me!"

"What are you boys going to do this evening?" I said, without even looking at them, instead scanning the area for a taxi.

Dav laughed. "Well, I'm guessing we're not spending it with you. But we'll share your cab into town. If it all goes pear-shaped again, we'll be close by to sort something out."

"Great. Ta, lads." I muttered, my mind now firmly fixed on making sure I managed to get to La Capsule before Colette disappeared. After a team effort, Matt managed to persuade a reactant driver to forgo his late passengers and take us back into the city centre, and we raced through the tight streets, past thickets of depressed Belgians wearing red, black and yellow wigs and delirious Welshmen ready to attempt to drink Lille dry. As the street lights blinked by one by one, I attempted to repress all the wonderful flashbulb moments Chris Coleman had orchestrated out of my mind for just a few minutes, and think about what I was going to say to Colette. I knew that as soon as I was confronted by those hypnotic hazel eyes and thick, instantly-kissable lips, I would invariably lose all my vocabulary. I re-read her last few texts over and over again, trying to decipher whether she wanted to meet up as friends, or just spend another night together before kicking me out of her bed and life again the following morning. I tried to construct a couple of good opening lines, but it was useless; between replaying how we left things in Toulouse and reliving the Robson-Kanu goal on loop, I came to the conclusion that it was as pointless as an Englishman buying semi-final tickets.

Eventually the taxi pulled up next to a passageway far too narrow for it to navigate through, and after some gesturing and haphazard French speaking from four Welshman without a GCSE in the language between them, I jumped out alone and began plodding nervously down yet more cobbled streets. I spotted the sign of the bar dangling in the distance, and there was a crowd of people gathered outside the entrance which was situated directly on the corner. Straight away my sight was drawn to a woman within that group - about five and a half feet in heels and short black hair wearing a red top. My heart, which had only just recovered to resting levels, began to beat furiously once again.

Colette must have seen me coming, as before I could get to within 10 feet of her, she had broken away from the crowd and started trotting towards me in her boots, clip-clopping along the stony ground to give me a cuddle. As soon as her body pressed up against mine, my speaking capabilities, as expected, amounted to a caveman-esque inaudible grunt as the infusion of her vanilla-scented perfume wafted around our vicinity.

"Scott! Oh my god, what a game!" she said excitedly in that sultry French accent of hers that I had been dying to hear one more time for the past week or so. "Wales were brilliant weren't they? I was supporting them all the way."

"Yeah, incredible, I can't believe it!" I replied, realising I sounded exactly like one of our victorious players being interviewed post-match, tiredly rolling out fatigued clichés to escape the media glare.

"Right," she said, "let's get those celebratory drinks, shall we?" She grabbed my hand before marching us into the crowded bar. Dying for some booze after going cold turkey for just a few hours, I pushed my way to the front of the bar and, spying some bottles of champagne, I enquired as to how much one was. When faced with the prospect of shelling out 100 euros for the privilege of France's finest, I quickly selected a much more reasonably priced bottle of prosecco instead - after all, it all tastes the same anyway. I still had the pleasure of popping the cork to toast Welsh football's greatest day, and handed Colette a glass and poured her some bubbly as we sat in a dimly-lit corner of the bar at a table for two.

"What are we drinking to?" she asked, once again looking unexplainably sexier wearing my national team's colours.

"Surely you know the answer to that?" I said, mischievously.

"Yes - to meeting up again," she replied, and lent her lofted glass towards mine.

"Yeah… that's it," I replied. The correct response would of course have been "Hal Robson-Kanu," but I let this slide as we touched chalices and sipped at the sweet nectar of victory. "So, where are your friends?" I enquired, now beginning to finally loosen up after a whirlwind hour that had left me incredibly tightly-sprung.

"They're in Paris; they didn't fancy a trip to Lille to watch a team they didn't care about."

"Ahh - so you care about Wales that much that you wanted to travel all the way up here to see us on TV?" I said slyly, implying there was more to her motives than football.

"Well, yes, of course!" she giggled and began to twiddle her straight hair through her fingers. "I wanted to see you, obviously. How's the rest of your trip been?" We proceeded to discuss my time in Paris the previous week as we glugged the contents of the bottle pretty quickly. Conversation flowed as quickly as the waiter could refill our glasses from a fresh supply. Knowing my terrible track record of handling sparkling wine or champagne (the bubbles making me lose my head faster than Craig Bellamy armed with a putter), I should have stopped after the second bottle was no more. But I was so preoccupied absorbing every soothing French-sounding syllable that I wasn't paying attention to how much alcohol I was knocking back. In great detail, we worked our way through everything we had been up to since I had shuffled out of her bedroom 11 days earlier, tip-toeing around the reasons why I had been forced to make the walk of shame through the streets of Toulouse, and we landed at the topic of my living situation.

"…so then I went around to my flat and my ex-fiancée was gracious enough to move out, so I've managed to get my place back."

"Hang on - ex-fiancée?" said Colette, stopping me in my tracks. "You never told me you were engaged?"

"Oh… well, yeah. Well I was - before I came out here actually. Not when we met up or anything," I quickly clarified.

"Don't worry about it; I'm engaged right now," she responded calmly, looking at me straight in the eyes while she lifted her flute to her lips, nearly causing me to choke on a mouthful of wine.

"What? Really?" I gasped, my body suddenly tightening, a bit like when you see a defender step forward to take a sudden-death penalty in a shootout.

"No, silly," she laughed, touching my hand as she gave me another sighting of that sexy wink of hers.

"Thank god for that," I sighed, chuckling to myself as I hoped that little beads of sweat weren't forming upon my forehead. I then revealed all about Victoria - from the university infatuation right up to the messy break-up less than a month earlier. It was a long story, and as such a third bottle of prosecco was ordered. By the sad conclusion of the tale, Colette had gone through her full repertoire of supportive faces and was now clutching my outstretched hand, the free pair allowing us to continue to swig mouthfuls of fizzy booze as we leaned closer to each other; the intimate conversation drawing us emotionally, as well as physically, closer together.

"Oh, Scott - I didn't know," she sympathised. "Still, better to find out now before it's too late, I guess."

"Yeah true - never mind, hey. Right, I'm just going to pop to the toilet. I expect to see none of that wine left when I get back," I said, trying to lighten the tone - after all, Wales had just made it into the semi-finals of Euro 2016. It still felt weird to say it, knowing it was actually true.

I pushed out my wooden chair and headed to the loo, closely followed inside by a tall man in a leather coat, who insisted on standing next to the adjacent urinal to mine despite us being the only two people inside a large bathroom.

"Champagne! Celebrating tonight?" the local said in broken English.

"Yeah," was my uncomfortable response. I hate speaking to randoms in toilets; it's a weird place to communicate unnecessarily with someone you've never met, especially when you suffer with bouts of stagefright like myself, despite being in my mid-30s. I didn't correct him about the prosecco

- I quite liked the fact he thought I was a high-roller, despite actually being unemployed and dining out on my ex's stash of money.

"Getting married to that woman?" he continued, pointing back towards the door in Colette's direction and not sensing my conversation-ending tone.

"No, just friends. Celebrating Wales' win," I said slowly and loudly as my stream began to turn into a trickle.

"She is beautiful. Très bien," was his response, not understanding a word I had just uttered. I relented, "Thanks. I'm very lucky," and he exited without washing his hands. As I went to do just that, I looked at myself in the mirror and laughed that he thought that Colette and I were getting married only based on the fact that we were drinking what looked like champagne at a bar together. Then a subtle, sudden thought darted into my mind: I really wished that he was right. It was a strange feeling that only entered my consciousness for a second, but like a lighting bolt it made an indelible mark and was now spreading through my nervous system like electricity. Did I like Colette enough that I wanted to marry her already? I splashed some water on my face and stared at the mirror, watching it drip down my cheeks and off my chin. I ran through the signs: I had been struck by her beauty from the moment I met her; I was at my happiest in a long time when in her presence; I struggled to shift her out of my mind when she wasn't there. I thought she was funny and intelligent, brimming with artistry and talent, and had an infectious charm that made me want to slip a ring on her finger. I breathed in deeply - there was no denying it. I was in love with Colette.

Suddenly, the toilet door was barged open and a couple more natives walked in, so I hastily retreated and returned to my seat opposite the most beautiful girl in the bar, the street, the city. I stared at her straight in her gorgeous eyes, and double-checked all those symptoms again whilst watching her break out a smile. Yeah, I was certain. We had not said a word before she suddenly broke the silence with a hiccup, and we both laughed.

"The prosecco is going down well then I see," I said, feeling my head spinning slightly, but not just from the liquor consumed.

"Yes, definitely. You're getting me very drunk," she chuckled. "I think we need to go outside and get some fresh air." I agreed and with that we swigged the last of bottle number three and headed out the door onto the cobbled streets. This time, I reached for Colette's hand and she interlocked her fingers with mine. We had only walked about 50 metres from the bar when the tone of her slightly-slurred voice suddenly turned serious.

"Can I ask you a question, Scott?"

"Fire away."

"Do you believe in fate?"

I hadn't been expecting that particular musing - especially given that the consumed alcohol was beginning to eat away at any pertinent conversations at this time of the day. Her request took me by surprise, almost as if she knew that everything this summer had hinged on moments out of my control.

"Why?" was my diplomatic excuse, not wanting to reveal those revelations just yet. She let go of my hand and suddenly began fumbling through her handbag before pulling out her phone and tapping away on the screen, which illuminated her face in the dark of the night. She looked concerned, and the cheeriness of the past couple of hours had been washed away as she concentrated. Eventually, she held it up to my face, saying, "I've been working on this for the past week or so."

As I began to process what I was looking at, I quickly gauged that it was the development of her latest artwork. Sketched out was a curved section of a football stand, with the pitch in the distance, and swashes of blues, reds and yellows created a dramatic-looking skyline punctured by some unfinished floodlights. It was the view from our seats at the Russia game - exactly as I had suggested she should attempt. It looked to be a masterpiece in the making, and it was well advanced given the short timeframe since we had born witness to that glorious sight on a magical evening.

"You were right, Scott - that photograph was a great inspiration for a painting, and when you left that morning I began to work on it, so it was fresh in my mind. I have spent hours working on it already, and with every brushstroke I put into it I have been thinking about you and what an amazing night that was - during and after the game." I wanted to interrupt to tell her the feeling was mutual, but I didn't want to stop her when she was in full flow.

"That's when I began to think about everything, and how random it had been that we had met just 24 hours earlier and suddenly I'm going into that ground for the first time ever, and I see this breathtaking sight. It was almost as if something didn't want me to go there until that certain evening, with a particular person that I had yet to meet. When I began to think about things a bit deeper, I remembered I wasn't even supposed to be out the night before; I was meant to be babysitting for the people I work for, but the mother was ill and they rang up to cancel that afternoon. Had that not happened, I wouldn't have met you, and I wouldn't have been at the Wales game the next day."

"You don't think it's a coincidence, no?" I asked as we continued to stroll down the street, our pace quickening slightly due to my excitement of hearing these words.

"No, I believe in fate," she said. "I think that sometimes an unexplainable force in the universe just forces people together without them knowing. The more time and effort I put into that painting, the more I began to realise that I had made a mistake in letting you leave so easily. I watched the Wales v Northern Ireland game and all I could think about was you, and I was hoping that Wales would win just so that you would remain in France and I might be able to see you again. They did, and then my friends asked if I wanted to travel to Paris for a weekend, at the same time that you happen to be nearby, only because Wales are still in the tournament, against all odds? You don't have to believe me, but it can't all be a coincidence."

By now we had stopped dead in our tracks inside the grounds of la Cathedral Notre Dame de la Treille that Matt had taken such a liking towards when we were previously in the city for the England game. I led a nervous Colette to the steps leading up to the entrance and sat her down.

"I don't think it's a coincidence, either," I began, probably about to make the most important speech of my life, my heart racing at a million miles per hour. "If you had asked me a month ago, I would say the notion of fate is nonsense. But, I sit here in front of you, a mere passenger throughout the craziest few weeks of my life. I said to myself that if Wales won our first game, I would leave Victoria, and I did just that. Then I quit my job because my boss wouldn't let me watch the Russia game in a pub. A day later, I'm watching it in the stadium with you after an impulsive trip to Toulouse."

"See, you understand!" she smiled.

"I really do. And since I've met you, I've been waiting for Wales to get knocked out, but they refuse to, and that means I get to create more memories and share experiences like this with you. To me, as stupid as it sounds, it feels as if the players are trying to stay in the tournament long enough for my life to change for the better, and I know that if it's to do that, then I somehow need to find a way for us to stay together, because I'm pretty sure I'm in love with you."

My body seized up, but it was too late. I didn't want those last few words to slip off my tongue, but my emotions were pouring out of me like water out of a dam, and all I had to hold the floods back was my finger. I had nothing to lose, because I had already lost it back in Toulouse. I looked at Colette, awaiting any reaction, good or bad. It took a few seconds, but she threw herself towards me and kissed me tenderly, before adding, "I think I love you, too, Scott."

"I know it's a bit crazy -"

"It is! It is crazy!" she laughed, and kissed me once again. "But if it's how we feel, we can't help it. All the signs are telling us to try and make something work, so I think we need to. I just don't know how."

The world seemed to stop turning for a second as I said, "I think I do." My hands were shaking as I slid my right one into my back pocket and pulled out my wallet. I carefully opened the coin compartment and found what I was looking for. Pulling out Victoria's engagement ring, I shuffled off the step and down a few levels so I was looking up to a shocked Colette, and bending down onto one knee, I held the ring out in front of me.

"Colette - will you marry me?"

CHAPTER 13

Her face was a picture that, despite her talent, she would not have been able to paint. It was a mixture of shock, excitement, panic and confusion. She stared at the diamond glistening in the street light, and looked back at me in disbelief, but her hesitant demeanour meant that I was still in possession of the ring.

"I know it's a bit sudden, but every hour of every day that I have spent in your company has been amazing. I just don't want that to ever end," I said, in a slightly desperate tone. She smiled and stroked my face, and then closed my fingers up into a ball with the ring inside in the exact same way that Victoria had done earlier that week.

"Oh, Scott," she said ruefully. "I don't think I can. I mean, there's following fate and then there's just being reckless. We live in different countries, we have different lives, we've never properly dated…"

"All valid points," I laughed, despite the situation. "But if we never take the leap, I guess we will never know how the story is meant to end." It was one of the most poetic things I had ever said - especially when drunk - and it certainly resonated with Colette who continued to weigh things up.

"OK, you're right - I'm not going to say no," she said. "However, I'm not going to say yes, either. If we're leaving this to fate, then we have to let this decision follow the same path that brought us together in the first place. We'll let the football decide."

"How is that going to work?" was my confused reply. I was also very intrigued. At least she hadn't ruled out the possibility altogether.

"Well, Wales are in the semi-finals, and France will be, too, if they win on Sunday. If we are destined to end up together, then our teams will meet in the final. If that happens, we'll get married. How does that sound?"

If I thought leaving my fiancée because of the result of the first game of the tournament had been big enough, then the last game of it could be the one that shaped the next half a century of my existence. The stakes could not have been any higher, but I was never going to fold now. As Wales had somehow gotten me to this point, I was willing to bet the rest of my life on them.

"You've got a deal!" I said, and we kissed on the steps of the cathedral as it seemed a more pertinent way of accepting the agreement than shaking hands.

"Wow - I didn't think I would be proposed to today!" she gushed, and I laughed too. "Where the hell did you get a ring from?"

"Well, it's the one I gave to Victoria. I was going to sell it over here when I got a chance, but it seemed poignant to give it to you. I was a bit caught up in the moment."

"It's OK," she laughed. "We'll have plenty of time between now and the final to pick out something more to my taste." I appreciated the humour and helped her to her feet. We began to walk aimlessly again, so I put my arm around her waist and tucked it into her back pocket.

"Voulez vous coucher avec moi ce soir?" I attempted in my best Gallic accent, which just came out as corny, but she burst into hysterics.

"Haha, yeah I guess so," she said. And with that, we continued to stroll through the charming city until we found a hotel to allow the final embers of the most magical day to burn out.

Maybe it was because I was in France, but when I awoke a few hours after my adrenalin levels had finally lowered enough for me to fall asleep, I had a sense of déjà vu. It felt like the same perfect start to the morning as when Colette and I last lay naked together back in Toulouse; however, this time I knew that the sounds of bicycle bells and the smell of freshly baked pastries weren't about to be rudely interrupted by tears and heartbreak. It would be football which decided how many more times I would enjoy this moment, and with France's game against Iceland the following day, I knew I had at least two mornings to savour so I was going to make the most of them. I shut my eyes and pretended to be asleep, but a few seconds later Colette had rolled on top of me and was kissing my neck.

"Bonjour, monsieur" she breathily whispered.

"Bonjour, mademoiselle" I replied.

"Wow, très bien!" she sniggered.

It took us a good couple of hours to finally get out from under the covers, but once our discarded clothes were back on and we had checked ourselves out of the hotel, we crossed the street to the wonderful little bakery that had provided the splendid aromas to my daybreak. Over cups of coffee and tea, we began to discuss our next movements.

"Shall we go to Paris today?" I suggested.

"Do you want to? What about your friends?" She did make a valid point - I had abandoned Dave, Ieuan and Matt the previous evening, and now I was thinking of running off to another city without consulting them. Would they mind? Surely not, given the circumstances.

"I don't think they would be too bothered if we spent a few days apart," I stated. "I don't think we should tell them about our little plan, though. Don't want to jinx it."

"Definitely," said Colette.

"Besides, if we have just two days together before France go out and ruin this for me, or if I get a few more up to the semi-finals, I want to make each one matter. If I only get to spend a small amount of time with you speaking like this, being the way we are, then I would rather have that than nothing at all."

She smiled - "I agree, Scott. I think we should sneak off to Paris together now, just the two of us. I will tell my friends that I'm arriving on Sunday afternoon, so it can just be me and you."

"Sounds wonderful," I exclaimed. I wasn't too keen on meeting her friends at that particular moment anyway; the usual new-boyfriend question and answer sessions that led to an evaluation on whether I was right for their mate could wait. "I just need to get my suitcase back from the hotel and then we'll make a move."

Once back in my original hotel, any awkward conversations with the boys were also put on ice, as when I quietly opened the door in expectation, they were all still fast asleep. Half-drunk cans of lager were scattered around the room and the smell of stale Kronenberg wafted around the air; still clad in their red shirts, all three of them were splayed across their beds. The result had meant it was always destined to be a heavy night, but the sight suggested it had been a heavy morning too. My case was located closest to the door, so didn't have to encroach too far in to grab it and begin my escape to Paris.

For the next 24 hours, Colette was all mine. Rather than hating on the same loved-up couples that I resented seven days earlier, we were now one of them. I attempted to spot someone displaying my same crushed demeanour, as I wanted to show them that I was living proof that everything would come good eventually - well only if you supported Wales that is. My hands barely detached from hers during that time, and we spent more time with our lips locked than actors in an American teenage drama. Unlike my time with the boys, we didn't seek out attractions, but instead we lived like Parisians: lounging in parks watching the cloud slip by, sipping red wine and eating bread at restaurants, and walking along the banks of the Seine watching the boats chop alongside us. We spoke openly and freely about ourselves, even at one point joking about where we were going to live together once the tournament was over and what pets we would have. Despite it holding my destiny in a vice-like grip, that Saturday I was as far removed from football as could be, and it was enlightening. As much as I loved Gareth, Aaron and Hal in a purely ridiculous platonic way, my love for Colette was much more fulfilling. Over the previous few years, the game had filled a shortfall of excitement in my life, but now she had taken over that role, and the healthy release of frustration that I unleashed at the TV or on the terraces during the Victoria years also seemed superfluous.

But just as it seemed that I had allowed football to become less of an importance in my daily life, Sunday arrived and the first of three hurdles had to be cleared. France hadn't been convincing in the group stages; they had scraped through thanks to last-minute goals in their opening two matches and then edged past the Republic of Ireland by a single goal despite facing 10 men for the final 25 minutes. Iceland, meanwhile, like Wales, were having the time of their lives. Their impressive defence had already frustrated Portugal to claim a draw in their opening game before holding firm against England. But surely the hosts would manage to make home advantage count - after all, I needed them to.

With so much personally riding on a match that didn't involve my actual country, I began to suffer the same stresses and strains as I would when building up to a Wales match. I picked away at a pretzel as gravel crunched underfoot and we made our way through another of the city's gorgeous little green areas. I eventually tossed two-thirds of it in a bin, when it wouldn't fit in my stomach due to the amount of butterflies scurrying around inside there.

"You're anxious, aren't you?" said Colette.

"How can you tell?"

"You haven't spoken for 10 minutes," she smiled. "Look, you can't worry about it. That's the beautiful thing about fate - it's already been decided."

"You're right," I said. "So where shall we watch the game?"

"Well, my friends and I have tickets, but we need to watch it together somewhere don't we?"

"Yeah, or if France lose I might never see you again," I nervously tittered. "I'm sure we could get tickets if you wanted to be in the stadium?"

"That's sweet of you, but, Scott, we're in Paris and every Frenchman here is going to want a ticket, too. I've watched every France game so far in a bar, so I think I'll keep that tradition, and I'll get my friend to sell my ticket. I think I'll need the money to go to the Wales semi-final anyway."

"Hang on - are you switching countries mid-tournament?" I laughed.

"I think everyone, even the French, want Wales to win if we can't," she said. "But when we play each other in the final, your fiancée will be wearing a blue shirt, sorry."

"If you beat us in the final, then we're definitely not going through with this - I'll never be able to like another French person again."

"Try and stop loving me if we get that far - there will be nothing you can do about it. After all, it's fate," Colette purred as she ran her fingers through the back of my hair. At that point, she got a text from her friends with their location, and we headed on the Metro to meet up with them. I spent the next two and a half hours drinking with Colette, Claude and Michel, and after the introductions, I had no understanding of the resulting conversation as their English was as good as my French. Instead, I sat quietly and worked my way through five or six pints, familiarising myself with the French team on my phone - after all it would be better to learn the names and faces of those men who would play a part in determining whether the woman sitting next to me would be my future wife, and if Claude and Michel would be guests at our wedding in the near future.

Eventually, they left us to it, but only after I had received some evil stares when, I presumed, they were discussing Colette's decision to forgo her ticket to spend time with a random Welshman - one of the only French words I had picked up on this trip was 'billets,' which cropped up often - and made their way towards Saint Denis and the Stade de France - a journey I was certain that I would be making in exactly one week's time as Wales took their place in the Euro 2016 final.

After a swift costume change in the toilet, Colette re-emerged in the same low-cut version of Les Blues' current strip that had been the first thing that caught my eye when we had made acquaintances. To get into the mood, and get a cheap laugh, I nipped outside and paid 10 euros for a fetching blue beret with a gold cockerel stitched into it. I could imagine the jokes coming from Dav's direction if he had been there.

Colette and I found a prime position to view the bar's biggest TV screen, and with hands held we awaited our fortune to be told. It was answered in extraordinary fashion: Olivier Giroud, Paul Pogba, Dimitri Payet and Antoine Greizman quickly assured themselves a place in my heavily-crowded heart alongside the entire Welsh squad and, of course, Colette, as they all scored to send a riotous France into the half-time break and also in the semi-final. As each goal went in, Colette and I hugged a little tighter, and when the impudent Greizman ran through to chip in the fourth, we were kissing passionately in front of everyone cheering on the team in blue. A thriller ended 5-2, but we weren't to know, as we were back in our hotel room before the full-time whistle had peeped, confirming what we already knew - we were two results away from a lifetime together.

***

"Where the bloody hell have you been?" shouted Dav, whose booming baritone had ripped through the tranquillity of a stunning Tuesday afternoon in Lyon. He approached Colette and I as we each sat with a glass of red wine, enjoying the calmness as we gazed up to the Fourvière hill and the basilica of Notre-Dame, with its golden statue of Mary watching over the city. This particular corner of the south of the country was gradually becoming awash with replica Bale shirts as my fellow countrymen began to descend from aeroplanes, alight from trains, and even found a place to abandon their cars for the next day or so. That number included Dav, Ieuan and Matt, who had finally tracked me down after three days in hiding with my new beau.

I got out of my chair to greet them and gestured to a nearby waiter for three extra beers. "I should think so," was Dav's playful response. "I thought you would have something to do with it," he continued, turning his attentions to Colette, before giving her a big cwtch. "I love your hair, Dav," she said politely. His locks were now displaying a slight hint of green as the peroxide began to lose its impact. "Cheers, Colette," he responded, not sensing the falseness before adding, "So, what have you guys been up to since we got the semi-final?"

"Well, you know - this and that," I said bashfully, not wanting to go into too much detail about how incredible the past 72 hours of my life had been. After celebrating the French victory on the Sunday night, we had reluctantly decided to leave Paris behind and rattle along the train tracks to Lyon to take in the delights of this gorgeous city before the biggest game of football in Wales' history, well until the final at least. We spent the rest of that day taking in some magnificent Renaissance neighbourhoods - as Colette enlightened me - by bicycle, which had been the first time I had gotten on a saddle since I had parted with my BMX as a teenager to afford attendance to a nearby Young Farmers barn dance. We meandered through the petite passageways of the stunning old city and along the top of the lofty walls containing the Rhône and Saône rivers, and even watched the sun dip down over the horizon perched in a Roman amphitheatre. I had only discovered France three weeks earlier, but its wealth of culture, history and architecture had really made an impression. I felt like this trip had seen me grow as a person; more in tune with being in their mid-30s and finding an appreciation for the finer things in life, although it did help that I was spending my time with a woman with an eye for art and local knowledge, rather than the regular rabble that I normally keep acquaintance with, whom I would not swap for all the cheese in France.

"What about you guys?" said Colette, also keen not to delve too deeply into our affection-filled few days. "How was your time in Paris?"

"It was proper Lionel," said Ieuan.

"What?" said a perplexed Colette as I shook my head in dismay.

"Messy!"

"You're not a cockney, so leave off the rhyming slang," said Matt.

"What are you talking about? I say that all the time."

"I have literally never heard you say that in all my life," said Dav. "And please never say it again."

Colette giggled at the absurdness of our little group, and Matt began recounting a few tales that took so long that we were all beginning to go a little bit pink from prolonged exposure to the scorching rays. Following the Belgium game, they had attached themselves to a group of fellow Welsh fans celebrating, and somehow Dav had successfully managed to chat up a girl from Swansea, after she had pinched his hat. Left alone in the corner of a bar, they began kissing - much to the hilarity of Ieuan and Matt as she was at least 10 years his senior - but just as they began to dance together, she instructed Dav to be careful because her husband was in the next room. According to reports, Dav had bolted as quickly out of the doors as if he was about to be ambushed by a bunch of Russian - or indeed Slovakian - hooligans. The following night, Matt had been forced to haul Dav's dead-weight carcass home after one too many sambucas, nearly concussing the person he was attending after bouncing his forehead off a lamppost as soon as they left the club, distracted by an attractive girl trying to entice him to a burlesque show. He then somehow allowed Dav to get bitten by a stray dog on the way back to the hotel, before finally dumping him on his bed after an hour-long struggle. Meanwhile, Sly Ieu was on the prowl again and managed to work his magic with a local girl. Incredibly, he managed to persuade her that a night in a room with two other drunken blokes was a good idea. Once they had also made it back, and noticing that both were out for the count, messing around Ieuan picked up his new friend and tossed her onto his bed, only for Dav and Matt to be awoken by a girl screaming in pain. In transpired that Matt - in a rare display of immaturity - had hidden Ieuan's mattress and draped a white sheet over the wooden slats of his bed. With his dreams as battered as the poor girl's back, Ieuan was forced to call her taxi and spend the night fuming alone.

Somehow, after all of that, they were still friends, and thankfully Colette had not been appalled by their tales, promising them that when she got to know them better, she might tell them a few sordid tales of her own.

"Ah - so will we be seeing more of you in the future, then, Colette?" asked Dav intrusively.

"Well, we'll have to wait and see, I guess," she chuckled, shooting me a look that suggested that only I knew exactly what she was talking about. I smiled, but inside my nerves were jangling with just over 24 hours until 90 minutes that would have a huge bearing on the rest of my life. Whilst trying to solely enjoy three days' worth of wonderful company with my new partner, there was no hiding place from the football. A Coca Cola poster featuring the French team here, a bar advertising live games there, buses adorned with Euro 2016 livery, and even vending machines selling official merchandise popping up in random places - you couldn't escape the buzz that the final week of an international competition brings. As well as an expectant host nation, the final four contained Germany, Portugal and, incredibly, us. There was a 25 percent chance that we would win silverware, but - whisper it - more importantly the same percentage of a Wales v France final, and, thus, gold being slid around Colette's finger.

The Germans and the Portuguese stood in the way of that, but I was much more optimistic of Gareth Bale coming out on top over his fellow Real Madrid galactico Cristiano Ronaldo than France beating the tournament favourites in the other semi. Wales would have to do it without their suspended duo of Aaron Ramsey and Ben Davies. Portugal, however, had been one of the competition's biggest let-downs, yet to win a match in 90 minutes, scraping through their group after three uninspiring draws and winning in extra-time against Croatia, before requiring penalties to edge past Poland. They were a far cry from the sometimes-swashbuckling, pragmatic if required side set up by Chris Coleman, and by all accounts it seemed as though we were favourites - hype I, too, bought into. Having gone where no Welsh team had been before, I was sure that we were just one step away from reaching our first ever final, putting me a giant leap closer to marrying Colette.

The pair of us had managed to hold our tongue and not tell anyone about our little pact, but the secrecy was gnawing away inside me. With no springboard to bounce the idea off, I could not be sure if Colette and I were the only people on the planet who thought this was a good idea. As afternoon turned to evening, and eventually evening into night, a lot of wine had been knocked back by the five of us, and when Dav and I decided to head to the toilet, I couldn't hold it in any more - the secret that is.

"Mate, I need to tell you something, but you cannot tell anyone."

"Hang on - are we 15 again? Who do you fancy?"

"Very funny, but you're not far off, actually. It's me and Colette."

"Well, I guessed that - you have been gallivanting around France with her for quite a while. You even sacked me and the boys off for her!"

"Well, do you want to know why? I proposed to her on Saturday."

"You what?!" said a shocked Dav, turning towards me mid-flow.

"Woah - watch where you're pointing that!"

"Sorry - but Jesus, mate! Bit of surprise that. Why... I mean what did she say? You're not having me on?"

"No, mate, I really did - I used Victoria's ring and everything. But we said we would leave it up to fate."

"What does that even mean?" he asked, stepping away from the urinal.

"Well, I'm Welsh and she's French -"

"I never realised"

"Very funny. We were unsure what to do, so we said that if it is a Wales v France final, then we'll do it - we'll get married. But what do you think - is it crazy?" I realised there and then that I hadn't even unzipped my fly, due to my overriding desire being talking through this dilemma with Dav rather than performing a bodily function, so I moved away from the ceramic trough beneath my feet and nervously began to unnecessarily dry my hands.

"Mate - it's absolutely mental," said Dav, looking at me straight in the eyes via the reflection in the mirror in front of him, but I applaud you for it. I've seen the way you are around her; you've barely managed to stop touching her this evening - you're like a cat with a ball of yarn. But I remember what you were like around Victoria at first, and it was exactly like that back then, too. Hopefully this one doesn't go off the rails, too. But she seems pretty cool to me."

That was exactly what I had needed to hear, and why Dav was my best mate. "Cheers, mate - come here" and I got one of his massive bearhugs as well as, "Don't worry, I won't tell the other two, but for what it's worth, I really bloody hope we win tomorrow now for two reasons."

Our little moment came to an abrupt halt, when we heard the sound of a flushing toilet from one of the nearby cubicles, and having thought we had been all alone during our heart-to-heart, in fact, when the door opened, we realised that a man around 60 in age, with dishevelled hair, tracksuit trousers and a faded Le Coq Sportif t-shirt, had been privy to our conversation, and was now wheezing with laughter.

"I heard what you said - you are an eediot," he muttered towards us in his local accent.

"Sorry - did not know you were here," I replied in English, but copying Colette's dialect. "Do you think it is too fast to get married?"

The pensioner shook his head slowly, and as he shuffled back into the thriving bar, he replied: "No - France will not beat Germany!"

***

Despite being full of alcohol and turning in at an early hour, I barely slept a wink that night. Even with the fall of the sun, the temperature was too sticky, and as happy as I was that I was sharing a bed with a hot woman, it did not make things any cooler. Unable to drop off, my trail of thought was never too far away from the Portugal game as I constantly envisaged Robson-Kanu, Bale, Vokes, and even the marauding Neil Taylor, banging goals past a helpless Iberian goalkeeper. Thoughts then turned to the final, and a showdown with France. Colette and I would be perfect for the TV cameras to capture during the anthems as we held hands as a newly-engaged couple, wearing our contrasting red and blue shirts and singing our respective anthems at the Stade de France. Then Bale pops in a 30-yard free-kick and I experience the ultimate high as Ashley Williams makes his way through the stands to lift the trophy into the Parisian sky, red, green and white ticker tape fluttering all around Dav, Ieuan and Matt and I before we all live happily ever after.

I don't know during which point of that daydream that I fell asleep, but I was awoken by Colette seductively kissing my chest, indicating that she had grown bored of waiting for me to stir and was now trying to get me up - in more ways than one. However, it just wasn't happening. From the moment I had become conscious that I had arrived at the day that would determine whether Wales would either make the final of Euro 2016 or go home, and if mine and Colette's future would either flourish or perish, I simply could not concentrate on anything else - even sex. She gave up after a couple of attempts, and concerned about my lack of libido, she simply said, "You're nervous again, aren't you?"

I bashfully nodded and thankfully she understood - I would have hated for her to take it personally; after all she did still look breathtakingly good as the early morning sun glistened on her sweaty olive skin.

"Sorry," I said. "I just can't stop thinking about the game; I barely slept last night imagining different scenarios."

"How did Wales do?" she smiled.

"They won tonight, and they also beat France in the final," I laughed.

"I'll ignore the second part, but the first - that's a good omen, isn't it?" she suggested, running her fingers through my greasy hair and inadvertently making it stand on end as last night's wax reformed with horrid consequences.

"Well, yeah, but I hope I'm not setting myself up for a fall if tonight all goes horribly wrong."

"We'll just have to wait and see - it's not in our control, remember?" she hushed, and put a finger to my lips before I could suggest that I might sing a little louder, or gather outside the team's hotel and offer motivational words as they boarded the coach on their way to the stadium. I was desperate to have some sort of impact and make the tiniest bit of difference that might swing a close defeat into an edgy victory.

We were staying in the same place as the other three, and once they had eventually risen for breakfast, Colette was treated to two solid hours of intense football chat over crepes and coffee, as if we were on *"Sunday Supplement."* We debated who should come in for Ramsey and Davies; would we change tactics to cope with Ronaldo and if the tag of favourites would be too heavy a millstone around our necks? These were questions for a few hours' time, so instead we decided to focus on the matter in hand and began our quest to find ourselves some tickets to see what happened for ourselves. We had around 10 hours until kick-off, so began in the city centre, near the train station, in the hope to spot people with expensive tickets but no intention of watching some tiny nation take on Portugal.

As we hopped from café to restaurant to bar in the heart of Lyon, Colette clocked a shop advertising that it would buy any spare gold, and would act as a go-between between myself and the owner as I attempted to part with Victoria's ring. After some hard bargaining, he caved at 1,150 euros, which wasn't too bad seeing as it had set me back nearly a grand many years previously. Before he changed his mind, I stuffed a substantial wad of notes into my wallet to help the semi-final fund. But tickets were proving to be more elusive than Ryan Giggs at a 1990s international friendly.

We eventually turned our search towards the ground, having exhausted every barman, Welsh fan and even those that looked like a shady tout. We rode the Metro out to suburbs, and found ourselves in the middle of a housing estate filled with affluent abodes, with the hard-edged, brutal exterior of the Parc Olympique Lyonnais looming menacingly in the distance, encircled by a vast amount of lush green fields. Pretty to admire, yes; but the lack of touts, or indeed anywhere to drink whilst we whittled away the four hours until Bale and Ronaldo's showdown, meant we were stuck with very little options. A friendly dog-walker eventually rather bemusedly pointed us in the direction of some nearby hotels, and soon after striking up a conversation with a barwoman, she informed us she had spoken to a number of men over the past few days who were all going to the game as they worked for various tournament sponsors. Immediately we knew there was a chance to get uninterested neutral fans to part with their little slices of gold dust in return for hard cash.

But even though we seemed to be in the right place, we were still a million miles away from the game that was happening just across the road. When the minute hand struck eight on the large clock behind the bar, we were pretty much resigned to our fate - we would be watching the game on TV, and in an hour's time we would probably hear the roar of the Red Wall in the distance. It was painstaking to see dignitaries and guests all suited up, going to watch a game they had no vested interest in, denying die-hard fans the chance to witness history as they gorged on canapés and champagne at another networking event in their calendar. I then caught a glimpse of a tall, white-shirted man in trousers and shoes exit a lift and pull some tickets out of an envelope, I could see the hologram blinking away at me, like a temptress urging me to do something out of my comfort zone. I decided enough was enough, and scraped my barstool along the floor as I marched over and tapped him on the arm.

"Hi there, sir - do you speak English?"

"Yes, I do," came a quintessential British accent. "What can I do for you?"

"Sorry to ask, but I'm guessing you're not supporting one of the two teams are you?"

"No, I was hoping that England would be here," he said with a chortle, his pig-headedness not improving my anger towards corporate greed taking control of football tickets.

"Look, me and my friends are desperate to go to the game - we've been to all the other matches and we can't miss this one; it's the biggest game in our country's history. What would you sell your tickets for?"

The man smiled and said, "Well they're not just for me - they're for me and my three colleagues over there, too. I can't really sell them. We work for Adidas - that's where I got them from. Sorry, pal."

With one last roll of the dice and in sheer desperation, I ripped my wallet out of my pocket and held out all the money from the engagement ring. "There's around 1,150 euros there - would that change your mind?"

The man from Adidas took stock of the wedge of rainbow-coloured notes quivering in front of him as my hands shook. "You'd really buy them for all that?" he asked, and I gave him a firm nod of the head that indicated I was being deadly serious. "Hang on, I'll go and ask the others," he replied and strolled off towards three other men slumped in leather chairs next to an electronic display of a fireplace. As I breathed deeper than the Welsh defence of the Toshack-era, the businessmen deliberated, shooting me concerned glancing from time to time, before the white-shirted bloke returned.

"OK, mate, give us all of that and you can have the tickets." In sheer joy, I took a step forward and inappropriately grabbed him tightly, Dav style, and gave him a massive hug. "Thank you. Oh, thank you, mate! I'm so grateful," I gushed as I pressed all the money into his hand, and he gave me the tickets in return. "Enjoy the game," he said, looking at me as if I had a third eye; they must have thought I was mad to pay that much money to watch a game of football. "We're going to use this cash to enjoy some of Lyon's finest strip clubs tonight."

He could have blown it all on Panini stickers for all I cared. And with the tickets secured from a sleazy businessman, I triumphantly returned to my group to pile-on celebrations echoing the ones after the goals scored against Belgium.

"How many did you get?" said an excited Ieuan, picking himself off the floor after some over-exuberance.

"Four!" was my excited response as I fanned them out as proof of my achievements. "And, guys, don't worry about paying me back for them."

"Mate - no way, we can't do that!" spluttered Ieuan.

"I insist! Call it Victoria's treat." I looked around and, apart from Ieuan, the others were suddenly looking pretty uneasy; their mood altering within a second or two. "It's fine, guys, I don't mind. It's the least I can do."

"No, it's not that, Scott," said Matt. "You seem to be forgetting - there's five of us now."

For some reason, I had to look at every person as I counted them, and every time I reached five. After spending so many weeks always looking for hotel rooms with four spaces, or trying to acquire four tickets to matches, it had become second nature. When the Adidas bloke had suggested he had four available, I paid everything I had because I instinctively imagined witnessing history in front of our very eyes as a foursome. Ordinarily, I would have expected Colette to just forego a seat, but we had vowed to watch the games that would decide whether or not we got hitched together, and I couldn't face not having her there by my side when my dreams came true - be it watching Wales reach a major final, or my wedding day.

"Scott, honestly, I don't mind staying here," came her expected response.

"No, Colette, if you stay here, then I'm staying here, too."

"No way," she stated forcefully. "I would feel terrible if you missed the game because of me."

"I don't care - we said we would see how things panned out together, and that's what we'll do," was my emphatic response. At this point, Ieuan and Matt were shooting confused looks in each other's direction, not understanding the situation Colette and I had put ourselves in; however, one person knew exactly what we were going through.

"Guys - don't worry, I have a solution," said Dav. "I will stay here, and the rest of you can go."

"No way, Dav, you have to come," I said, also not wanting to deny my best friend a seat at an event he had waited his whole life for.

"Nope, mate - you go with Colette. I know what this means for you guys - besides, Colette got me a ticket for the Russia game, so I owe you. Ieu and Matt have been to all the other matches, so I don't want to ruin that, so I'll be fine here. Trust me, it's OK."

It was probably the most gallant gesture I had ever witnessed from anyone in my life, and I was proud it had come from my best friend. Dav had received so much stick over the years for being so unreservedly selfish, but now here he was, giving up a free ticket to the biggest game he might ever attend to allow his best friend's girlfriend to go in his place. Years of scrimping out of rounds and managing to avoid shelling out for meals had been repaid and more by this one incredible gesture, and I had no idea how I could show my gratitude. He touched me on the shoulder, as if to say that he understood what hinged on the result for me and the girl that stood next to me, and for the second time in a matter of moments, I had wrapped my arms around another man blurting out my eternal thanks. Colette kissed him on the cheek, while Ieuan and Matt didn't say a thing, knowing that if they didn't then their seats were secure, especially with Dav's track record. Dav took his bucket hat off and dumped it unceremoniously onto Colette's head, covering her eyes in an almost symbolic gesture of the temporary passing of the torch.

"You keep that for now - it'll bring you luck," he chuckled. "Now get yourselves over there before you miss kick-off," he continued once I had withdrawn from his clutches. "But remember, if we only get one ticket to the final, I think we know who will be watching us win the whole thing." And with that, we left my future best man sitting at the bar all alone, staring into his pint with a painful expression on his face, wondering if he had done the right thing. I knew exactly how I would repay him, but it would mean Wales getting to the final first and foremost.

CHAPTER 14

Since I was seven-years-old, I've been to a lot of matches. But game number one stands out vividly among the masses of memories; that first time you are confronted with the view of the pitch as you excitedly make your way up never-ending staircases, the loudness of being a number, as part of a vast crowd, as your unbroken voice squeaks along to unfamiliar chants and having to make commentary up in your head to make do without the television and John Motson to guide you through the action. Because those first memories are just that - first memories - you never forget them. But when you get the opportunity to go again, you do so knowing what to expect. The pitch becomes just another lawn, the crowd don't seem as boisterous as before as they sing the same old songs, and you aren't as captivated the second time around. Hundreds of games later, and it all just becomes a ritual; the small things that used to be so special reduced to humdrum.

But, as I entered through the Parc Olympique Lyonnais' turnstiles, I could have been seven again. This was unchartered territory: Wales in the semi-finals of the European Championships, the smallest nation ever to do so. Working on logic, which had long been discarded, it simply should not have happened, and therefore definitely would not happen again. So this was the first and last time I was likely to enter a football stadium with this jumble of emotions bubbling inside me, not knowing what the next couple of hours would have in store; it felt like game number one all over again.

Just as I had with my dad all those year ago at Villa Park, I held Colette's hand as I began my ascent up the steps, just in case I was overcome by the sight of all that green grass. I thankfully managed to remain vertical as I saw our players warming up opposite their Portuguese rivals, encircled with a thick red ring of supporters from both sides. We took our places in one of the middle tiers, saved for affluent 'fans' and members of UEFA's "football family" such as the Adidas bloke, but it seemed other freeloaders had also been persuaded to spend the evening experiencing the city's gentleman's clubs, as we were surrounded by Wales fans who had shunned a shirt and tie to instead proudly display their colours and their game faces. To think that some people say that football is "just a game" - we all felt that we were on the verge of the biggest moment of our collective lives.

"Are you ready?" said Colette as the big screens showed the players - glassy eyed, fully in the zone - in the shadows of the tunnel, awaiting their cue to be thrust into the spotlight. I nodded unconvincingly, as it still hardly seemed real and I could not fathom whether to laugh, cry, be serious or embrace the moment. We were so close to winning the tournament, yet, on the other hand, we had already won. Regardless of how the 90 minutes ended up, it had been an unforgettable summer for anyone privileged enough to have a Welsh birthright and cared about the result of any one of our matches, be that watching in a stadium, fanzone, pub or at home. I quickly thought about Arthur, no doubt sat at home next to Bethany with a glass of scotch, beaming with pride along with the rest of the nation.

I felt a tap on my arm, and Matt was leaning across, holding out his phone. "Look at this," he said, and showed me a photo of thousands of fans inside the Millennium Stadium, watching the game on a big screen erected on the pitch. "There's 27,000 people there, watching it on a bloody telly!"

I could only shake my head in disbelief - a stadium nowadays only associated with rugby had been taken over by football fans. The whole of the country truly was behind us.

An ear-splitting roar broke out as Ashley Williams and Cristiano Ronaldo led out the 22 protagonists, who assembled in two lines facing us, standing proudly for the anthems. We followed suit, with myself between the still-hatted Colette and Ieuan, with Matt taking the seat to his left. It did seem strange to cheekily allow my right hand to pop itself onto Colette's pert bum as the anthem started, rather than groping away at Dav's moob, continuing our long tradition of linking arms. But despite the more pleasurable squeeze, I genuinely missed my best friend when Hen Wlad Fy Nhadau began. Despite a large presence being missed, we still binded tightly together to serenade a continent one more time, and even Colette joined in with the gwlads, meaning she got a big smooch at its conclusion. The Portuguese support was also pretty vocal, and having been so close to winning tournaments before without success, they must have felt the same blend of trepidation and hope that all football fans know so well. As a shrill blast of the referee's whistle got us underway, I was still confident that this summer of miracles had at least one more up its sleeve.

Searching for early omens, my self-belief was knocked as we were once again adorning the tainted black kit that should have been consigned to history after the England game, while Portugal were wearing some pistachio number, despite the game kicking off bathed in a background of rouge hues. But when the two captains met for the first time since the toss as the orange-skinned waxwork that is Ronaldo charged goalwards, Williams clattered into him to take both man and ball with a fierce challenge that brought huge cheers from the Welsh support. An early psychological battle had been won, and in no uncertain terms, Williams had told Ronaldo what he thought of his reputation.

The first 15 minutes saw Portugal timidly stroke the ball around for the sake of it, scared to try and get it into a dangerous position for fear of the now-famous Wales counter-attack. But having gotten bored of soaking up pressure, our own galactico seemed keen to make something happen. With the platinum-haired Ramsey conspicuous by his absence, it meant that Bale had to shoulder the hopes and dreams of three million people alone, but he took it in that quick-step stride of his. Two shots from distance failed to trouble Rui Patricio in the opposition goal, but allowed us to exert tension-filled oohhs and ahhs into the still-warm summer air.

Further strikes at goal were difficult to come by during a quiet, but definitely not dull, first half, with both sides knowing that they couldn't win the match at this stage - but they certainly could lose it. Had it not been for the sheen coming from the amount of gel applied to his jet black hair, Ronaldo would have been anonymous, mainly down to an unlikely ginger hero in James Collins; a man I had pilloried in the past for being a disaster waiting to happen was giving the world's best player as good as he had got. However, in the final minute of the half, the man known as CR7 displayed his deadliness when finally freed himself from Collins' attentions and soared upwards, hanging in the air for an age until he made contact with a cross from the left flank; his header, though, thankfully ended up ballooning over. But a warning shot had been left, and gave Chris Coleman something to drill into his players at the break, which was signalled shortly after.

"It's going OK," Matt shouted down the line at the three people adjacent to him. "I reckon we'll sneak this."

"Me too," said Ieuan. "We're looking good at the back and Bale is on it yet again."

"It looks as though both teams are playing for penalties," I suggested. "But I think one goal will do it. I'm still confident."

"Me too," smiled Colette, kissing me on the cheek, and forced me to realise that we were 45 minutes closer to overcoming our penultimate hurdle. Devoid of action during the interval, I became tetchy and anxious, wondering how many weeks of my life would be shaved off by the jaw-clenching nervousness of extra-time and penalties, so it was a relief when the players re-emerged from the stadium's bowels to resume the semi-final.

But just five minutes later, my world and my summer was turned on its head - from which it seemed it would never recover. Portugal won a corner on the left, and knowing all about his aerial ability, my eyes were immediately drawn to Ronaldo. He buzzed around the penalty searching out the slightest slither of space, and typically found it. He once again towered above the defence and this time planted a textbook header into the top corner of a helpless Wayne Hennessey's goal. Half the ground fell silent, and half the ground erupted.

The ball had barely stopped bouncing in the net when a dark veil fell over me and my mood turned sour. The wrong kind of red and green flags were props in nearby celebrations, and Ronaldo's characteristically obnoxious carousing caused me to put my head in my hands and begin to dread the reality of the scoreline. Usually, this stabbing-like feeling would be hard to recover from, but in unlikely fashion, the figurative dagger was released via some gentle words from the pretty woman next to me - "Don't worry, it's not over yet." I honestly hoped she meant the game, rather than our blossoming relationship, but her soothing tone patched me right up and I instantly believed her. It was as though Colette had some sort of magical presence over me; if she said there was still hope, then that was gospel.

Her supernatural ability was seemingly rubbing off on the rest of the Welsh contingent inside the Parc Olympique Lyonnais, as they instantly rallied behind their players, encouraging them to take the kick-off and get at their opponents. For the next three minutes, positivity flowed from us towards our players, who were now in need of some inspiration. Their favourites tag had been taken off them, and they were free to scrap away and try and come back, just as they had against Belgium. After everything we had seen throughout the tournament, it just had to happen.

But history will tell you that it never did, and after three minutes of cajoling, nothing seemed to shake the Welsh players out of their anguish at falling behind, and before you knew it, we were two goals down - Euro 2016 was slipping away from us. The second, decisive goal, is still painful to watch now - a scuffed shot by Ronaldo looked to be trickling harmlessly well wide of the target; however, it crossed the path of Nani, who stretched out a leg and managed to modify its path. The diversion wrong-footed Hennessey, who could only watch in hopelessness as the ball cruelly trickled into his net.

Instantly, Colette's hand sprung onto my knee for comfort, but it was no use; 2-0 meant there were no magic words or power of positivity. Almost childlike, I slammed my eyes shut to try and block out the scenes around me, but that only heightened my sense of hearing and amplified the Portuguese cheers that sounded like those certain they were now going onto the final. Having felt like I was a seven-year-old kid again an hour before, now I wanted to burst into tears in Colette's embrace and be taken away from the scene. It was heartbreaking, in more ways than one.

When I could finally bring myself to do so, I glanced at a glum-faced Ieuan and Matt. Instead of red shirts, it would have been more apt to be wearing black ties as we mourned this particular loss, as it seemed certain there was no life left in our challenge. We all remained silent as the game just continued in front of us, only because it had to. Thoughts of Liverpool's night in Istanbul and Manchester United's Treble-clinching comeback danced fleetingly through my mind, baiting me to cling onto some strand of hope, but I had accepted my fate: Wales were finally going out of the Euros, and I wouldn't be going out with Colette for much longer. The mood, like Wales' performance, had been flattened.

The men in black were rocked by 180 seconds that they will file in the "what if?" folder of their lives until death, always wondering what would have happened if they had managed to keep things tight at the start of that second half. After five gruelling matches to get this far, the sixth had been beyond them. It almost seemed as though each encounter until this point had been a bit of fun, with no-one expecting them to scale such glorious heights. Suddenly, they had found themselves in the final four, and the realisation of what could be achieved had proven to be too great a burden to carry any further. As the minutes slipped agonisingly by, Portugal exploited the sombreness in the Welsh side and only some good fortune and goalkeeping by Hennessey managed to keep the score at 2-0.

A glimmer of hope came with seven minutes to go when Bale lined up a free-kick from 30 yards out, just as I had dreamed about the night before. Our last chance had fallen to the one man who could suddenly provide the elusive spark. My heart practically bursting out of my chest, I gripped Colette's hand as he stepped back, composed himself and then hot-stepped towards the ball, but the weight of a nation had forced itself from his shoulders onto his magical left foot. The free-kick struck the wall. It was well and truly over.

With our dreams dashed, suddenly a much-needed moment of catharsis broke out. Accepting that our time was up, the Red Wall had burst into song, in tribute of our heroes' achievements. "Don't Take Me Home" had never been sung with so much meaning, before "Wales, Wales, Wales" rang out. However, an a capella rendition of the national anthem, sang with such poignancy, meant there was barely a dry eye in the house. That was the point it all became too much.

Having bottled up a myriad of contrasting emotions for the best part of a month as my personal life intertwined with footballing fortunes, the overwhelming pride towards the players mixed with the uncertainty of what would happen next with Colette, and there was a reaction. My eyes filled with tears, and when the weight of them became too much, they fell down my cheeks and splashed onto the concrete beneath my feet. I sat still and quiet, trying not to draw any attention to myself. A few other fans had their heads in their hands; others possessed bloodshot eyes having started welling up well before me. We were all hurting, but I felt like I was losing much more than a football match.

I couldn't bring myself to join in with this display of defiance, so I sat back and listened to our splendid supporters instead, which stirred up warmer emotions of this incredible tournament. The magnificent, against-all-odds victory over Belgium was the highest of highs, and the crushing defeat at the death against England the polar opposite. Nail-biters against Slovakia and Northern Ireland had helped us on our way, and that evening when we exorcised 13-year-old demons against Russia had been sweeter than nectar. There had been so many positives: players had developed into stars on a massive stage, with fans from the Rhondda to Rome and Bangor to Bucharest fully aware of Sam Vokes, Hal Robson-Kanu and Neil Taylor. Wales was at the forefront of the world's conscience once again, with non-Europeans adopting us as their second-favourite team, as Brits back home unearthed imaginary, long-lost uncles and aunties from Caerphilly to qualify their allegiance. Off the pitch, the camaraderie we had enjoyed with fellow supporters as we made our way around the various cities had been entertaining and enlightening, and we had been welcomed with open arms by warm hosts. Long-time friendships with my three fellow travellers had developed a new lease of life, and Euro 2016 had given me an escape route from the domestic misery that had engulfed me just a month ago.

But as the clock on the big screen approached 90 minutes, the fourth official's board indicated that there would be three additional ones to play before the cold, harsh hand of reality would appear to slap me in the face and send me home alone.

Without looking at her to conceal my emotions, I fumbled my hand into Colette's one last time. Three minutes of this match had seen our chances of getting married vanish as swiftly as the ring I had proposed with, and now I just wanted to spend the last few injury-time minutes of this trip alone with only her, not the 55,000 others surrounding us. She spun towards me and buried her face into my chest, clinging onto me for what seemed like her life. I knew that she was also crying, as I could feel my shirt getting damp. I put my hand on the back of her head and consoled her. Looking for Ieuan and Matt's reactions, their slightly redder than usual faces wore astonishment at this crestfallen French woman weeping at Welsh pain; they too gave her reassuring pats on the back as we embarked on a melancholic group hug.

Colette stayed coiled up next to me until the referee at long last brought proceedings to an end. It was all over; our fate carved in stone. The fairytale had reached its conclusion, and Wales were out of Euro 2016. Our warriors crumpled to their knees whilst those wearing green raced around, their shattered bodies drunk with victory. We applauded our heroes for a good 10 minutes as they took in their final images of what had been career-defining weeks, collecting enduring memories that would be recalled time and again at anniversary dinners and television documentaries until they were grey and old. Their tournaments over, the squad seemed to transform from professional teammates to personal friends as they comforted each other while slouching desolately around the field, graciously thanking us for our support by wearing bilingual t-shirts emblazoned with "Diolch" and "Merci." There was no need for that; after all, we were the ones eternally grateful for their efforts in giving us a summer the entire country would never forget.

For many, the realisation that our magical journey had reached its conclusion began to subside, instead allowing for feelings of celebration of what had been achieved. Thus, with rueful expressions, the Welsh support began to filter out of the stadium to reflect in the bars of Lyon, before saying their au revoirs to the country that had treated us so well. But I couldn't shake the fact that as per the terms of our agreement, Colette and I were not about to get married anytime soon, or indeed ever. We remained rooted to our plastic seats as the players returned to the privacy of their changing room and the chance to freely express their disappointment.

"Shall we head off?" asked Ieuan to myself and Colette, whose face was still turned into towards my torso as I held onto her shoulder. "I think I need a beer or two after that."

"I'm just going to stay here for a bit longer, mate," I said, desperately grasping for extra-time in my extraordinary French adventure. "I'll catch up with you in a bit. Send me a text."

"OK, see you later, guys," he replied, waving goodbye with Matt as they joined the queue of people snaking out of the ground. Having craved a chance for solitude, finally Colette and I dwelled in the silence for a while. This time, though, we seemed incapable of talking, for fear of saying the words that triggered the end of our brief but beautiful union.

Eventually, it had to be done, and by the time I came up with, "So, what do we do now?" there were probably only around a hundred or so figures scattered around the stadium, which was as lifeless as the action taking place on the pitch at that moment.

Colette turned to me, continuing to defy beauty as she looked stunning despite having bawled her eyes out for the best part of 15 minutes; even her sniffles as she tried to clear her sinuses were moments I decided to treasure in case this was indeed the end of our road.

"Well, I guess we're not getting married then," she struggled through, her voice cracking slightly at the final few syllables.

"Well, yeah, we did leave that up to fate, and that plan backfired," I said, trying to make her laugh. While the very corners of her lips arched upwards for a fraction, she still seemed devastated.

"Yeah, you're right. I guess it's not meant to be," she said.

"You don't actually believe that, do you?" I stated. "Because I don't."

After an agonising pause, she shook her head. "No, I do want to be with you. But it's so difficult and complicated given our situations."

I pulled away from her, shuffling backwards so I could properly face her. I had a sense that she was desperate to find a get-out clause to our agreement, and I was determined to find one.

"I know, but it seemed so simple when we wanted someone else to take the matter out of our hands and decide it for us. Just because it's now back in our control, it doesn't mean we have to throw it away."

"So, what are you suggesting?" she said.

Without hesitation, I declared, "Come back to London with me. Stay with me for a couple of weeks; we can talk about everything, take our time and see if we can make things work."

"Oh, Scott, if only it was that simple."

"It is that simple, Colette. It's as simple as you want it to be. I'll even move to Toulouse if I have to because I'm madly in love with you, and I will do whatever it takes. I can tell that you feel the same, or you would have run a mile when I proposed. These past few weeks that I have known you have been incredible, but why should they end because Wales have been knocked out and I have to go home? Over the last four days or so, I've got to experience what life would be like if we were together, engaged or otherwise, and you're the person that I want to wake up next to every day. You're the person that I want to eat my breakfast with, or spend time just lounging around with. It's been amazing having a holiday romance with you, but what I really crave is all the day-to-day stuff. You're probably the only person that I've made two of these embarrassing speeches to, but I'll keep going until the floodlights get turned off and we get kicked out of here if you need more reasons to see if we can make it work."

The passion poured out of me, and she reciprocated with a long, tender kiss that I was powerless to curtail, as I wasn't sure if it was goodbye or an acceptance. Eventually, when we came up for air, she said: "I was hoping you'd say something like that."

I laughed and we kissed again, before the final two relived souls left the cavernous stadium bowl and Euro 2016 behind. That night, we would laugh amongst friends, including Dav, who amazingly managed to get himself into the stadium halfway through the first half by squeezing over a fence and sneaking past a couple of negligent stewards.

The knowledge that his sacrifice had not caused him to miss out on our final breaths of a wonderful championship meant a lot, and in the way it was the perfect ending. But as I boarded the Eurostar home the following day, arm in arm with my gorgeous Gallic girlfriend, it actually felt like the beginning of something special.

CHAPTER 15

Despite the passing of two months, it seemed like nothing had changed. Here I was, stood alongside friends inside a football stadium filled with red-shirted fans, blaring out our national anthem with new-found vigour and watching Wales play a sparking brand of football. It was now September, and we were thrashing Moldova, 3-0. The 2018 World Cup qualifiers had started, and it was all beginning again; after all, it was still 58 years since we had qualified for the World Cup. New goals had been sought, and with them expectations were heightened.

As the 80th minute approached and the game a mere walking-paced procession for our princes of the principality, I had a chance to take stock of what had happened to me since that night in Lyon. Having heard there had been hastily-made plans for an open-top bus parade for the squad through the streets of Cardiff, having barely returned to London, Dav, Colette and I had raced down the M4, Tom Jones blaring out as we crossed the Severn Bridge, to see it for ourselves. The capital was an outpouring of nationalism as red, white and green flags fluttered in the sunshine while the players were made aware of the galvanising effect they had had on their fellow countrymen and women. School bells rang early so their pupils could enjoy the occasion, and shopkeepers abandoned their premises for a minute or two to show their appreciation. In total, around 100,000 people lined the route to the Cardiff City Stadium, where they received a warm homecoming, and the Manic Street Preachers were on hand to put the full stop on an amazing summer.

Back in our homeland, Dav and I decided that we should give Colette an impromptu tour of the country, to fully educate her as to what Welsh life was all about. After spending a few hours strolling around the city, showing her the crown jewels of Cardiff Castle and the Millennium Stadium and recalling university tales, we headed north through the valleys and rolling hills to spend a day or so back home in Llandrindod. Enjoying my mum's home cooking, Colette was introduced to my parents as we spent the night squeezed into my childhood single bed, before sampling the peacefulness and tranquillity of life in mid Wales the following day.

When it was time to leave the fresh air and clean water behind and return to London's polluted pavements, we were just about to join the motorway again when I spotted a road sign for the Cotswolds. After a quick gander at Google Maps, I persuaded Dav to take a detour.

"Where do you want to go to?" he said, intrigued.

"Great Rissington," I replied.

"Where the bloody hell is that?"

"It's not too far away. I just need to see someone really quickly."

Around 25 minutes later, Dav's battered old Transit's tyres were crackling over gravel outside the same Tudor stately home that I had been so unwilling to have visited just four weeks ago, but was now actively going out of my way to be at.

"Why are we here?" said Colette and Dav, virtually in unison.

"This is where Victoria and I attended that wedding reception that clashed with the Slovakia game," I said. "I met a guy here called Arthur who I watched the match with and he was brilliant, he helped persuade me to leave Victoria and go to France. If it wasn't for him, this summer would have been pretty crap, and possibly the rest of my life."

Colette broke into a smile. "Aww, that's sweet. I want to meet him, too."

"Pffft. I'll wait in the van," smarted Dav, anxious to get home in time for a Saturday night out back in London.

It was a strange feeling, walking hand in hand with Colette along the same route to the main reception, especially when we walked over the exact spot I had seen Victoria kissing that random bloke in what seemed like a different lifetime ago. As I opened the doors, I was in familiar surroundings, although slightly more underdressed in a t-shirt and jeans rather than suited and booted like everyone else I encountered enjoying the festivities of another wedding reception.

Walking up to the desk, one of the receptionists took an interest in us and asked if there was anything she could help with.

"This is a random request, but is Arthur working today?" I asked. Screwing up her face slightly, the young woman replied, "Sorry, who?"

"Arthur. He's a handyman who works here. Old bloke, white hair, glasses?"

Her brow furrowed deeper. "Hmm, I'm not sure who you mean. Let me ask someone else." She walked away and began chatting to a couple of colleagues nearby before returning momentarily. "No, sorry, have you got the right place? We've never heard of anyone called Arthur working here."

"Sorry, I was here about a month ago and I got talking to him. He's an old Welsh guy, married to a woman called Bethany. Likes a drink."

"Hang on, let me ring the manager," politely replied the receptionist, and I listened into her conversation. "There's a gentleman here who wants to know if someone called Arthur has worked here in the last month or so.... Oldish man, white hair, glasses.... Welsh.... Drinks a lot.... Haha, OK I'll let him know." She put the phone down. "Sorry, there's definitely no-one here called Arthur, or ever has been."

I was so confused. "Umm, OK, thanks anyway," I replied, and began to walk slowly out of the building, a little shaken.

"Are you alright?" said Colette.

"No, I feel very weird right now. He was definitely here, he spoke to me for hours."

"And it was definitely this place?" she said.

"Yeah, definitely. We watched the game together in a bar. How do they not know him?"

I got into the car and was pretty silent for the rest of the way home, trying to explain the unexplainable. But as I stood watching Wales attack the Moldovan goal for the umpteenth time that night a few months later, I still had no explanation, and probably never will.

Regardless of Arthur's existence or not, what was not in doubt was how much my life had improved since returning from France. After our little trip back to Wales, Colette and I enjoyed spending ample time together in London, seeing all the sights, dining out and chatting long into the night about how we could make things work. Many options had been mooted, including me looking at jobs in Toulouse, but after two weeks we still had not discovered a definite solution. But instead of jumping on a plane home, Colette stayed put for another week, and then another. Slowly but surely she began to build up a collection of Primark clothes and regularly raided Boots to stock up on supplies. After a few weeks, I made a joke that she had already moved in without me asking.

"Well, I was waiting for you to ask properly, so I thought I would just do it myself and see what you said," she laughed.

"OK - well, do you want to move in with me, here in London?" I asked.

"Finally! Yes!" she squealed, and that was that. A few days later, I was back in Toulouse helping her pack up her belongings, and after spending one final night in her tiny apartment, where the magic had begun, we returned to Britain with as much stuff as we could physically drag over with us in an assortment of suitcases.

Once Colette had settled in, I could then focus on finding new employment, especially as the constant travelling had blown right through the money that Victoria had given to me from our joint bank account. After a few interviews, I managed to land a role at a small marketing company in Stratford who had been looking for a studio manager to look after a team of three designers, tasked with providing branding for a number of clients in the sporting sector. My knowledge and passion towards football helped swing the decision in my favour above my fellow applicants, and my early ideas - aided by design discussions with my artist girlfriend - had received high praise by my new boss, Craig. He had welcomed me to the company by treating me to a Fulham game in an executive box - a far cry from life under Graham. To top it all off, the money was far better, too, helping me quickly repair the hole burned in my wallet from the summer of a lifetime.

Since the previous May, my life had been turned upside down, which is not a bad thing when you are facing rock bottom. I may have started Euro 2016 with a fiancée, a job and a flat, but now I had a girlfriend who I loved, a career with prospects and a home that I wanted to get back to each night. But there was one thing that had not changed. As Bale slotted home a late penalty right in front of me, Colette, Dav, Ieuan and Matt, we celebrated far too overenthusiastically for a routine 4-0 win against minnows like Moldova. However, a generation ago we were losing to these footballing outposts. For so long, Wales have had great players but not a great team, and therefore a nation was deprived of representation in international tournaments, condemned to decades of ridicule. The lack of support for soccer in a rugby-dominated land was hardly helped by the lack of success on the pitch, but now Euro 2016 had well and truly changed that. With the glass ceiling not just smashed but obliterated, and the relative youthfulness of the squad but masses of experience gained, hopefully things bode well for many more summers spent following the fortunes of this fantastic group of boys in red over the coming decade, and hopefully longer. Hopefully by the time I introduce a new generation to the wonders of Welsh football, they will endure much less of the suffering that supporters since 1958 had grown accustomed to and thought would never change, until Coleman, Bale, Ramsey et al came into our lives.

"Shall we start looking for flights to Russia yet then?" said Dav as the final whistle sounded. "If we book now, they might be a bit cheaper."

"Hold your horses, Dav," I said. "Nine more games to go now."

"Well we're definitely going to get there, aren't we? We're bloody amazing these days!" he laughed.

"I really hope you're right, Dav," said Colette, who gave me that same look back that she had offered up when talking about reaching the final of the Euros, followed by a wink.

"You never know how much our lives might change if we go to the World Cup."

"Well, we'll just have to wait and see, won't we," I said, nodding in agreement at the silent deal we had telepathically just agreed. "We'll just leave it in the capable hands of Coleman, Bale and company - it all worked out alright last time, after all."

ABOUT THE AUTHOR

Jonathon Rogers is a sports journalist who was born and raised in Llandrindod Wells in mid Wales. He studied sports journalism at Staffordshire University and graduated in 2010, and has since gone on to work for Crystal Palace Football Club. Currently residing in south London, Jonathon is a passionate football and rugby fan, and was in attendance at Euro 2016 following the fortunes of Chris Coleman's side, which paved the way for the inspiration for this, his debut novel.

www.jonathonrogers.com

Twitter: @jonnyrogers9

21381765R00154

Printed in Great Britain
by Amazon